The Decision

by

John Sills

The first part of the HOPE trilogy

ISBN: 9781731233851

Previous titles by the author:

I Was There – A Musical Journey. 2016. A personal story of music since the early 1970s.

Growin' Up – Snapshots/Fragments. 2017. A book of poems about childhood and youth.

Both books are available on Amazon and Kindle.

This book is dedicated to my three children, Kieran, Isabelle and Rebecca – and their generation.

I hope they will have the chance to put right the injustices that their predecessors – my generation included - are leaving them with. I hope they will be strong enough to combat the hatefulness and the prejudice that today's leaders have unleashed, even in the heartlands of freedom and democracy. I hope they will end the pursuit of profit to the detriment of everything else, including the planet. I hope they will not need HOPE.

John Sills
March 2018

Chapter One. The Message
(10-05-27)

Eight-thirty. The office was deserted. The buzzing holos had fallen silent. The earphones and comms glasses lay abandoned on the grey desks. Worn blue chairs rested at various angles underneath the surfaces. Each space carefully calibrated - the bare minimum that a worker needed to function. Enough room for the holo, or a laptop for those workers who still preferred the old ways. It wouldn't be long now before the choice was removed. No reason why anyone couldn't use the holo, or the glasses, these days.

Grey, blue, blue, grey: the Department for Education, Leisure and Engagement - DELE - knew nothing else in its drab, decaying headquarters in Westminster.

Susan sighed as she looked around. So depressing. Couldn't the department whose motto was *FULFILMENT IN LIFE* do just a little better for its own staff? She switched her holo to web mode to check the news and the tube before she left. She had been preparing for her visit to the Wash the next day, to see how the refugee education centres were doing. This was her project, the thing that kept her going amid all the internal politics, the cuts and the policy reversals, as ministers came and went and the Authority slowly rooted out anything that smacked of the old leftism. She was surprised that the Authority had allowed the project to continue, but guessed that it had concluded that the distraction of education stopped people from going crazy and rioting on the Bases. That was enough to save it; and Susan wasn't about to ask any questions that might make them change their minds.

Delays on the District Line - some things never changed - and her mood dipped a little further. She moved to the BBC News. The BBC: still hanging on, still the best, although the Authority had started to make some very threatening noises about balanced programming. Flood levels in the Wash had subsided after Base Two had been on a red alert. Germany was frying in unseasonal heat. They were rioting over water - in Germany! The US was threatening Mexico with sanctions if people kept blowing up the wall. The NATO-Russia standoff in Ukraine continued. Susan wondered how her brother Will was doing, stuck in Kremenchuk, with nothing to report, but no chance of getting out before the next rotation, whenever that was.

She scrolled through a bit more, checked the train schedules to the Isle of Ely and the Hydro times for the Wash. All seemed OK. Time to go home, get some rest. Tomorrow was going to be a long day. But as she watched one last news story, a message flashed across the bottom of the image. It made no sense.

Cabinet Office, 08.30, 11 May, Room A. Code: Bolingbroke. Subject: HOPE kidnap attempt. 15.00 Saturday 15 May, Wembley. Mowbray C aka H5 leading effort. Objective: termination. Purpose of meeting: agree next steps.

What the…? Susan gazed perplexed at the holo-screen. She instructed her wristpad to expand the message. The recipients were listed. She recognised a couple from the Home Office, but the rest were Cabinet Office, No 10, Treasury, Defence, and more people who meant nothing to her. Except one. Her boss. Chris Yorkminster. A man she hated with every fibre of her being. The most arrogant, self-important, scheming bastard she'd ever had the misfortune to come across. Even worse, he fancied her, and made it obvious. Always suggesting a drink after work to discuss the refugee project *in a bit more detail than we have time for in the office.* No way! Whenever he came near her it made her teeth grind. She had to smile, talk sensibly, stay business-like. He was her boss. But every time she declined a drink he'd call her the ice maiden, *Siouxsie Sue,* who Susan knew was a punk singer from her Dad's era. Quite how Yorkminster thought she, Susan, resembled Siouxsie was beyond her; how in fact, he'd even heard of her was a mystery. As far as she knew, he just liked all the robo-pop stars with the biggest breasts and the least clothes. And she was happy to leave it there. Music was something she had no desire whatsoever to discuss with Chris Yorkminster, although he often liked to probe her about her preferences. Way too personal. The thought of going there just made her cringe.

But Yorkminster was on the copy list and somehow she'd got the message. She wasn't on the list. She'd never heard of Code Bolingbroke, or a kidnap plan, or a termination plan, if that was what it was.

But she had heard of HOPE and knew the leader, Charlie Mowbray. It was her brother.

Chapter Two. Base One
(11-05-27)

Susan rose at 6 o'clock, to catch an early train from Liverpool Street to the Isle of Ely. Back in the pre-Wash era that was just a name for the local council; derived, yes, from an ancient description, when the Fens were still marsh. The area had been drained first by the Romans. From the 17th century onwards, the task was completed, creating some of the richest soils in the country. Dark and fertile. It had stayed that way until the early twenties, when decisions had to be taken about how to fight the rising sea levels, after a surge in 20/21 had frightened the hell out of everyone. There was speculation about whether Kings Lynn, out there facing the Wash, would have to be sacrificed. Lobbying was heavy. The Labour government hadn't a clue: this sort of thing just wasn't on their political compass. They'd been swept to power in 2020 when years of economic stagnation, the confusion over Brexit - were we in or out? - and the Corbyn cult, which had begun in earnest in 2017, convinced enough people that the opposition, whoever they were, had to be given a chance. Maybe the promises about fair treatment at work, fair wages, fair taxes, no student fees, would make a difference.

The first couple of years of Labour government had been chaotic. Taxes were raised, the markets targeted the pound brutally, workers in all parts of the public sector went on strike as expectations of wage increases weren't met. New trade deals outside Europe weren't finalised. There were savage defence cuts to pay for the NHS, Trident was cancelled, and the refugees started coming in, in ever larger numbers. France ended any controls on its side. Britain, despite new border controls, couldn't keep people out, especially when the lorry queues in Kent lengthened after Brexit formally took place and the inspectors couldn't cope with the demands.

The Establishment rallied. In early 2023 a coalition of Conservatives, bankers, industrialists and the military, with the tacit support of King Charles, put it to the Government that there needed to be a vote of confidence, and there could only be one result. There was a feeble attempt by Prime Minister McDonnell to rally support against what was a coup by any other name, but half of the Labour party in Parliament deserted him. The Government fell, and a national coalition was born. The *Authority for National Stability*. With a mission to restore order and economic stability, and deal with the growing environmental and refugee crises. Despite attempts by a few comedians on the web to name the new Government *the Anus*, it soon just became known as *the Authority*. And the wags learned to keep their mouths shut when the threats started coming.

The Fenlands were central to the responses by the Authority to the environmental and refugee crises. A decision was taken to allow parts of the region to be flooded, to relieve pressure on other coastal areas. The Fenlands became an extension of the Wash, and took on the name. The western version of the Norfolk Broads, but larger. Many villages and small towns were sacrificed for the greater good. The larger towns - Wisbech, Downham Market, Kings Lynn, Ely - were spared. Walls, channels, deep moats were built to protect them, and the A47 and A10 were reconstructed as elevated roads. It was an impressive achievement, completed in three years. The Authority got things done.

The flooding also created an opportunity to address the refugee problem which had overwhelmed Kent. Makeshift towns had grown up there, with conditions even worse than those that had existed in France. The Authority acted. Two island bases were constructed in The Wash. Both were located on the sites of old military camps. The housing was preserved, facilities to make living conditions tolerable were constructed, and people were shipped in. Once there, they were trapped. Access was only by Hydro - there were no road connections. Security patrols around the Bases were extensive - providing plentiful job opportunities to local people, if they wanted them. In fact most of the jobs were taken by the same people the locals had objected to when they voted for Brexit in 2016. The Poles, Lithuanians and Estonians. Likewise in the camps themselves: the shops, the clinics, the schools. Not many volunteers from the English population, although the project attracted idealistic students from around the world, who spent their holidays helping out. This was an international operation in post-EU, post-UK England.

Susan was uneasy about the origins of the Authority, but had seen from the inside that something had to be done. She told herself that elections in 2025 would give a stronger democratic basis to the government, were it to win. And win it did, by a landslide. She'd argued with both her brothers about this. They agreed not to fall out about it, but it was hard. They felt she had sold out; she argued that, as a civil servant, she could see what was going wrong and what needed to be done. Serious problems needed serious solutions, not futile political gestures.

And so she was heading for Base One in the Wash. The biggest camp. Accessible only by Hydro from the Isle of Ely. Or jet copter - but only the military, VIPs and emergency supplies came in that way. Anyway, she rather liked the journey across the flooded marshes. They were often very beautiful, the light mists mingling with the weak sunlight: pale greys and yellows merging with the pure green of the reeds that grew everywhere that hadn't been cut away for the channels. Herons perched on invisible mounds, otters swam alongside the Hydro, hoping for titbits. All nature was here; and a beautiful silence hung in the air, broken only by the rumbling of the Hydro's engine, and the swish of the prow cutting through the thick marshy waters.

Susan wasn't thinking too much about the journey as she got on the tube at Ravenscourt Park. Her mind was a mess of big questions: *what crazy stunt has Charlie got himself mixed up with now? How am I meant to know about this? Who put that message on my feed? Why is Yorkminster involved?*

What am I going to do?

Charlie was quite possibly going to die on Saturday 15 May unless someone told him what was waiting for him and his gang. And Susan knew. Surely the answer was obvious - she had to get a message to him. But, but... why had she been told? What were the motives of whoever had told her? Was it someone with Charlie's interests at heart? Was it someone who wanted to trap her in the conspiracy, someone who wanted her out of DELE? Yorkminster? Someone who wanted to trace her communication with Charlie, through the lo-fi? Or was it just an accident, a rogue message? Questions, questions, and no answers.

She was so preoccupied that she didn't notice Liverpool Street as the tube stopped there. She got off at Aldgate East, crossed over to the westbound platform and resolved to concentrate on getting the train to Ely. There was plenty of time to think it through on the journey up there. She made the train, and, armed with coffee and croissant, she settled in for the slow trudge up through the East Anglian wastelands. The fast trains from Kings Cross to Cambridge had been suspended due to lack of funding - everything to East Anglia was now from Liverpool Street. Susan's Mum said that was just like how it was in the 1970s. Back to the future.

The train, the 7.50, was pretty empty. A couple of pallid young men in ill-fitting grey suits - probably from the Ministry of Resettlement, Susan thought - and a couple of refugee families, kids climbing all over the seats and whining about things she couldn't understand, accompanied by an avuncular looking man in the dark blue uniform of Immigrant Control. With a stun laser of course, and a pair of high capability glasses hanging from a side belt buckle. People were usually bussed up to the Wash, but maybe these people had paid for the premium service. Yes, capitalism had even made its presence felt in entry levels to the Bases of the Wash. It was possible to buy a VIP travel and accommodation option. A bit like glamping at a music festival - without the entertainment. Sterling or dollars, cash only. Early release guaranteed. Susan was outraged by this, but as ever, as a good civil servant, accepted there was probably a good reason for it, and concentrated on her own responsibilities.

And this attitude, which was essential to do her job, complicated her reaction to the message the night before.

Her brother was at grave risk. It was of his own doing, but she couldn't just let him walk into a barrage of lasers. If only he hadn't got himself involved with the fantasy politics of the HOPE movement. *The Holistic Organisation for the People and the Environment.* Really! Susan shared their concerns. Inequality was even worse now than it had been in the mid-tens, before Brexit. London continued to thrive, but those parts of the country that voted to get out of Europe to get the much-vaunted control back soon realised that all that meant was that that the Government could ignore them with even greater impunity. It was the greatest act of self-harm ever perpetrated by the English people (the Scots said their goodbyes in the referendum of 2020). The environment had been pretty much left to itself after a brief flurry of hope following the Paris agreement in 2015. At least in England, where profit continued to drive everything. The flooding of The Wash was one of the consequences - earlier than predicted, but a demonstration of what nature could do if humankind messed with it enough. Yes, all this worried Susan as much as Charlie, or Will or any other person who cared about the whole of society and not just their own little bubble. But there were ways of addressing the problems, through democratic argument and then government action. Not letting off smoke bombs outside fracking plants, or spraying right wing politicians with manure. At least HOPE hadn't yet graduated to real bombs, although there were news reports that they were developing links with the INSF in Ireland and the Northern Islamic Self Defence League.

Now, it seemed, if that message was real, that Charlie and his gang were planning some kind of kidnap at Saturday's European Elite League final between Stratford Olympians and Barcelona. And the Authority knew.

And Susan knew they knew.

But what if it was a hoax? What if it was some kind of test for her? The Authority knew she was Charlie's sister. No-one had ever said anything directly to her, but Yorkminster had made some pretty marked jibes about HOPE and their motives in her presence, inviting a response from her. She always gave the same answer: she understood some of their concerns, but opposed their methods. Only democratic action could provide long term solutions. *So sensible,*

Siouxsie, he'd reply, and Susan would just give him a thin smile. He'd move on to a bit more name-dropping about the committees he sat on.

But he'd never mentioned being part of the Cabinet Office group that was planning a warm welcome for the HOPE delegation on Saturday. If it was true, she guessed Yorkminster was representing DELE because football came under the department's remit. They had to have someone there. The fact that a mere Director from DELE was invited showed the department wasn't that big a player. He'd just be there to keep DELE's ministers informed; and he would hate that. He'd put a big spin on his involvement when he reported back, though Susan wouldn't normally hear about such top secret matters.

So why now?

Why now?

She couldn't figure it out. It just made no sense. Top secret messages didn't just flash randomly across people's screens. Susan wasn't involved in the sports side of Yorkminster's responsibilities at all. Her role was all in *engagement*: finding ways to involve the people with no organised voice in decision-making. And, with the creation of the Bases for refugees, seeing that they had a chance to make it in English society, if eventually they were allowed into the mainstream.

Susan loved this side of her work. It was inspiring to go up to the Bases and see children, adults, learning English and other basic skills. It was inspiring to see the volunteer teachers, people of all ages, though mainly recent graduates, giving so much to these communities. Giving them hope for the future. It pained her that Yorkminster always required her to report back on any signs of extremism amongst the pupils. That meant spending a bit of time with the security services inside the Base - never a pleasant experience, as they talked of bribes, drug deals, infiltration. Suspicion and more suspicion: they needed to find problems, and Susan suspected they'd manufacture them if they couldn't. There were targets no doubt, always targets. Pointless, fake targets, that only drove fake evidence and perverse behaviours. But Ministers liked them, needed something to measure, achievements to parade. How did you measure the fact that a young refugee girl could read and speak enough English to make her way in the world, receiving an education for the first time in her life? Discover there was an alternative to drudgery and compliance, even in the confines of the Base? Susan could see hope, liberation ahead for this generation of refugees. It was a fragile thing, but flowers were ready to bloom. If only the Authority would allow it to happen.

As the train pulled in to Ely station, Susan told herself to focus on the job ahead. Feel that inspiration. Try to provide some, in return. Worry about Charlie later. There was nothing she could do about it anyway, until she got home and had access to the lo-fi.

***

The huge Fenland skies, silver grey and intimidating, loomed over the Hydro as it glided through the reef channels en route to Base One. They passed outgoing ferries, taking the refugee men and boys to work the local fields on the edges of the Wash. The low cost workers so disliked by the Brexiteers back in '16 were nothing like this lot, as Susan's Mum said. The East Europeans who had been allowed to stay were now complaining about being undercut by government-sponsored slave labour. But the Authority was unmoved. The men, young and old, needed work to safeguard them from the extremists, it said. And no-one could really argue.

Susan thought about the little girl, Amla, or Amie as she liked to call herself, who had been so shell-shocked when she arrived at the Base that getting her to speak her own language was hard enough, never mind English. But six months on, she'd run up to greet Susan with "Susa!" And hug her with childish delight. Susan crumbled every time. And she couldn't wait to crumble again.

The Hydro was held up at the Base One docking station; two boats laden with supplies were taking their turn. Normally they would have gone to the cargo dock, but this place was beginning to boom. The men and boys had money to spend from the fields; there were eager suppliers wanting to meet their needs. The Authority was pumping money into the bases too. It wanted them to be a success, trouble-free. Some of the residents would be living there for a long time. The Authority wasn't completely heartless. It didn't send people back blithely, irrespective of the fate they faced back home. It was willing to integrate most of the refugees into mainstream society. But at a steady pace, a pace that was manageable and not disruptive. This enlightened attitude gave Susan hope. She hadn't welcomed the coup, although she carried on working, like the rest of the senior civil service, out of a sense of duty and an acceptance that while it *was* a coup, it had been executed through parliamentary means. The progress being made at the Bases helped, as it allowed her to reconcile the authoritarianism of the government with her own conscience. It was still possible to be doing good. And she had a job that was doing good, notwithstanding Yorkminster's obsession with extremists.

A little late, she stepped off the Hydro. Immediately the smells of the place aroused her. The docking station was surrounded by eating joints that seemed to cover the cuisine of the world. How they got all their ingredients was a mystery, but the Docks had become the place where people came to eat, if they had money. Susan would often buy a snack for lunch - an Indonesian rendang perhaps, or some Syrian kebabs with vine leaves. Or just a Chinese duck wrap. There were no Chinese refugees, as far as she knew, but the entrepeneurs had made their way into the camp. The human spirit was irresistible.

She had put on her boots before getting off the Hydro, as not all the pathways had been paved yet and there had been a lot of rain in recent weeks. The side streets were a quagmire - *just like Glastonbury most years*, Susan thought. But a permanent fact of life. A lot of kids ran barefoot as it was the easiest way to get through the mud. The schools had hosepipes and paper towels at their entrances to help the pupils clean their feet before they entered the classrooms.

She started in Zone A Academy, as the Authority liked it to be called. There were four zones on The Base, plus the Docks. Children from the age of six to sixteen were receiving an education.

The focus was on the basics: language and writing, maths, and an Authority-approved history module to integrate the children into English society. For the older children with good prospects of mainstreaming there were a few skill-based courses like brick-laying and carpentry, but take-up of these was still low. Most of the boys over thirteen were out in the fields with the men. Susan couldn't understand why this was allowed - surely proper integration into society meant observing the norms and not exploiting child labour. She'd heard it was the refugee parents who wanted it, but it still seemed a flaw in a system which otherwise seemed to have the right motives.

Zone A Academy was a cluster of prefabricated huts, which looked like old RAF issue. They were dry and had heating in the winter. Keeping them cool in summer was more of a problem. Inside they were decorated by the work of the children, like any other school. Except some of the paintings were starker, as the young refugees expressed their emotions, memories, through art. Susan gulped every time she saw another depiction of destruction, blood, loss, anguish. She felt a desire to take the paintings, the sketches away, and demand they be displayed in the House of Commons: anywhere that could remind people of what so many of these kids had been through.

She observed a brick-laying class - mostly girls - before moving on to the Year 5s, where Amie would be. She entered the classroom silently and sat at the back. The teacher acknowledged her with a smile, and carried on. The children were learning English for shopping. They were playing the parts of shopkeeper and customer. Little Amie was looking for carrots and garlic. Susan choked with emotion as Amie said, with her Arabic lilt, "Could I have a kilo of carrots please? And do you sell garlic?" So plaintive, like she hoped against hope that they sold garlic. She looked around and saw Susan and beamed the biggest smile in the world. And Susan crumbled.

At the end of the class, Amie ran to Susan and hugged her around the waist. Susan looked to the teacher for confirmation it was alright. The teacher nodded approval; Susan lifted Amie up and kissed her on the cheek. "You're doing so well, Amie, I'm so proud of you."

Amie brushed her hair against Susan's face. "I'm so happy here Miss Susa. One day I speak perfect English, and help my mother go mainstream. We have a shop selling vegetables and bread and fruits and snacks and maybe beer."

"Beer?" said Susan.

"Yes," said Amie. "My friend Sula says you need to sell beer in England for people to come to your shop. Is that true, Miss Susa?"

"Oh, maybe sometimes," said Susan. "But not always. If your vegetables are the best, people will come".

"You promise, Miss?"

Susan choked again. "Yes, I promise, Amie".

Amie smiled a sunny, uplifting smile and rushed back to her friends, who had been waiting for her. Susan stood, still at the back of the class, momentarily feeling rather foolish. She was here to observe progress - and detect signs of extremism - not to get emotionally involved. The teacher saw her unease and came up to her. "Amla's making great progress. And she's so sweet and popular. But sometimes she just cries. She's working through some dark moments in her life."

"What chance does her family have of mainstreaming?" Susan asked.

"Right now, it's still limited," the teacher replied, "Her mother has no English to speak of, and is still deeply traumatised. Amla's brother works in the fields, but is an angry young man and has become involved with some of the Zone A gangs. That won't help them. The Authority likes to move whole families out, and won't do it if there are any obvious risks. I've spoken to Social; they say they are aware of the brother and are looking to get him on a programme. But it will take time. With no father and an errant brother, Amla's prospects aren't too good."

Susan shrank inside. She wanted to take Amla, her Amie, away with her, give her a good, a happy life. But for now she knew she could only watch and hope. Rather depressed, she moved on to Zone B, recovering her spirits when she watched a group of Year 8s

17

– 12 to 13 year olds - rehearsing "Oliver!" Songs and all. In Zone C, a group of Year 9s were tackling some equations that Susan would have struggled to remember; and in Zone D there were seven year olds who could name all the colours of the rainbow. Susan came out of it all, as ever, truly inspired. Just one more thing to do. The obligatory visit to Security, to hear the latest on the gangs and extremist infiltration. She found most of the extremist trails unconvincing, though some of the gang culture was more worrying. Not least because Amie's brother was clearly at risk. It meant the visit ended on a bit of a downer; but as the Hydro pulled away from Base One, Susan tried to think about all the good things she'd seen, and to dream about how she could help little Amie make her way in the world.

Back on the train, Susan put on her comms glasses and ran through her messages. Nothing more on HOPE and the Saturday ambush. She flipped back to the rogue message. It wasn't there. She hadn't deleted it, but it wasn't there. She checked the deletions folder just in case. No sign. What was happening? Work messages never just disappeared.

She tried to figure out possible explanations. Maybe it had been a genuine error and someone got the controllers to go into her system and expunge it. Someone in authority. Maybe the message was on some kind of self-destruct loop. Not normal at work, but common enough in private life. Maybe someone was just playing with her, seeing what her reaction would be. Looking to drive her a bit crazy, at which point she might deliver Charlie into their hands. Maybe it was just fake and the perpetrator thought better of it. But again, how did he or she get into her system?

Maybe, maybe, maybe. How, how, how? What was happening?

Susan tried to switch off. She called up some music footage she hadn't seen. But it just didn't do anything. Her mind was a swirl of Amie, her brother, and the missing message. She took off the glasses and went up to the bar for a large gin and tonic. She found herself talking to one of the pallid men in grey suits that she'd seen that morning. He was interesting - knew about the protocols for mainstreaming. Susan probed him about the chances for a family

18

like Amie's. It wasn't impossible he said, if the girl showed enough promise and the boy could be reached by one of the programmes. It was accepted that some of the older people would never master the language or the culture, but as long as they lived a quiet life and the kids looked after them, anything was possible. He enquired whether there was any extended family already mainstreamed. That might help. Susan didn't know, but she felt a bit better, and bought the man a beer when she topped up her gin and tonic.

She'd work out what to do about Charlie when she got home.

***

Susan sat at her desk in the living room, in semi-darkness, just a side light beaming on to her keypad, as she sketched the outlines of her report on the visit to Base One. She could fill in the detail tomorrow, but just wanted to get it on the network before she became completely preoccupied with the question of Charlie. Radiohead wafted on low volume in the background - Susan still liked the music of the tens and even before. Her Mum and Dad had both been big music fans: Susan went to her first festival at the age of three. Latitude: she still had the photos of her on her Dad's shoulders, with her giant pink earmuffs, hands in the air, like all the teenage girls in front of her. Will was there too, clinging on to his Mum's arm. Happy days.

Susan knew she couldn't write about Amie - she had to remain unspecific, except where she'd identified any signs of extremism. She plotted a narrative about the genuine progress across the Base, but a progress that disproportionately benefited the girls, as the boys were being sent out to work so early. She'd noted this before, in all the Base reports, but it hadn't got much traction yet. The belief back in London seemed to be that if the boys were working the fields, and earning a bit of money, they were less susceptible to extremist influences. To Susan this didn't make sense: education, the acquisition of life skills, was the key. Boys from the age of fourteen were missing out.

With a heavy heart, she mapped out the Security section. No significant evidence of extremism, but a solidifying gang culture. Based around ethnic origin, but not exclusively so. Certain gangs were cooperating, to gain control of particular products: drugs of course, but also gambling, and, inevitably, girls. Often young girls: there was always a market. It wasn't good, but the Authority tolerated all these things, as long as it thought it could keep a lid on them, and the extremists were kept out. If it was just about money and gratification, and no-one was getting badly hurt, it was deemed containable. Badly hurt was a relative concept. The Authority was thinking only of obvious physical harm. Susan hated this attitude: girls like Amie would be highly vulnerable in two or three years' time if she was still on the Base. Susan knew she would have to do something to help her and her mother and brother get out.

But that was for the future. The here and now pressed down hard on her. She couldn't put it off any longer. What about Charlie?

Her little brother, the wayward one, and the genius. The charmer. The chancer. The one who caused her Mum the most anxiety, but also the one she truly adored. Susan and Will both knew that, and accepted it. They both loved Charlie, in their different ways, as well as finding him deeply frustrating at times. And now he had really landed himself in it, and Susan still didn't know what to say to him.

She fidgeted with her iPhone 8 - the route into the lo-fi. It was eight years old now, but still functioned on the basic level. No-one really knew whether or how the Authority monitored the lo-fi. There were no examples of people getting caught out when on the lo-fi. Maybe the Authority just let things pass, or maybe it was just too focused on keeping up with the latest technologies, where the big criminals, terrorists and hostile governments would be operating.

So, with a couple of encryption codes for safe measure, Susan keyed into Charlie's network. She still wasn't sure what she would actually say. But she just wanted to hear his voice, sense where he was at. The phone buzzed, two, three, four times: maybe he wasn't there. Then he picked up. The signal was weak. "Hey, Suze, what's up?"

"Oh, Charlie, I just wanted to know how you are."

"Yeah, just fine. Just fine. Not like you just to call for no reason. What's happening?"

"Nothing in particular, but it's getting heavy right now. People are worrying about HOPE. I'm never sure whether they think I'm connected."

"You saying that's because of me? I thought they knew you despise my methods."

"Don't say that, Charlie. I can't agree with what you are doing, but I don't despise it. That would mean I despised you. I could never despise you."

"You sure?"

"So sure, Charlie. So sure. I love you so much Charlie, I could never despise you."

"Hey Suze, this isn't like you. Something's troubling you, I know it. Tell me. You never talk that way. Tell me."

"Oh nothing, Charlie. Just I'm so worried about you. And Will too, in those trenches. My two brothers, both in danger. Me just sitting here. It's tearing me up."

"Hey Suze, stay calm. I'm in control. We're in control. We've got plans. All cool. No worries. You'll see. You'll be proud."

"Will I?"

"Sure, I hope so. Really proud. You'll be surprised. And feel proud."

"When, Charlie?"

"Soon, big sister. Just wait and see. No-one hurt, but a good gig. High impact. Remember that Suze, no-one hurt. No-one ever gets hurt."

"But everyone says you're in with the INSF and the Northern Islamists."

"Hey, are you on some kind of work tip here?"

"No, Charlie, no. I'm just worried. Those connections will make you more dangerous in the eyes of the Authority: they'll want to know more about you."

"They asking you?"

"No, not yet."

"Not yet?"

"Charlie, they'll know we're related."

"So why haven't they asked you?"

"I don't know."

"Maybe we shouldn't be speaking."

"No, Charlie. But yes, I need to tell you something..."

"Yeah, like what? This is sounding like a set up. See you, Suze."

"No, Charlie, please, it's serious..."

He was gone.

Hung up on her. Didn't trust her - his own sister. Shut her down. She'd totally messed up.

Just worried the hell out of him, without helping him at all.

A total fuck up.

She slid the iPhone across her desk, put her hands over her eyes and just cried. And cried. Sobbed and cursed herself. Fucked up. Left her brother to die. Couldn't even tell him. He wouldn't speak to her now. She was going to let him die.

Maybe she could talk to Will. Too late tonight. Tomorrow. Yes maybe he could help. Always took the rational view. Yes Will, tomorrow. Not Mum, she'd freak. And, Dad, when had she last spoken to him? What money launderer was he sucking up to then? No, she didn't want to do that. It had to be Will.

She poured herself a glass of white wine and lay on the sofa. She summoned the music station. *Mellow please*, she whispered. An old Joni Mitchell track came on. "Little Green". It caught her mood and she lay there with the tears rolling down her cheeks. She didn't try to stop them. She felt them on her neck. Tears of helplessness. There was nothing she could do...

An hour or so later she woke up. She'd drifted off, drained by the worry. The mellow music still played - another oldie, "Protection" by Massive Attack. She cut it off, gathered up her things, put the glass in the dishwasher, and headed to the bedroom. She was exhausted and just needed to sleep. Tomorrow was going to be difficult. She needed to re-energise.

In the bathroom, as she combed her hair, her wristpad buzzed. Urgent holo. *At this time?* She couldn't ignore it. She said OK, and the message flashed up: *Say nothing about HOPE at senior team meeting. CY.*

Fuck him, fuck him, fuck him!

Chapter Three. Glastonbury

James had been surprised when Olivia said yes, the first time he asked her out. They'd met at a party in Kennington - one of his friends, Davey, had bought a place south of the river to everyone's amusement. *Great value*, he said. It was a big place, much bigger than any of them could have afforded in Notting Hill or Islington, right at that time in their careers. It was 1988, barely two years after Big Bang. The money was rolling in, but people were still getting used to it. James still had a place in Shepherds Bush. He was happy enough there. It was near his old haunts in Chiswick, where he'd grown up, close to Notting Hill and Hammersmith, and not too far from Chelsea, who he still went to see most home games. That season they were back in the Second Division, and had made a slow start. James was feeling a bit low the night of the party, as Chelsea had bombed at home, 3-1 to Man City, and hadn't yet won a game. Bleak.

He'd been talking football with a few of the lads when three women he didn't know arrived. They didn't look like the City types or Sloans you normally got at these parties. They looked, how to put it, a bit more *Bohemian*. Looser fitting clothes, more interesting colours. Hair a bit more natural. *Less means more*, thought James. He liked their style, and especially liked the girl with long, dark hair and hazel eyes. Every time he looked her way they seemed to pierce right through him. And yet he couldn't even be sure she was looking at him. Why would she? He was just another banker in a sea of bankers...

In the kitchen to get another beer he bumped into Davey, getting wine for a few people. He asked who the three women were, the ones who looked a bit different. "Oh, local arty types. There's loads round here. Studios under railway arches, that sort of thing. Got talking to them at an exhibition just round the corner a few weeks ago. I bought a few pieces there – they're on the walls in the living room if you want to take a look. Nice stuff. Different. Never know, could be worth a bit in future. Quite fancy this investment-in-art lark. Especially when you get to meet interesting women at the same time."

"Sounds alright," James said. "What're their names?"

"The blonde's called Miranda. Got my eyes on her, so keep your hands off, Arnold. Short red hair is Angie. Not 100% sure about the dark one - might be Ellie or Livvy."

"She's nice."

"Oh yeah? Don't think she's taken. Quite shy. Want an intro?"

"Well, maybe, yeah, if..."

"Now c'mon Jimmy boy, you can't tell me you fancy someone then try to wriggle out of it. Time to shake off those Chelsea blues."

They were introduced. The next day James could hardly remember the next hour or so. He just recalled gabbling a lot, wincing at some of his own attempts to talk about art. He liked it - loved it - but wasn't sure how to express himself when the person he was talking to had studied History of Art at Cambridge and was now lecturing at art college, while working in a studio cooperative, some nights and weekends. He felt awkward, embarrassed almost; but she didn't walk away, and those eyes shone brighter than ever. She seemed interested in his work, and when they got onto music they discovered they had a lot in common: reggae, the Smiths, the Waterboys, Kate Bush even. He loved it when she stated that she would refuse to dance to a Kylie Minogue record on principle, when they heard the beats of "I Should be so Lucky", thudding from the adjacent room. His heart sank when she had to go to another party with her friends at ten-thirty. But they swapped phone numbers, and she seemed genuine when she said *give me a call.*

And he gave her a call the next day. And she said yes, she'd love to go for a drink and a bite to eat. And the rest, as James always liked to say to the kids, was history.

***

James Arnold and Olivia Mowbray were married in Ealing Abbey, near to where she had grown up. It was a beautiful October day in 1990. James was doing well at the bank by then, and they invested in a lovely old house in Chiswick, within an easy walk of the river, where they spent blissful summer evenings - when James wasn't stuck in the office, on a deal - walking down to Hammersmith, along Chiswick Mall, where the majestic houses were still out of James's reach; *but not for long*, he said. They'd stop at The Dove, or Old Ship, or stroll down to the places by the bridge. There was no better place in London, they both agreed.

They started a family quite soon after they were married. Will was first, born in 1992. Susan followed in '94, with Charlie making it three in 1997. Will was a serious boy, always questioning things. He shared his Dad's love of football, but deserted Chelsea for Arsenal at an early age. James blamed it on Thierry Henry, but Olivia reminded him that Will developed an independent streak when James was so often at work late. *Keeping us in this place*, James would say to himself, but he stayed quiet about it. It was true that the higher he rose, the more he seemed to do. He'd thought it might start to work the other way at some point, but if that was right, he hadn't reached the point yet.

Susan was thoughtful, creative. Quiet like Olivia, but not shy. Concerned for others. Serious about church - unlike either of the boys. Serious about her friends - intensely loyal. At primary school she was already showing a real interest in history, and in working for good causes. She loved to turn history into everyday stories, and Olivia would help her illustrate them. Together they helped make the Year 5s' play about King Alfred and the Cakes a huge success. At Christmas in 2004, Susan won a special drama award and got free tickets to see Swan Lake in town. *My greatest artistic success,* she'd joke in later years.

Charlie was the wildcard. They hadn't initially planned a third, but Olivia felt, especially when James was away so much, that the family wasn't quite complete. She worried about Susan and Will, especially, becoming too self-absorbed at an early age. A younger presence might bring them out of their shells. And in Charlie, they certainly got what she wished for. Impulsive, reckless, brilliant, fearless, wild. All these words were used to describe Charlie - often by disapproving neighbours or teachers. Will found him a pain, but didn't shirk his big brother duties on Playstation and the football field. Inevitably Charlie was a star at football and athletics, cricket and rugby coming later, but he was unfocused. Training was a bore, the coach was wrong. Even at age seven he was telling the PE teacher who should play where, and how he had to be in the centre, in control. And then he'd spend all his time up front. He demanded that he should be Alfred in Susan's play, but was told firmly that the most any seven year old was going to be was a Viking soldier. Charlie refused to appear.

Susan doted on him though. She'd spend hours with him, telling him stories, helping to build the den at the bottom of the garden, where he'd bring his friends and they'd pretend to be Jedi Knights, or Pokemon. Many a child retired hurt after receiving too many light sabre hits. Charlie always won. Charlie had to win.

Olivia's adoration was mixed with worry. Too many of Charlie's reports were the same. Massively talented, but undisciplined. Great potential, but could he channel it, resist the next thing that came along? She worried about what he'd be like in London, as a teenager. Mixing with the rich kids of West London. He was one himself. Olivia couldn't even see the disciplines of a good secondary school having much influence on Charlie. He was too strong-willed. If there was a drug to be taken she was sure Charlie would be at the front of the queue to try it. And she was worrying about him like this when he was eight!

James played down her concerns. "Much too early to worry. He'll grow up. Admire and nurture his talent. He'll be head boy one day at senior school, you'll see. Needs to decide what his best position at football is though..."

Olivia's worries about Charlie came together with a growing dissatisfaction about her own life. It wasn't so much James's absences - she accepted that their lifestyle depended on him earning the money that he did. It was more her own work. She was still lecturing, she still enjoyed it, but it wasn't really going anywhere. She was still painting, and selling a few bits and pieces, but the cooperative had broken up, and most of her time was inevitably spent caring for the children. Yes, it was fulfilling, but, creatively,

27

she was stagnating. Susan's Saxon play was the most exciting thing she'd done for ages.

In the early 2000s they'd started going to a place just outside Glastonbury for the New Year, with their friends Tony and Mary, and all the kids. They stayed in refurbished farmhouses, and walked over the Tor to get into town. Magical moments: standing at the top of the windswept Tor, gazing over the Somerset valleys; drinking local ciders and eating veggie food in the cafés with names like Crazy Gekko and the Purple Parrot; the New Year's Eve party, when the kids danced to their favourite records and the whole group played hilarious charades. On New Year's Day they'd walk into town and the kids would play hide and seek in the ruins of the old monastery, destroyed in Henry VIII's brutal purges. Tony and Olivia would fantasise about escaping it all and starting up their own café, maybe even a good old-fashioned fry up, as there only seemed to be one at the time, and it was always rammed. James called it fantasy week. Live the dream and then return to reality. Hippies for seven days. Better than nothing at all.

But for Olivia it wasn't just fantasy. A plan started to take shape in her mind. Make a go of the café, sell some art, get the kids into the local private school - its reputation was good. Take Charlie away from London before it captured him. Give Will and Susan plenty of time to adapt before the big exams came calling. She mentioned it to James, tentatively, expecting a push back. But he didn't object. He confessed that the City life was getting to him. He worked his arse off, earned a lot money, but he'd lost the cause. Some of his colleagues had that *belief*. The power of capitalism. The wisdom of the market. The cleansing pursuit of profit. If he'd ever had it, he'd lost it. Pride in the job, his firm, kept him going, but that belief wasn't there. He spent a lot of time thinking about university days: arguing the case for socialism, revelling in punk, new wave, reggae. Drinking, playing football, dreaming of changing the world. And how had he changed the world? By charging huge commissions on obscenely large deals that usually ended in tears for the workers and the ordinary shareholders of the companies they merged, broke up, re-merged, asset-stripped. All in the name of the visceral power of profit. The market. Only the market mattered. Returns on capital. Not identity, loyalty, pride in the product, respect for the community, for history. History was dead. Nothing mattered except tomorrow's profit.

And so James was more amenable to a change than Olivia had ever dared to imagine. They started to look at properties in and around Glastonbury - somewhere to live and a location for the café. They found a refurbished farmhouse just outside the town, and put down a deposit on it. Then they heard that the owner of the Purple Parrot had decided to move on. They took on the lease. Everything was in place to live the dream.

They told the kids when they were in Glastonbury for New Year, 2005. Figuring that while they were enjoying the place, they'd feel better about the change. Will seemed OK, once he knew that he'd be going to a decent school. It washed over Charlie, who was intoxicated with walks over the Tor - he was the fastest up there every time - and preparations for the New Year's Eve dance with his mate John, Tony and Mary's boy, who was a couple of years older, and a hero to him. Susan was different. "What about my friends? Will I ever see them again? I thought I was going to St Paul's, like Alicia and Charlotte. I'll have to make new friends. What if they don't like me?" She ran to her room and cried.

Olivia gave her a couple of minutes and then went up to her. "It will be fine - honestly, darling. You'll stay in touch with Alicia and Charlotte and all the others. They can come down for holidays. You'll make loads of new friends. It's a nice school. We've checked it all out. You'll like, it, really like it. I promise."

"You promise?"

"I promise, I so really, really promise. And we can make our own café. Decorate it together. Make it the best place in Glastonbury. Friendly to schoolchildren. You can bring your friends there and we'll give them a special welcome."

"Really, Mum, really?"

"Really, I promise, from the bottom of my heart, my darling. You'll be so happy, I promise."

29

***

And so, in July 2005, the *Marquee Moon* cafe opened on Glastonbury High Street. James's choice of name. He'd always loved the Television record of the same name, and it sounded right for Glastonbury. The Marquee Moon had all the healthy food and drinks like all the other cafés, but you could get a bacon bloomer too, or the all-day breakfast, with all-local produce. It was quickly a success. People loved the music - carefully selected by James and Olivia - and the food, and the atmosphere. The school kids kept the place lively at three-thirty until five every weekday afternoon, and in the holidays, when it became the place to hang out, with Susan in her element. Olivia adorned the walls with her paintings, with a new line that expressed the vibes of Glastonbury and exalted the centrality of the Tor in a world of ley lines and mysticism. They sold well, better than anything she had ever managed in London. James started by managing the café, as well as frying the bacon, but soon got someone in to help, as he wanted to keep some fund management interests going. Keep his oar in, make some money. He teamed up with a few guys based in Oxford and played the Far Eastern markets, exploiting the imperfections that remained. He hired a graduate from Bristol, who'd applied to their advert in the Guardian, to help run the café. Her name was Emma Westcliff; she was 24, she'd studied English at Nottingham, but had drifted for a while afterwards. She'd had a job at Pizza Express in Bristol which could have led to management opportunities; but after going to Glastonbury festival a couple of times, she felt the pull of the place, and found a job waitressing at the Crazy Gekko.

That was her CV for the management job at the Marquee Moon. Pizza Express and the Crazy Gekko. And an English degree. She was also very beautiful. Wavy blonde hair, dark eyes, slim, dressed in an indie style. Green Doc Marten boots, black jeans, black T-Shirt with Joy Division's "Unknown Pleasures" album cover on the front, the day James interviewed her. Leather jacket hanging off her shoulder when she arrived. He was immediately smitten. She had real potential, he told himself. She was intelligent, feisty, and had a nice manner with the customers - he had seen her in action at the Crazy Gekko. The job was hers.

And Emma was a success. She quickly took on the day-to-day management, kept the other staff happy and motivated, and was welcoming to Susan, who liked to get involved at weekends and in the holidays. (Will refused to have anything to do with the venture). James watched from the food counter with admiration as she charmed the customers, from old hippies to local mums with their kids at lunchtime, to the American tourists making an excursion from Bath, and the surge of teenagers in the late afternoon. He loved the way she had a smile for everyone, the way her T shirts rode up as she served the food, giving just a glimpse of her pale midriff. And, most of all, he loved it when they got together after the café closed at seven and counted the takings together. Olivia would join them sometimes and help plan the menu for the next day, but usually she went back home to attend to the kids. Taking stock at seven o'clock became the highlight of James's day. Cracking open a couple of bottles of Orchard Pig cider - dry for James, medium for Emma - and watching her frown if the numbers didn't add up first time. They started to share stories about their past lives with each other, and six months after Emma's appointment, James suggested a visit to the local pub to celebrate the success of the Marquee Moon. They asked Olivia, but she had an art club to go to after feeding the children.

The evening went by in a whirl for James. They had four or five pints - he'd lost track in the bliss. It felt like that evening when he first met Olivia. Time stood still. He offered to walk Emma home and she accepted. She took his arm: he felt a warm glow of protectiveness. When she stumbled, he held her firmly and wanted to kiss her. *Not yet, not yet.* They got to her place and they hesitated. "Thanks for a lovely evening," she said, smiling one of her ice-melting smiles. "Thank you for being such good company," replied James, touching her shoulder as he dared to kiss her cheek. She turned to face him full on, and so he kissed her on the lips. They held each other and kissed again, longer, slower. And then they just held each other close for what seemed like forever.

31

James pulled away. Then hugged her again. And kissed her again. And then she said, "I'd better go in. Thank you so much James, for everything." James just smiled and said, "See you tomorrow then."

"Yeah, tomorrow..."

***

On the first of April, in 2008, James and Olivia hit their family with a bombshell. Will, of course, said it had to be the worst April Fool joke of all time, but it was no joke. James and Olivia were separating. James was moving to Bristol with Emma, to start a new venture there. Olivia had found a new manager for the Marquee Moon. His name was Michael, an Irishman who'd settled in Glastonbury. Olivia had got to know him through the Glastonbury arts network. Olivia and James both promised the kids it would be alright. They wouldn't fight. There'd be enough money. The Marquee Moon would stay in business. No-one's schooling would be disrupted.

Dad just wouldn't be around much anymore.

They told the children just after dinner - James skipped his stock-taking with Emma, which had become a bit of an opportunity for cynical jokes for Will over the years. James made the announcement. Olivia looked tearful, then tried to reassure them all about future plans. There was a long silence, then Susan ran up to Olivia and just sobbed, holding her tight. Charlie ran up to his bedroom and put a chair up against the door. Will sat tight, then said, "You might as well go and take stock with Emma, Dad."

"Don't you want to talk?"

"Not really."

Then he got up and left too.

Susan looked up from her Mum's arms and cried, "Just go, Dad. Just go and see your little girl. Don't worry about us. We'll cope..."

"But, I ... wanted to expl..."

"I don't need your explanations, Dad. I've seen it for years. Go and make Emma happy. You can't make us happy anymore."

"I'm so sorry..."

"Just go, Dad. Please."

And so James left. And spent the night with Emma. And never stayed with his family again.

Chapter Four. Lost for Words
(12-05-27)

Nine-thirty, the Directorate of Arts, Sport and Outreach - DASO - Senior Team meeting. Normally Susan didn't mind these meetings. She liked most of her colleagues, especially Millie, who headed up the Urban Outreach team, and Mark, who oversaw the arts. All the arts. The Authority wasn't keen on funding people who then just complained about the government, but it hadn't given up completely. Mark did what he could to help new, young artists, as well as the big institutions. Susan and Mark had been out a few times - films, dinner - but she wasn't looking for anything more than that. She'd started a relationship with a good friend, Ed, in her final year at Sheffield, where she'd studied history. They'd stayed together for six years after university, both working in London, but then he'd been posted to Paris, and Susan wasn't sure she wanted to give up her job and follow him. Not least because she still felt a close bond with her Mum, who'd soldiered on after Dad left with Emma: keeping the Marquee Moon going, with the help of Michael. Susan helped out as much as she could too, school permitting. She was wary of Michael at first, as she thought he fancied her; but she warmed to him, realising his familiarity was just his natural style. A good Irishman, with time for everybody.

And it was as well that she did warm to him, as Olivia certainly did, and eventually Michael moved in with them. Will had gone to university by then - LSE - and didn't seem too bothered when he came back in the holidays. That was Will really - not bothered with anything, or anyone, it seemed. Except Dad. Of all the children, Will stayed closest to James. Ever rational, he'd say to Susan, "It takes two to tango. I don't see why everyone should demonise Dad." Susan would argue that it was Dad who went off with someone else, but Will just came back to his tango point, and Susan would give up.

Will and James would watch Bristol City together, and occasionally they'd get the train up to London to see Chelsea, or even Arsenal, Will's team, if James could wangle the tickets. Susan didn't have any interest in football, but always remembered the disgust Will expressed when West Ham and Tottenham merged in 2022, to form the Stratford Olympians. He was even more disgusted when the inaugural English places in European Elite League in 2024 went to Manchester Purples, Liverpool Atlantic, the Midlands Tigers, Stratford Olympians and the Wembley Warriors. The latter were Chelsea, QPR and if they wanted to join, Arsenal. They declined, settling for dominance of what was left of the English Premier League.

The break up with Ed had been pretty messy, especially as they had so many mutual friends, and Susan was cautious about entering a new relationship. Mark, she thought, was keen, but whenever he suggested anything that hinted at commitment - like a weekend away - Susan always found an excuse not to do it. Usually that she was needed back in Glastonbury - even now, when Olivia and Michael had taken a back seat at the Marquee Moon and got a younger pair in to keep the old institution going. Mark took it all with equanimity, and they remained good friends. Maybe one day...

Yorkminster kicked off the meeting with an announcement that he'd be out of the office most of that week, working on something he couldn't tell them about, at the Cabinet Office. Security-related. Old colleagues from the Home Office. Important. He glanced at Susan as he said it, to confirm that she'd seen his message. She looked down at the table, unwilling to make eye contact. That meant yes, of course. Probably no-one else noticed this interchange, not even Mark. Why would they suspect anything?

They talked for a while about a Directorate-wide awayday they were planning, to get everyone up to speed with the latest objectives of the Authority, and to take the temperature of staff morale. Civil servants hadn't been too welcoming of the coup, but accepted the democratic mandate of the 2025 landslide and carried on working with diligence if not enthusiasm. There were exceptions of course: true believers. Yorkminster was one for sure; so was the rising star in DASO, Peter Edmondson: straight out of private office and given the plum post of Head of Elite Sport Relations. Elite Sport, including the new European Elite League football teams, was very important to the Authority. Sporting success made a lot of people happy. A happy nation was a compliant nation. Edmondson was heading to the Cabinet Office or No 10 in a couple of years' time, no doubt at all. One to keep the right side of. Susan was polite to him, even supportive, when he asked her about the management issues he had in his division. But she was careful what she said to him, especially about her background. Mark hated him, thought he had no talent other than a gift for sucking up to the right people; but Susan urged him not to let it show. He just about managed.

Finally they got around to updating each other on what was happening on their patches. Yorkminster orchestrated the contributions. He kept Susan waiting until the last. *Just no need to do that*, she thought, as the tension grew inside her. Normally it was no big deal, but she felt Yorkminster was taunting her by leaving her until last. Her turn came. She talked about the visit to Base One, and her worries about the boys missing out on a proper education. Her colleagues nodded supportively, but Yorkminster challenged her. "Susan, that's what you tell us every time. It's very generic. What exactly are you worried about? Give us specifics. Is there a risk of extremism? Are there vulnerable individuals? That's what we need to know Susan."

Susan felt a rage swelling inside her. What did he want? Names? Without evidence? She wasn't sure what to say. She wanted to tell him to fuck off. Get out of her life, her family's life. "It's not about individuals Chris. It's about lost opportunities and risks. Not terrorism, but there are gangs. The usual semi-criminal sort. The boys are going to gravitate towards them if they don't have alternatives. Picking strawberries, or potatoes, isn't an alternative."

"Why not, Susan? It's work, they get paid. Better than sitting in a class learning about Shakespeare."

"No it's not, it's just not! If you could see the progress children make just by reading stories, learning how to express themselves, you'd understand."

"Understand what?"

"The transformative effect of language, of description, of interaction, that's what."

"OK, that's better. Give me an example. A real example. One from yesterday."

"You want one. I'll give you one. Let me tell you about a little girl called Amla..."

Oh no, she'd said it...

"Yeah, tell me about Amla, Susan."

"You want to know about Amla do you? A girl so shell-shocked when she arrived, she couldn't speak any language, not even her own. A girl who rushed up to me yesterday, and hugged me and wanted to tell me everything about her life since I last saw her. A girl who calls herself Amie now, because she wants to be English. Who worries about her mother, who still suffers from the nightmares of her past existence, whose husband died as they escaped. Whose brother works the fields instead of finishing his education, who..."

"Who's heading for a gang?"

"Maybe, I don't know; but we could save them, keep them together. Amie's strong enough to help her Mum."

"Sounds like you've fallen for them, Susan. Careful."

"No I haven't! I can just see a family that needs to make a new life. We could help them. Get them out of that camp. It's served its purpose for them."

"And you've fallen in love with little Amie."

"No, don't say that, why are you saying that? Don't you have any compassion?"

"Anyone else have any questions?"

Susan shuddered and tried hard not to cry. Mark went up to her and pulled up a seat. "It's OK Susan, just let it pass now."

"Thanks, Mark, I'll try, but he's such a bastard."

"Would you like to share your conversation with the rest of your colleagues?" said Yorkminster.

"Not really," said Mark.

The meeting broke up. Susan went back to her desk. Yorkminster came up to her shortly afterwards.

"Can we speak for a moment?"

"If you want."

They found an empty meeting room. Yorkminster spoke as soon as they sat down.

"I expect you're wondering why you got those messages."

"You could say that."

"Ah, passive-aggressive, just like you, Siouxsie."

"Don't call me Siouxsie."

"OK, Susan, I won't beat about the bush. We needed to know whether we could trust you. Your brother is a terrorist."

"No he's not, he's a..."

"Terrorist, Susan. Terrorist. No other word for it. We had to know where you stood. The only way to find out was to bring you in on the secret and see how you reacted."

"And?"

"Until that emotional outburst just now, I was feeling pretty confident."

"What do you expect? Have you ever been to one of those Bases?"

"As it happens, no, but that doesn't mean I don't know..."

"It means you don't know."

"As you will Siouxsie, sorry, Susan. But look, I value you, I don't want to move you out just because of your brother. I know you've been a loyal civil servant since the Authority came to power; you're one of my best people. I just need one thing from you."

"Which is?"

"Silence, Susan, silence."

Susan almost said, *and let my brother die?* But she regained her self-control just in time. Instead she just said, "And what do I get in return?"

"Safety, Susan, for you and your family. And little Amie and her family, maybe we could do something for them. Something that saves her brother."

"You bastard."

"That's no way to talk to your boss, Susan. But I'll take it as agreement, unless you say otherwise. Anything else to say, Susan?"

"No, nothing."

"Good, Susan, I knew I could rely on you. Always knew."

He got up and left.

Susan went up to the window and stared out at the backs of the nearby offices. She could see people at their keypads, seeming to stare into space, where the holos were. Over the rooftops, the trees of St James's Park poked out. A formation of geese flew over the trees, descending onto the lake. Susan imagined the tourists walking through the park, carefree. The kids crying out for an ice cream, people taking photos on the bridge. Ordinary life, going on in its ordinary way. Susan so wished she could have a bit of that life right now.

***

Mark suggested a sandwich at one of their favourite cafés that lunchtime, and Susan couldn't really say no. And she found his presence, his calmness, comforting. He didn't probe, just offered to help if there was anything that she needed help with. She assured him it was OK; she'd just been upset with Yorkminster's line of questioning, when he knew that visiting the Bases was an emotional experience for any normal human being. And yes, it was her job, but it didn't stop her being moved by the experience. Mark was understanding - sensitive as always - and Susan opened up about Amie and her family. It felt good to share her feelings with someone who cared. It seemed so natural. Mark never pressed, he just let her talk, putting in a question when it seemed right. Susan started to think that Mark was right for her, but now was not the time to start down that line. But she did want to let Mark know how much she appreciated his support. As they left the café, she turned to him and said, "Mark, I really just need a hug." He grasped her readily, and there, in broad daylight, they just swayed together for a while, and Susan allowed the tears to roll down her face. Mark offered a tissue from his pocket and wiped her cheeks for her. She rested her head on his shoulder, and he held her tight. They looked up and smiled.

No kisses in front of all the passers-by. But a future had started to unfold.

***

Susan left the office at five-thirty. Yorkminster wasn't there to look up disapprovingly, which helped. There were so many things to think about, people to talk to if she dared. She got home at about quarter past six, changed into T-shirt and track suit bottoms, poured herself a gin and tonic, with more gin than tonic, and lay on the sofa. She called up the music system and asked for James Blake's latest. There was something in its gentle anguish, and those disjunctive bursts of electronica, that suited her fragile mood right then. She took a sip of her drink, closed her eyes and let the music wash over her. She stayed that way for about half an hour, thinking but not thinking, just letting the random thoughts collide; maybe something would click, make sense. Not much did at the moment.

She was jolted out of her reverie by a buzz on her wristpad. *Mowbray, Olivia,* it intoned. "Answer," she instructed. The holo shot up. It was her mum, looking anxious. What did she know? Nothing surely. "Hi Mum," she said, sitting up, "Everything alright?"

"It's all fine here, darling, but I'm worried about Charlie. I've tried to call him a couple of times, and he's not answering. It's not like him - even when he's campaigning he normally talks to me. I just wondered if you knew anything."

"No, we've not spoken for a while. He doesn't really trust me much. The government sell-out..."

"That's so wrong, Susan, so wrong: you're just doing your job. And you do so much good up at those Bases. I saw a programme on them the other night. So much better than those places they used to have in France in the tens."

"I know, Mum, but that's not how Charlie thinks. He's still righting the wrong of 2023. Fighting the old battles."

"Not fighting, I hope. He said he was just in the political wing. I hope that's true."

40

"I'm sure it is, Mum. He doesn't tell me much, but when he's in the news, it's always political. I'm sure he knows what he's doing."

"You would tell me if you knew anything, wouldn't you, Susan?"

"Of course, Mum, of course I would."

"It's just that Jack Oldfield is back in town, and I've heard he's not saying good things about Charlie."

"What sort of things, Mum?"

"That there's some kind of plot, and Charlie's disowned him, doesn't trust him anymore. After they'd been friends for so long. He says the power's going to Charlie's head. I'm really worried, Susan. Oldfield could make trouble for him. Knows a lot of gangsters."

"Yeah, he's always been trouble. Could never see why Charlie thought so much of him. Just enjoyed the hero-worship, knowing my little brother. I can't help much, but I'll try to talk to Charlie soon. And you let me know if you hear anything more."

"Alright, darling... sure you're OK? You sounded a bit strained when you came on. Looked it too."

"I'm fine, Mum. A hard couple of days at work. Went up to Base One yesterday. Always moves me, makes me want to do a hundred things to make their lives better. I feel so frustrated sometimes, even though I agree things are better there than the old camps."

"Well, keep believing Susan. That's what's always driven you along. A belief in what's right and good. Keep that, Susan. Don't let anyone take that from you."

"I won't, Mum."

"Promise?"

"Yes, I promise. Love you, Mum."

"Love you too, darling. Take care of yourself now."

"I will. Bye for now."

"Bye, my love."

The holo faded. *So now I'm lying to Mum,* thought Susan. *Who shall I let down next?*

She knew what she needed to do. Contact Will. See if he'd heard from Charlie. Get his take on matters, though she could guess what he'd say.

Just a bit more James Blake first...

***

It was after eight when she stirred from her slumber. She entered that exhausted but blissful daze when the music fades in and out of your consciousness, as you drift in and out of sleep. It seems unreal, a dream, but also deeply affecting. A sound that reaches deep into your soul. As she awoke, Susan tried to remember what she was supposed to be doing. It took a moment or two.

Shit! Will! It'll be past midnight in Ukraine. Oh, I'm so stupid, should have called him as soon as I got in. Stupid, stupid, stupid...

Will was awake when Susan's message appeared on the lo-fi. Will was usually awake. The Ukrainian front line may not have been quite as bad as the First World War trenches, at least not in the journalists' quarters which were located half a mile from the front, but it was never easy to sleep. The missiles went off at all times of the day and night. And in Media Camp, Central Front, there was a constant buzz of chatter, holo calls, shouting, as people came back from the front. There were press and TV from around the world, so someone was always getting ready for a shift. This was world entertainment; although, from day to day, almost nothing of significance happened.

Will was out there for the Financial Times. He'd convinced them they needed a front-line reporter. While he towed the NATO line - he had no choice - he was trying to accumulate evidence to expose this fight for the farce - tragic farce - that it was. Working for the FT, a respectable paper that generally tried to report the agreed facts, which inevitably were the ones fed to it by NATO, or the Authority, gave him cover. Meanwhile he tried to talk to soldiers returning from the front, or to missile operators, or even the few Russian prisoners taken as the battle wore on.

It was badged as the *Battle for Freedom*. When Putin's militias encroached once again on the eastern cities of Ukraine in the early twenties, the Ukraine government called on NATO to guarantee its protection. President Obama, just into her first term, was in no mood to allow the Russians to make any more gains in Ukraine, after Trump had given them carte blanche. The EU was surprisingly united in support of the new US position. The loss of Britain from its ranks had, after some turbulence, led to a determination to act together. Germany, Poland and Lithuania in particular were adamant that the Russian advance had to be resisted. It was agreed that the cities on the Dnieper, among them Kiev and Dnipropetrovsk, would have to be protected, by armies to the east, preventing the Russians from getting close to the river at any of its strategic points. It was a huge undertaking, with ramparts, trenches, new settlements growing up along the key points in the forthcoming battle. The unemployed of Europe poured in to create the defences and form the necessary armies. Critics suggested that the defence of Ukraine was really just a way of breaking out of the recession that had plagued Europe since the crash of 2008, and to keep the increasingly restive young male population under control. It became a primary destination for the refugees still flowing into Europe from the Middle East and Africa. It was truly an international effort.

The Russians responded by building their own fortifications within shooting range of the NATO forces. It was clear what was going to happen - a prolonged struggle - but there was no appetite to find a solution. There were too many short term advantages for the participants. Apart from the Ukrainian people of course, whose destiny was now completely out of their own hands.

England, in the early twenties, was a bit part player. The Labour government was fighting too many other battles to pay much attention to a border dispute in Eastern Europe. But the indecision played a part in the growing support for a change in government. The military was losing patience at not being able to do its bit for NATO, to which the country remained committed after Brexit. And so, once the Authority assumed control, England became one of the most enthusiastic supporters of the defence of the Ukraine.

Will was deeply sceptical about the whole thing. For him, the conspiracy theory was perfect for this situation: this was both superpowers, assuming Russia was a superpower again, pitting themselves against each other for reasons that had little to do with what was best for Ukraine. This was all about the other advantages: the states of emergency that allowed for suspensions of normal democracy, the building projects, the transportation of troublesome population groups to the conflict zones. He wanted to go there and find out for himself.

He'd been with the FT since 2020 - just after Labour was elected, to the consternation of most of the establishment. They had been exciting times, as the government lurched from crisis to crisis. Its economic policy, based on higher taxes for the rich and big corporations and borrowing that no-one liked when it led to hikes in interest rates, started to increase inflation. That was no bad thing, as it added life to the economy, but it was greeted as the apocalypse by most of the media, and led to a rapid loss of confidence in the government's ability to manage anything. The pound was fair game for the speculators, which added to inflationary pressures. It was the best time Will had ever had as a journalist, excoriating the Government's economic incompetence, without offering any real alternatives. It was an easy target, and when the coup occurred, Will and his contemporaries couldn't really complain. They had helped to undermine the one government that had tried to break free from the stultifying economic orthodoxy of the tens.

He didn't see it like that of course, and now vowed to get behind the facade of the Authority, and expose what was really driving it. The defence of the Ukraine seemed like the perfect opportunity.

Unfortunately for Will, the war got real. Measured destruction. But real fighting nonetheless. Over-the-top incursions that seemed like carbon copies of the First World War; missile strikes that mostly missed their targets, but caused great anguish and kept the front on alert most of the time. And then the rains came, rains like they'd never experienced in this part of the world. Part of the global tantrum, the Earth fighting back against its exploiters. Trenches were flooded, ramparts collapsed. Armies were forced to regroup in the cities themselves until emergency reconstruction could take place. The Russians launched a few sallies to take advantage of the turmoil, but in the first major fighting of the war they were pushed back. The stalemate was resumed.

And Will was stuck in the media camp, not far from the city of Kremenchuk. The arse end of nowhere, as far as he was concerned. A long way from Kiev, where all the news was. He'd been promised Kiev in time, but somehow that time hadn't arrived. Even worse, the Russians clearly saw the central front as a weak point in the NATO defences, so there were more incursions, more missiles. There was just nothing going for it, except a more authentic depiction of war. Will wrote some stirring prose about the miseries inflicted on the local population and the young boys (they were almost all boys) in the trenches, but got nowhere nearer what he was looking for. Something that exposed the motives of those in control.

And so, when he got Susan's message on the lo-fi, he wasn't in the mood for sibling affection.

"Will, can we speak?"

"Bearing in mind we may have an audience."

"On the lo-fi? OK, I'll keep it short. Have you heard from Charlie?"

"No, have you?"

"Well, yes, I spoke to him. He cut me off. Doesn't trust me."

"Why not?"

"I'm government."

"Yeah, you are. Why am I talking to you?"

"Oh Will, please don't joke. This is serious. Charlie's in trouble."

"What sort of trouble?"

"Like he-might-die sort of trouble."

"What? How do you know?"

"I just do. I can't say exactly. But can you tell him that they know about Saturday?"

"Who's they?"

"You know. Don't ask more. Can you tell him?"

"I can't initiate contact. We are too closely monitored. Incoming lo-fi is all I can risk. Even that, who knows? You might just have given the game away."

"Please don't say that."

"Sorry, but it's true."

"So you can't help."

"Not really. But if it's so important why didn't you tell him yourself?"

"I tried. He cut me off before I could tell him."

"Why?"

"Like I said, he doesn't trust me."

"Sort it out, Susan. He's your brother."

"Yours too."

"Yeah, but I'm stuck in a Ukrainian hellhole. Not much I can do from here."

"Alright, forget it."

"Sorry, Suze."

"Yeah, me too. Speak to you again sometime."

"OK. Maybe when you don't need help I can't give you."

"Yeah maybe."

She cut off.

Will sighed. *Oh man, why did I say that? She didn't deserve that. What did she mean about Charlie? Nothing I can do. But fuck, she deserved better than that. What am I turning into here?*

Oh God, forgive me, please. Yeah God, get me out of here. Please. And not in a coffin...

***

Susan stared into space. Two calls. Deceived her mother, blanked by her brother. She was on her own. Risk all to save Charlie when she wasn't even sure that anything was actually going to happen? Or play along and hope something might happen before Saturday that would tell her what she needed to do? *Oh God, help me, how do I solve this? What am I going to do?*

She went into the kitchen. *Better try to eat something, though I feel sick. Just some rice or something.* She poured herself a glass of white wine and gulped down half of it in one go. *Careful, careful.* She gulped the rest and refilled the glass. *Take it easy now. Easy. Eat something. Relax. Think things through.*

Her wristpad buzzed. It was Mark. She put him on.

"Hey, Susan, hope you don't mind me calling. Just wanted to see how you were, after lunchtime."

"Oh Mark! I'm so mixed up right now. Sorry, I'm just so... could you come over? I so need someone sensible to talk to. Sorry, I don't mean like boring, just someone who might understand. Sorry Mark, I'm talking nonsense, I just mean..."

"It's OK, Susan, I'm coming over."

***

Mark was there in half an hour - he lived in Fulham, not far from Putney Bridge. When he arrived Susan clung on to him, tears again flowing. Apologising, apologising. "I'm so pathetic, sorry, it's not me."

Mark, as ever, was calm itself. He sat her down, asked if she'd eaten. When she said no, he called up for some pizza - he hadn't eaten either. He poured a couple of glasses of wine, and said, "Tell me everything Susan. It's all safe with me."

And she told him. Everything. The rogue message. Yorkminster. Amie and her family. The calls with Charlie and her Mum. The exchange with Will. Some family history, in fact a lot of family history. It made no sense without that. Made not much more sense with it. Mark listened, built on what she said. She rested her head on his shoulder, his arm around her. She felt like at last she had someone who could help her. Someone who understood. They ate pizza, drank some more wine, and Susan sank to Mark's chest and then just lay with her head on his lap, talking, talking. He stroked her hair, listened and offered his thoughts from time to time. Susan lost all sense of time. She remembered Mark saying that he

47

was sceptical about the message, that it could all be a con by Yorkminster to test her loyalty, but she couldn't remember what he thought the solution was. She woke up in her bed at five, alone, but heard someone breathing heavily in the living room. Mark was on the sofa, under a blanket he'd found somewhere. She must have fallen asleep and he'd put her to bed. And then just roughed it on the sofa. *Gentleman* wasn't a word she'd ever used much, but Mark was the ultimate.

She went up to him and tapped him on the chest. He opened his eyes and smiled. She took his hand and led him to her bedroom...

Chapter Five. Charlie's Journey

Charlie's first encounter with Jack Oldfield was in the school playground in 2005, when Jack came up to him and asked him if he wanted a cigarette. Charlie declined, and when Jack questioned his virility and mocked his long hair, he offered to take Jack out with one punch. Jack liked that, and Charlie quickly became part of the gang. In fact, within a few months Charlie had become leader of the gang, and Jack his loyal sidekick. It stayed that way all through schooldays, even though Charlie and Jack went their separate ways at the age of eleven, when Charlie started at the local private school. They'd meet after school, and sometimes at weekends, although Charlie was often tied up on Saturdays, playing rugby or cricket. Jack knew all the local dealers and became one of the main suppliers of weed and ecstasy to Charlie's schoolmates - with Charlie taking a cut of course. Jack could usually round up the best looking local girls too, if Charlie and his mates from school were thinking of having a party.

"Jack mate, you're a great factotum," Charlie would say, and Jack would glow with pride. He was never quite sure what Charlie meant by that, but it sounded like approval, and Jack craved Charlie's approval. Charlie had that effect on people - an effortless charm, a way of talking to you that made you feel like the centre of his universe. The darkness only descended if you asked him about his family, or the Marquee Moon. "Private matters, I don't discuss them," was all you could get out of Charlie. Jack learned to avoid the subject - his mission was to please *the Boss*, as he started to call him.

At home, Charlie was attentive to Olivia, but didn't tell her much about school, and nothing at all about Jack. Naturally that worried her, especially as she and Michael picked up a bit of gossip in the café about Jack Oldfield's links to Bristol gangsters as the boys hit their mid-teens. Charlie tried to reassure her: "Don't worry Mum, he's a good lad. People are just being snooty about him because he's a local lad who doesn't care much for school. You know I'm not going to get myself in any trouble, with him or anyone else." Which was exactly her concern, of course. But in fairness to Charlie, he did seem to stay out of any real bother - it always seemed to be Jack who'd have the police round his house. (Some local wags suggested that was because they fancied his mother.)

Charlie clashed a bit with Michael as he saw him getting closer to his Mum, but for her sake he usually held his tongue. His biggest rows were with Susan, who knew more about his nocturnal activities and continued to try to persuade him to see his father. Charlie steadfastly refused. "It was his choice to leave us, and he can fuck right off for all time, as far as I'm concerned," was one of Charlie's more measured responses. Susan, after a difficult start, had grown used to seeing James with Emma, and actually became quite friendly with her. After all, the age gap between her and Emma was less than it was between Emma and James. She'd go over to Bristol once or twice a month, and even help out at their café. It became an important routine in her life; together with Michael's steadying influence, it allowed life to be as normal as she could hope it to be.

Charlie, rather against Olivia's expectations, shone at pretty much everything at school. Not just the academic side and sport - where he would have been a shoo-in for rugby and cricket team captain had he not continued his primary school habit of arguing with the coaches about team selection, tactics, and just about anything else - but also in drama and debating. He was a massive hit - especially with the girls - in the sixth form production of *Henry V*. The drama teacher said he'd never seen a seventeen year old throw himself so much into a role. To get Henry V right, Charlie went back to both parts of *Henry IV*, walking round the house quoting Hal and Sir John Falstaff to no-one in particular, as Susan and Will were both away from home by then. He started calling Jack *Sir John*, which bemused but pleased him: it seemed like an upgrade from *factotum*.

So it was no great surprise when Charlie got into Oxford, or that he would study PPE - Philosophy, Politics and Economics. It seemed only a matter of time before he climbed onto the student political ladder. But Oxford bored him, and especially the politics. *Feeble posturing by political wannabes,* was his take on it. He campaigned for *Remain* in the run up to the referendum in 2016; but after the vote for Brexit, which, like so many of his fellow students, he found devastating, he completely lost interest in politics. Drama was his thing - he wondered whether he should have done English - and his social life coalesced around Oxford's thespian community. The College was desperate for him to play rugby and cricket - a Blue in both seemed inevitable - but after the first year, when his fly half skills had the coach alternatively purring and cursing (as Charlie once again broke free from the agreed game plan) he lost interest, and focused on acting.

He met a girl called Francesca - Fran - playing Hamlet to her Ophelia, and that set the seal on his priorities. Fran was from West London, and knew some of Charlie's old friends from Chiswick. She had use of a place in Notting Hill - the basement of her father's huge town house - and London became so much more interesting than Oxford, apart from the drama. PPE seemed largely pointless: the economics bore little resemblance to what was happening in the real world; the politics, equally, seemed too conventional and behind the times. Philosophy interested him, but he never seemed to have the time to get to the bottom of it.

London meant parties and drugs of course. Jack would come down from time to time and quickly established contacts. Fran didn't much like him - *the Oik* was her name for him - and she and Charlie started to row about him. Then, in the third year she gave up drama to focus on her studies - she *was* doing English and wanted to get a First. She and Charlie drifted apart, but he'd got the London bug and ended up staying on friends' floors when an essential party was taking place. After splitting with Fran, he lost the love for drama too. Too many people were friends of Fran's and he knew he was getting the blame for their break up. Or more precisely his relationship with Jack was, and what that was leading them into. But they didn't know, just didn't know. Charlie would send Jack out to get the drugs, but he hardly touched them himself. He boozed, like anyone else, but stayed away from the hard stuff. He liked to stay in control. Always in control.

It was towards the end of his third year at Oxford, when he was making a late effort to salvage a decent degree - for his Mum's sake more than anything else - that he met Rosa. She was doing a post graduate degree in East European Politics. Her father was Czech, mother English. They got talking at a reggae evening round a college friend's rooms. He'd banned Jack from this one. This was going to be a seriously cool evening and Charlie wanted to play the part. Jack dutifully supplied the *ganja*, before retiring hurt to Somerset. Rosa wasn't just cool, she was serious. She was with some political friends: lefty environmentalists. Of course they liked reggae. But so did Charlie: he'd grown up swaying to the beats of Bob Marley, Augustus Pablo, Gregory Isaac. Reggae had been one of his Dad's favourites - Charlie still remembered being lectured at a young age about how the Clash's "Police and Thieves", which he loved, was a cover of a Junior Murvin song. The four track twelve inch of Junior's original was one of Dad's prized possessions. He remembered dancing with Susan to Althia and Donna's "Up Town Top Ranking" as Dad cranked up the volume - and the bass, yeah that bass - when Mum went out to the supermarket. And as he remembered, he felt a pang of something that he didn't understand, something that made him choke, brought a tear to his eye. A sense of the missing years, the years without his Dad. He brushed the feeling aside - now wasn't the time to get nostalgic about his Dad, or anyone else. Because something in Rosa's dark, serious eyes fascinated him.

That night they only talked in the group: about music, art, about Charlie's acting and why he'd given up. He couldn't really explain it. He felt unserious, immature. Rosa and her friends talked passionately about the impending doom facing the planet, if governments didn't act much, much faster. They talked about a protest they were planning outside the Radcliffe Camera and a lot about *hope*. Charlie couldn't quite figure it out, against the pulsating bass lines and the hubbub of party conversations. But he found out a bit about Rosa's past: growing up in France, the US, Islington. Studying politics at the University of Sussex, protesting against fracking. Just as she was leaving, he asked if could see her again.

She smiled, a warm but modest smile - there may even have been a blush in the dim light - and said *of course*. Rosa Skvorecky - he could find her on Facebook.

As soon as he woke up that Sunday, half way through the afternoon, he looked her up, friended her, and, after she accepted, sent her a message. They met in the Turl a couple of days later and realised quickly that they were drawn to each other. Charlie couldn't figure out why - on the surface, they didn't have a lot in common - but he recognised in her a determination, a sense of righteousness, that he understood. And it turned out that her father had also left his wife for a younger woman when she was eleven. They talked about their feelings of bewilderment, anger, loss - and how they'd felt it impossible to compromise. Even now he could see the anger blazing in Rosa's eyes as she described the impact on her mother. He took her hand and said, "I've never told anyone about this before." "Neither have I," she replied, offering her other hand to him...

***

That first night together, Charlie also discovered why Rosa's friends had been talking about hope so much. It was HOPE - the *Holistic Organisation for People and the Environment* - an embryonic group that Rosa and her friends had just become involved in. It had been started up by some of her old Sussex contacts. Initially inspired by the Greens and the new leftist movements that had sprung up around Europe, especially in the Mediterranean countries, it soon transformed into more of an underground affair. The Corbyn mania that took hold of the English left following the 2017 general election, when Labour surprised everyone, including themselves, with the strength of their support - especially from the young - seemed too superficial to the HOPE followers. And the environment seemed to be slipping back into obscurity, as English politics returned to the two party *capital v labour* clash that the establishment found so comfortable. The Greens' attempt at political respectability, with a manifesto for every aspect of a government which they could never form, just seemed like a journey into the

53

mainstream, where all became a bland variant of the established norm. For HOPE, the priority was to shatter the norms, not cleave to them.

Charlie wasn't sure about all of this - it seemed like a path to earnest obscurity, something to debate in the pub, or over a spliff in someone's back room, but not much else. But it meant a lot to Rosa, and that was good enough for him - for the time being.

***

"It's the best comeback since Man United v Bayern Music," Will commented, when Charlie got his results that summer. "And just as undeserved." With some hard graft, focus and confidence in his own ability, Charlie had managed to scrape a First in his PPE finals. "Probably knew the examiners. Charmed them, or more..."

"Will, you're so bloody cynical", said Susan, as they discussed Charlie's surprise news on the holo. "But yeah, I'm as gobsmacked as anyone else. Mum is so happy about it. It's a massive weight off her mind. All the socialising, associating with Jack and his mates, it really worried her. Thought he was letting his talent go to waste. And splitting up with Fran too. She saw her as a stabilising influence. But now they're back together, and she's staying in Glastonbury over the summer. It's all a dream come true for Mum."

"And they all lived happily ever after... can't see that happening. Mum better enjoy it while she can."

***

Charlie and Rosa hadn't launched into a full relationship after that first night together. Their discussion in the pub had felt pretty seismic; and without really talking it through, they both sensed that the time wasn't right to take things further. They both needed time to process it, figure what it was like to share feelings on that level. They saw each other from time to time as term wound down (and party time wound up). It was always in the company of others, but they knew there was something special between them. For now they

54

were fellow conspirators, the only ones in the know. Charlie didn't feel inclined to go to any HOPE meetings - there was too much partying to be done to go along and debate how to stop the world spiralling into environmental catastrophe. Rosa seemed to understand. "Maybe in London, after the summer. When we all know what we are doing and have put some roots down. Until then, we always have Facebook..."

One reason why Charlie wasn't in too much of a rush with Rosa was that he had started seeing Fran again. They'd bumped into each other at an end of year Drama Society party and realised how much they'd missed each other. They agreed that they shouldn't let Jack be an issue between them. For Charlie he just wasn't an issue. More like a little brother. And always ready to do what was necessary, including disappear. Fran tried to start thinking the same way.

So Charlie went home for the summer, and Fran came over. She helped in the café and got on really well with everybody, including Susan, who often came down from London at the weekends with Ed. Olivia fell in love with Fran, and Charlie realised he was too. But still that discussion with Rosa lingered, and he started to think, for the first time, about getting in touch with his Dad.

He mentioned what he'd been thinking to Fran one evening, when they'd climbed the Tor to take some pictures of the sunset. As a pink grapefruit sun disappeared into the Vale of Avalon and the streaks of grey cloud became suffused with gold, Charlie opened up.

"All this beauty, Fran, and being with you, having time to think, it's making me wonder."

"What, Charlie?"

"Well, it's going to sound stupid."

"Tell me, Charlie. You know you can tell me anything. I won't think it's stupid."

"Even if I said I want to marry you?"

"Well..."

"No, just joking. Well, for now. No, it's my Dad. I've been thinking about my Dad. Like, maybe it's time. Maybe you see things less in black and white as you get older, develop your own relationships that aren't affected by other stuff."

"Maybe you do. You want to see him?"

"Maybe... fuck, I don't know, I just..."

"It's been a long time, Charlie."

Fran rested her head on Charlie's shoulder, and took his hand. The last strands of pink and gold were fading over the Vale as dusk set in. They turned to each other and kissed. Charlie trembled, and tears welled up in his eyes. A single teardrop broke free and slowly trickled down his cheek. Fran caught it with her finger, and pressed the moistness against her lips.

"Maybe you need to talk to Susan, Charlie. Your big sister. She still worries about you, you know? About you and your Dad. About what if anything ever happened to one of you."

"Yeah, I've thought about that too. But how can I talk to Susan about it? How can I even ask her? We had such massive rows about it in the past. We just about managed to forgive and forget. Forgive anyway..."

"I could help. I could mention to Susan that you want to talk."

"Could you, could you really? But what if I change my mind?"

"There won't be any turning back, Charlie, but you have to do it. Make a start with Susan, and see how it goes... Time to walk down now."

"Oh yeah, I forgot the torch."

***

The next weekend Fran mentioned to Susan that Charlie needed to talk to her about their Dad. Susan wasn't that surprised - she'd sensed something different about Charlie that summer. Something more reflective, serious even. She put it down to Fran, and the end of university. A big moment for everyone - the end of childhood in a way. Uni was the last stage in the transition. Time to grow up.

It was awkward at first, but then Charlie just let it all out. Apologies for his past behaviour. Sorry about the effect it had on her and Mum. Honest about how devastated he'd been. How it had shattered all the certainty in his life. All the trust. How sometimes he'd felt Jack was the only person he could trust. Susan listened mainly, but spoke of her own hurt - and Olivia's. Even Will's. Susan had always attributed Will's cynical wit as a defence mechanism, a way of hiding his true feelings. There were tears, long hugs, as Charlie crumbled, and became the younger brother again. Susan felt protective, wanted to make sure it would all be alright for her little brother, the one she'd always been so proud of. Charlie even talked about Rosa, and how their shared experience had triggered something in him that he couldn't keep to himself. He swore her to secrecy about that.

Charlie wasn't sure about what to do about Olivia, either. How would she react? Should he even tell her? Susan said that it was essential to be honest with Mum. Nothing could be worse than for everyone except Mum to be in the know. So this time, Susan set things up, as again, Charlie didn't know where to start. And this time the crumbling, the crying, was mainly Olivia's. Charlie became the dutiful son, the strong one, as Olivia talked of her anguish, how she was desperate to see James and Charlie reconciled, whatever happened in the future between her and James. Charlie hadn't really expected this - he'd assumed she'd be hostile to the reunion, even though Susan had said that wouldn't be the case. When he reflected on it afterwards, he realised that his reaction had been all about himself. A bit of anger about the treatment of Mum, but mostly about what it meant for the world of Charlie. He shared these reflections with Fran. "Boys," she said. "No emotional intelligence."

"That's unfair!"

"I know, but..."

"It's true. Yeah, I get it. I'll try harder."

"Don't worry, you're just fine. And I love you the way you are, Charlie Mowbray. Just get to know your Dad again."

***

They met in a little Italian in Kensington, tucked away in one of the side streets. Not so far from Fran's place in Notting Hill. She'd come down to London with him, to provide moral support and give him

57

someone to talk to afterwards. Susan had arranged it all - this was really important to her. She'd said to both of them not to expect too much from this first encounter. Just re-establishing contact would be something. They could decide what they wanted to do from there. It was still a little awkward. They both got there early - James was being shown to the table just as Charlie arrived. What to do, both standing there in public? They shook hands.

"Hey Dad, good to see you, how's it going?"

"Yeah, OK thanks Charlie, great to see you too. How much taller are you than last..."

James choked, and Charlie instinctively put his arm round his shoulder. He pulled it away quickly, and they both smiled.

"Hey, c'mon boy, we've got a lot of catching up to do."

They spent nearly four hours together. They got through a couple of beers each and three of bottles of Chianti. James thought he'd probably drunk most of the wine - it certainly felt like that the next day. The conversation went well for the most part. Charlie talked about university, his unexpected First (James insisted he knew he'd get one) Fran, the cafe, Susan and Will's embryonic careers (which James knew more about), even the latest exploits of Jack. It was trickier when they touched on Olivia - neither of them felt ready to go too deep on that. But there was a sense that it would be possible in time. James was impressed by Charlie's understanding of other people's feelings. "I owe it all to Susan and Fran," was Charlie's reply. "But I saw it in you when you were younger," said James. "Always a leader. Always the one who could talk to anyone." Charlie blushed a little, and moved the conversation on.

James talked a lot about work, and especially his new venture in London. He'd bought into a specialist fund manager with his Oxford partners and was spending a couple of days a week in London, getting back into the swing of things. He said he could get Charlie a job in the firm writing economic reports - a First in PPE wouldn't do him any harm - and Charlie said he'd think about it. He skirted around the details of Emma and their child, saying more about the café, which was struggling a bit. Heavy competition in Bristol.

Forcing the prices too low for the overheads. Charlie knew a bit about this from Susan - and knew too that Emma was feeling restless. A bit confined. She was reaching out to the alternative music scene in Bristol, and James, despite his love of music, and new sounds, wasn't someone she really wanted around for that. Charlie said nothing about this. *Dad's call whether he wants me to know.*

The evening flew by. When they got up to leave at just after eleven, it really did feel like they'd rediscovered each other. Outside the restaurant, as they parted company, James gestured to give Charlie a hug. Momentarily Charlie shied away, and then grasped his father with all his strength. "Don't ever let this fucking happen again, Dad," was all he could bring himself to say as tears streamed down his face. James could feel the hot tears, but didn't look Charlie in the eye. He just held him, and whispered, "Never again, my boy, never again. I promise a million times over."

***

By the time Charlie got back to Fran's place he could hardly remember what he and James had talked about. "It's crazy, Fran, it's all a blur already. We talked about everything, pretty much - not much about Mum or Emma, but everything else."

"So everything but the two most important things," said Fran, with a big smile. "Don't worry, two boys meeting for the first time in ages aren't going to plunge into their inner emotions."

"Not like girls?"

"Yeah, we'd probably be there within five minutes."

"Couldn't think of anything worse. But we will discuss those things, Fran. We vowed to stick together - forever."

Charlie choked as he said it.

"Come here, let me give you a big hug."

And for the second time in an hour, Charlie wept. In the arms of his love, his conscience. His salvation.

With a new life ahead.

The second half of the summer passed quietly for Charlie in Glastonbury, as he immersed himself in local life. Fran went travelling around Europe with a few of her girlfriends from college and Charlie got a job at a local farm, working the fields at harvest time. He struck up a rapport with the other farm workers, and happily spent time with them in the pubs afterwards, discussing the day's work, the changing seasons, crop prices, the government's incompetence, and who was seeing who in this community where everyone knew everyone else. Jack and his mates were around too, and Charlie found himself going back to schooldays, reviving the double act with Jack, to everyone's amusement. He even had a fling with one of the girls he'd been friendly with at the parties he and Jack used to arrange in the old days. Nothing serious: Fran wouldn't mind if she ever heard. Well, hopefully not. Jack was instructed to stay tight-lipped just in case.

He enjoyed the return to what he thought of as reality, and it gave him time to talk to Olivia - about his dinner with James, about her life with Michael in Glastonbury, about her pride in Susan who was doing so well in the civil service fast stream, and her worries about Will, who had landed a good job in journalism, but seemed so restless, so eager to find the wrong in everything. Charlie pointed out that that was the point of most journalism, and ultimately that had to be a healthy thing, even if it brought innocent victims with it. "Look at Trump", said Charlie, "Accusing anyone who probes into his affairs of fake news, trying to intimidate the press into acquiescence. Look at the Brexit lies, the press just swallowed them, deployed them as propaganda, and now we are heading for disaster. Will at least asks the hard questions, has some integrity. We need people like him right now. The boys I work with are worried about how the seasons are becoming more extreme - that's global warming, nothing else. That's on top of the uncertainty now of Brexit. DEFRA doesn't have clue. And the boys are beginning to wake up to the fact that trade deals with the US and Canada, Australia and New Zealand, are going to expose British farmers to way more competition. We need journalists like Will to wake up the nation from its stupor."

"You never worried much about these things before, Charlie. You were pretty damning about politics at Oxford weren't you?"

"Yeah, but the world has taken a crazy turn - and I met some interesting people late on at college. I like their way of thinking."

***

They'd hired a cottage just outside Devizes, not far from the Kennet-Avon canal. Charlie remembered it from the days just after they came down to London after university. Charlie and Fran had been cycling along the canal, from Reading to Bath, and hit some rough terrain in between Hungerford and Devizes, when cycling in the heat and absorbing the impact of the bumps and ruts in the drought-hardened ground started to take its toll, and they just craved refreshments, any refreshments. The scenery had been some compensation – the plant life along the canal's bank so verdant, lush and overgrown, shimmering in the gentle breeze. This was the west of England, but Charlie couldn't help but think of "Apocalypse Now", which he'd found himself watching with Will, on Christmas nights after his Dad left. It was that, or "Bladerunner", or "Lost in Translation". Dad's favourite films. Except he wasn't there. Only him, Will and sometimes Susan, although the only one she really liked was "Lost in Translation". The other two she dismissed as boys' films. And now the languid water, the undergrowth, the greenness of it all, the distant hills were taking him back. Anything could be round the corner. Eventually it would be Devizes. *Please, where the hell is Devizes?!*

Then, almost on cue, in an echo of "Apocalypse Now", when Captain Willard and his crew came upon the staging post where the guards sat in a bunker bombed out of their minds, listening to Jimi Hendrix's "Purple Haze", Fran and Charlie heard the faint rhythms, getting stronger, of a rock'n'roll song. It wasn't familiar at first, but then Fran got it. "This is weird, I can hear T.Rex. My Mum used to love Marc Bolan. What's going on?"

They cycled on, and came upon the source of the music. A pub on the river; a small beer festival, and a band. Two blokes – one on guitar, the other on a Roland keyboard. Marc Bolan, Elvis Presley, Mick Jagger filtered through a West Country accent. It was funny, but great too. In the middle of the afternoon, everyone having a good time; the mums and children dancing to the music while most of the men clung on to their beers. Fran and Charlie couldn't drink beer – they needed sugar. Coke and Mars bars. But they stayed for a while and loved the atmosphere. A sultry English country day. No pretence, just people enjoying themselves, with music at the centre of things. They could both relate to that.

They had plenty of time before the darkness fell, so took a diversion into the village. It was lovely. The high street was classic thatched cottage territory; elsewhere in the centre the local grey stone dominated. It was miles from anywhere else. A place to escape to, or hide. They vowed to return one day. But that hadn't happened, until now. *Wednesday, 12 May 2027.*

***

They'd been through the plans a couple of times. Rosa leading both sessions. This was the difficult time. Still three days to go. Close enough for the tension to build, not close enough to close out other thoughts and just focus on the objective. The mood in the room was solemn. What they were planning was audacious. It would be their biggest moment yet. But was it achievable? There was no margin for error. Timing was paramount. Speed and surprise. Synchronisation. Charlie said all of this as he closed things off. He was the leader now, the front man. Rosa did the planning, he did the rhetoric. He would make the speech to millions, live on TV. Then people would really know who HOPE were, and why their Cause mattered – for everyone. This was lift off. No longer just an irritant to the Authority. This was Charlie's big moment, his chance to show you could maximise impact without slaughtering innocent people. He would have none of that. Some people in HOPE had started to talk about necessary sacrifice, and Rosa was ambiguous

62

when they discussed it. Charlie worried about that, but hadn't challenged her directly yet. She was going along with his idea, and was helping to make it real. That was enough for now.

They'd dispersed over the previous week, and come together in a house in that village in the middle of nowhere which Charlie and Fran had discovered back in 2018. Old university friends getting together to discuss his ideas for a new play, Charlie told the owners. Inspired by Henry V at Agincourt. They liked that. *The days when England was great*, they said. *Not like now. All gone to the dogs now, though that Authority is doing its best to get things back to where they should have been before the Socialists got in.* Charlie nodded and smiled a lot and thanked them for the lovely place. The money was already in their account. The owners were happy, and that was the last they saw of them.

They were six. Charlie, Rosa, Luke, Gabi, Mike and Dan. Luke, Gabi and Mike had been around at Oxford, though Charlie hadn't known them particularly well. Dan had joined them on the recommendation of James. He was sympathetic to their ideals, but more important, he knew how to fly a jet copter. In fact, James had told Charlie, he was one of the best around. And they'd need someone good, if they wanted to get out without anyone getting hurt.

Rosa's talk through the plans was meticulous. Charlie had heard it many times; for the others it was the first time, although they'd practised the manoeuvres with the hover packs a few times on Wormwood Scrubs. That wasn't a big deal – hover packs were all the rage. The Scrubs was a great place to give them a go. Man really was starting to fly. But Charlie's familiarity with the plan allowed his thoughts to drift, and they kept drifting back to that call with Susan. His big sister. Who'd always cared for him. Why had she said what she said? So emotional. What was she worried about? Why did she mention HOPE's contacts with the INSF and the Northern Islamic Defence League? And why had he been such a bastard and cut her off? His big sister. The one who cared for him most through all the hard times. His rock. He didn't need this, but something nagged at him. What did she know? How could she know? Surely she would never be part of some operation monitoring him. Surely she would never do him down. Sure, she was part of the Authority, but he knew she didn't believe in it. Knew she hated her boss. Knew she was committed to making things better for people, especially on those refugee bases. Knew she was the best person in the world, and he'd cut her down.

Nothing he could do now. Had to focus on the mission now. Make it up to her later. Explain the tension, the stress, the doubt, the paranoia that came with being undercover, planning a massive statement to the world. Fuck it! So massive. So dangerous. But yeah, they were going to do it. Had to now. Everything had built up to this moment.

"The margins for error are tiny, Charlie". Gabi looked away from Rosa as she spoke. Rosa shot daggers towards her nonetheless. Charlie winced as he watched. "Won't take them long to see us leaping out of our seats," Gabi continued. "How much time have we really got to grab the players?"

"Enough," muttered Rosa. "We've planned this down to the minutest detail."

"I know – I'm not doubting that. I would never doubt that. But the place will be swarming with security. The slightest thing goes wrong and…"

"Yeah, Gabi, the best we can hope for is ten years in prison. But things aren't going to go wrong. It's all worked out. We looked good in practice. The kit was perfect. Wasn't it?" Charlie looked imploringly at Gabi, remembering how those pale grey eyes had sucked him in, cast a spell over him. Still did, but couldn't now. Time to focus. Only one objective now.

"Yes it was. But I just worry…"

"I understand, Gabs" – Rosa's daggers heading his way now – "But like Rosa said, we've worked it all out. We know the security is poor at pitch level, and we have the element of surprise. It's got to be perfect, I know, but it can be perfect. It will be. We are a team. We have a cause, a belief, don't we?"

"Yeah we do. Of course we do. I just want to be sure."

"I know. I understand. You are all going to feel apprehensive. Especially now. It's still three days away. Three days to sit around and worry. It's natural. But this is when we have to trust each other. Remember what we have to do as individuals and believe in our comrades. Do we all have that belief?"

Charlie looked around the room. Looking for eye contact. No-one was looking at the floor, were they? He felt a shiver down his spine as he saw the eyes fixed on him. The nods of affirmation. No words, just those gestures. The ones he needed. With a challenge to him: *we are with you, but we depend on you. Are you ready to lead us? Our fate is in your hands.*

"OK Rosa, take us through the escape plans one more time…"

Chapter Six. Lunch
(13-05-27)

Susan woke up at 7.30. She'd slept through her alarm. She'd been dreaming that she was with Mark, under the covers. She *had* been with Mark, under the covers. But he wasn't there now. She wasn't wearing anything as she eased herself out of bed. She had been when she went to bed. And Mark had been there, yes he had. She put on her dressing gown and went to the bathroom to freshen up. She felt really tired, but elated too. Things felt good, much better than they had the night before. Before Mark came round and changed everything. Her worries hadn't gone away, but she had someone to share them with now. Someone who wanted to listen, who understood. Someone who cared.

But where was he?

She shuffled into the kitchen. It felt stuffy; things were getting warmer. Unusually warm. She opened a window and a rush of thick air hit her. It was blowing a gale outside. The frame of the window rattled and she pulled it back – didn't want a broken window compounding her problems, or getting in the way of the pleasing memories of the night. She looked out of the window, out at the terraced houses opposite, without really looking at them. Just thinking, or not even thinking. Just dreaming, remembering. *Lost in a dream* – wasn't that a song? Another one of Dad's favourites. She choked at the thought; the tears almost came again. She looked up at the framed poster on the wall. *Planet Earth Fights Back – Water Stories. Tate Modern 21 April – 10 June 2026.* Floods, droughts, howling storms, sea surges. Captured in black and white. One of the most amazing, awe-inspiring, frightening exhibitions she'd ever been to. Beautiful images of calamity and profound change all over the world. Planet Earth reasserting its rights, teaching man a lesson for his transgressions and neglect, for the disrespect of decades. There had been speculation that the Authority would stop the exhibition happening. She was rather proud that her department had fought off the Home Office, who'd argued that it would stoke up anger, risk protests, encourage groups like HOPE to pull more stunts. DELE argued that it was important that the Authority showed itself to be enlightened, open about the challenges faced by the world, at the same time as it maintained public order and economic stability. Confident that it was doing the right thing.

Mark had played a blinder on this one – he'd persuaded Yorkminster to back the enlightened cause, against his natural inclination to suck up to the Home Office. And between them they gave their Secretary of State the arguments to win the debate in the Domestic Order Committee. Susan did her bit too. She'd pleaded with Charlie on the lo-fi not to use the exhibition for any protests. DELE needed a success if it was going to be listened to in future arguments. It was hard to face down the law and order lobby. She wasn't sure whether Charlie had listened – he was non-committal when they discussed it. But it all passed off peacefully – just a few demos from government-approved greens and world-peace campaigners. Harmless, and good for the Authority's image abroad.

For a moment longer Susan gazed at the watery haze and shadows captured in the image of the flooded Fenlands: a heron in silhouette, an elevated road on the horizon, rising out of the marshes. Beautiful. Tragic, but beautiful. *And Amie…*tragedy and beauty again. Hope rising eternal. Another tear came to her eye, and then … *uggh!* A blow to her chest, as an image of Yorkminster, smiling superciliously, intruded on her daydream. *Oh God, what will he be like today? What is he going to say next about Charlie? About Amie? Oh please, Mark, help me!*

There was a note on the kitchen table. *Thought I better nip home and change clothes before going into work. You looked so lovely lying there, so peaceful, I didn't want to disturb you. See you in the office, for the next battle. Lunch? Love, M xxx.*

And this time Susan did let the tears come. Warm, trickling over her cheeks. They felt good. She could face the day. She had Mark now.

Just before she set off for the office, her wristpad buzzed. She instructed the holo to bring on the caller, fearing it might be

Yorkminster. It was James, her Dad. When had he last called? The tips of her fingers tingled. Was there bad news?

"Dad, what…?"

"Sorry to disturb you at this hour, Susan. Sorry I haven't been in touch. I'm well, just sorry; but look, I need to talk to you urgently. Not on holo. Can we meet this lunchtime? Will called me. Sounded really nervous. Just said they know about Saturday. That's all. Said speak to you."

"Oh… Yes, of course. Where? How about St James's Park? On the bridge."

"Perfect. One o'clock?"

"Sure."

"Great. We'll catch up then. Better go now."

The holo faded. Susan's mind reeled. Looped. Will, Dad, Charlie, Amie, Yorkminster, Mark. And Mum, what about Mum? *Deep breaths. Stay calm. Glass of water. Planet Earth. Yeah, Planet Earth, bigger than any of this. This is just our problem. We can sort this. Just need to be calm. Talk to Mark. Mark will help. Must be about Charlie, but what? What did Will say? Just they know about Saturday? What did he say about Saturday? Calm. Go to work. Talk to Mark. Mark will know what to do.*

Oh fuck…

***

She got off the train at South Kensington. It was hideously crowded, and hot. She was stressed enough already. She could feel her breathing getting faster in the rank air of the tube, her palms getting clammier. And she needed time to think, before getting sucked into the demands of office life, and being Susan Mowbray, senior civil servant, a person that others looked to for advice, direction, reassurance. Team meeting at 10.30, discussion with Treasury at 11.30, about funding some new projects at the Bases. Dad after that. Needed to talk to Mark too. And the report, had to finish that. When? Afterwards, but what would be in her head after the meeting with Dad? *Oh my God, take it one thing at a time. The only way…*

68

The wind still blew hard as she came out of the station and made her way down past Onslow Square, along Sydney Street in the direction of the Kings Road. You could taste the dust, the dirt. Scraps of paper, food packaging and the remnants of old leaves swirled in the currents. People scurried along the streets, heads down in the blast of the wind, circumnavigating road works, trade vans, bin collectors, Chinese tourist parties. The daily ebb and flow of London life, oblivious to Susan's troubles. After crossing the Fulham Road, she cut through to the grounds of St Luke's church: a haven, a place for reflection. It was place she liked to come after work. The backstreets of Chelsea were restful, colourful, especially at this time of year, when the wisteria adorning some of the cottages bloomed a pale violet. She found an empty bench and gazed at the gothic tower, the arched windows of the old church, built in the 19th century, but homage to a mediaeval past. Timeless, a sanctuary of hope, beauty, mystery, secrets. Secrets. Susan had too many secrets. She needed to unburden herself of her secrets. She wanted to cry out to Charlie, the Authority: *Stop! Stop the madness! No-one is going to win. There's no point in any of it. Why can't we all work together for a better future? Why do people have to conclude that protest, subversion, is the only way? Why can't people listen to each other, respect each other? Why can't we focus on the needs of the dispossessed like Amie and her family, on the needs of our planet, rather than power, egos? Why do arseholes like Yorkminster rise to the top? Why are people's differences always a threat to the establishment? Why can't they be welcomed, nurtured, absorbed, instead of being crushed, rooted out? Why won't our leaders listen to the words of the Christ they still claim to act for?*

Why, why, why?

A group of young school children filed by. Smart in their dark green blazers. The boys' ties flapping around their necks in the wind, the girls holding on to the hems of their dresses. Chattering, pointing at the church, the resplendent flower beds, a squirrel scampering across the grass. Innocent, full of anticipation as they walked up to the museums, she guessed. Lucky children, the children of the moneyed classes. The people that the Authority was there to defend. They'd have a good life - a good start, anyway. Susan wanted Amie to have at least some of that life too. Imagine her delight in wandering around the Science or Natural History museums. Places of wonder and learning for people of any age. Glimpses into a prehistoric past and the unlimited potential of the future. If we didn't totally fuck up the planet and each other first. She sighed. *I can't do much about that today, but what about Dad, my family? How can I protect them all, sometimes from themselves? That's what I've got to do, and the only person I've got to help me is Mark. I must speak to him before the meetings start.* She got up, glanced back at the dark green blazers in the distance, the splendour of St Luke's, and headed through the backstreets to the Kings Road.

It was just before ten when she got to the office. Her team greeted her with smiles; she returned them. That was easy enough. A small step. She looked across the rows of identikit desks, the sea of grey and blue, hoping for a sight of Mark. She felt a jolt of relief when she saw he was there. After calling up the holo and checking for any urgent messages – there were none, thankfully – she went over to him.

"You made it." Mark looked up from his screen with a conspiratorial smile.

"Yeah. I walked from South Ken, just to clear my head. Can we find somewhere to talk about something?"

"Sure".

They found a small room that hadn't been booked out. It had a couple of rock hard grey sofas and a glass coffee table. DELE's *values* were stuck on the wall. *FULFILMENT IN LIFE*, of course. *RESPECT FOR ALL. DEVELOPING POTENTIAL. WELL-BEING. VALUING OUR CULTURE. PROTECTING OUR PEOPLE.*

Yeah, well, Yorkminster seemed to have jettisoned most of them as he'd clambered up the ladder, thought Susan. Just couldn't get him out of her head, even now, with more important things to talk about.

"You look troubled, Susan", whispered Mark. "Not about last night I hope."

"No, no, not at all. It was wonderful. You are my saviour."
Mark gulped as she said this; his eyes burned bright into her. It felt
like he was transferring some of his strength into her. She felt a
buzz of energy go through her, returned his look with one of
longing. Longing for peace.

"Tell me."

"Oh Mark, my Dad called just before I left the flat. Will called
him. Just said they know about Saturday. And probably that
Charlie's in danger. That's what I told him. I don't know why Will
called Dad instead of Charlie. He said talking to Charlie would be
too dangerous, but I don't know why he told Dad. And I've agreed
to meet Dad this lunch time." Briefly, there was a look of
disappointment on Mark's face, but he quickly reassumed his look
of concern.

"Where?"

"Just in St James's Park. I've got to go. Sorry, I wanted to be
with you, really wanted to be with you. But I have to do this."

"Of course you do. Do you want me to hover? You Dad doesn't
know me. I could."

"No, it's OK. I'm not worried about Dad doing anything, just
about why Will called him. It means he gets drawn in. I don't know
what he's going to say. We've hardly spoken these last few years.
And I'm worried about Mum. Will this all get back to her? I really
don't want her freaking out with worry. Oh, Mark, it's just a fucking
mess."

"It's OK. Be calm. One thing at a time. Talk to your Dad. See
what he says. Work it out from there. One thing at a time. I'd like to
be there, just in case. He won't know."

"You sure?"

"Totally. Just behind. He won't know. Where are you
meeting?"

"The bridge."

"Perfect. I can just be another civil servant taking a walk round
the park. Having my lunch."

"Oh Mark, I don't want to suck you into this."

"I'm in already. I want to be."

71

"Oh Mark…"

Susan looked down at her feet and sobbed. Mark put his hand on her knee and squeezed it gently. Enough to convey how much he cared. They couldn't do more – there was a window into the room. She closed her eyes and regained control.

"Thank you so much, Mark. I feel I can do this because of you."

"I'll do anything for you, Susan."

***

The wind had subsided a little by lunch time. The atmosphere was still heavy. It felt like thunder was brewing. Susan got there early and waited on a bench within eyeshot of the bridge. Mark, with his sandwich and a book, was two benches away. Geese wandered by, lords of their manor, searching for the scraps the human beings always left. Two squirrels danced by the railings and dashed off towards the trees. Tourists thronged on the bridge, taking their pictures of Buckingham Palace and the pelicans on their little island. And, shortly before one o'clock, James appeared on the bridge. Susan's heart thudded. She felt sick. Where was this going to lead? She got up and walked towards the bridge. She looked back and saw Mark get up and move towards her bench. *Don't make it obvious*, she couldn't help thinking, and felt bad about thinking it.

As she approached the bridge, James saw her. He moved towards her and they met just before the bridge began its incline. They both stopped. They stared at each other like friends who had forgotten what the other looked like. And then Susan crumbled. She shook, and James moved tentatively towards her. Susan looked up and implored him. It was time to be Dad to his little girl again. He moved to hug her and met no resistance. Just a sobbing, trembling child – his beloved daughter. They held each other tight for what seemed an age.

"My darling, I'm so sorry."

"Oh Dad, what are we going to do?"

"I don't know, Susan, but let's go somewhere and talk."

Susan looked back and saw Mark on the bench where she had been sitting.

"Oh, Dad, I just realised I forgot I was meeting someone this lunchtime. He's on that bench over there. There's so much to think about at the moment. Can I just go and apologise?"

"Of course you can."

Susan went back to Mark. "It's OK, Mark, really. You don't have to follow us. I just said I'd forgotten to cancel my lunch with you. He doesn't suspect anything, I don't think. It really is alright."

"You sure?"

"Yeah, really. We'll talk later. Tonight."

"Tonight?"

"If you want to."

"I so want to."

"Me too."

Susan closed her eyes and sighed. Mark just gazed lovingly.

And she went back to her Dad, staring out at the placid waters.

***

They went to the restaurant on the edge of the lake. They waited for ten minutes to be seated, eager to talk about Charlie, but unable to. Instead they talked about Susan's job, and the Bases, and Amie and her brother. James wanted to help. Was there a way of buying them out of the place? Susan said it seemed that way, but she was against people getting favours because they had money behind them. James chided her for that. "If you care, use the tools at your disposal." Susan had real problems with that. She had come upon Amie, but there were so many others in the Bases with similar backgrounds, similar stories. It would be wrong to favour one family just because she'd formed an attachment to them. Solutions for all the people there were needed. "That is not what happens in the real world," said James. "Think about it. My offer to help stands."

They were seated. They stared at the menus at first, and then stared at each other. James put his hands out on the table. An offering. Susan declined. Now was not the time. James withdrew the offer, feeling hurt, but knowing it had been a mistake.

"So Dad, what did Will say to you?"

"Just what I told you on the holo. They know about Saturday. He didn't say what about Saturday, except I needed to talk to you."

"Dad, how much do you know about Charlie and what he's up to?"

James sat back on his seat, ran his hands through his hair and sighed. "Can I be honest with you?"

"Of course you can."

"Everything. Most things anyway. I'm supporting him."

"How?"

"Money, mostly."

"Oh my God, Dad. Why?"

"I promised I'd never let him down again."

"Guilt then?"

"You can call it that if you want. I call it love."

"Love? Encouraging him in his crazy escapades? Do you know what he's planning for Saturday?"

"I do. Do you?"

A waiter came over to take orders. It helped break the tension. They scanned the menus and ordered, asking for a jug of water. No mood for anything stronger.

"All I know is the Authority knows that Charlie and his gang are planning a kidnap attempt at Wembley on Saturday. Of some footballers I assume. And that there's a termination order."

"Termination?"

"Shoot to kill, I guess. I don't know."

"How do you even know this?"

"I got a message on my work holo late one night. I don't know how or why, except that my boss is in on it. I thought it might be a hoax at first. Some attempt to tease some information about Charlie out of me. But it doesn't seem so. But I know my boss knows. He's such a bastard. He's on some committee planning the counterattack, I think. Dad, if you have any influence on Charlie, tell him to call it off and make himself scarce. He's going to die otherwise."

74

"I don't think that can happen."

"Why not?"

"There's too much riding on this. This is Charlie's mission. HOPE's mission. This will take them into the big time."

"Not if they are all dead."

"I doubt if the Authority knows that much. I don't know how they would have found out anything. The team is as one. The arrangements are watertight. There will be a strong element of surprise."

"How do you know?"

"I've made a lot of them."

"Oh fuck, Dad!"

"Susan…"

"Dad, what are you doing? Indulging Charlie because you deserted him for years?"

"Don't say that, Susan," James murmured.

"What am I supposed to say? My brother is going to die," Susan whispered, desperate.

The food came. They both picked at it. It gave them time to regroup, reflect.

"OK," said James. "Shall we just focus on what we know for a moment? What I need to tell Charlie?"

Susan, tears welling in her eyes, agreed. "Just what I said before. 3 o'clock Saturday. Termination of kidnap attempt. C. Mowbray known as H5. Code Bolingbroke. Some clever civil servant who's read Shakespeare must have come up with that. You have to tell Charlie, Dad. Whatever you've invested in this, personally or financially, doesn't count as anything against Charlie's life."

"I know."

"Oh Dad, how did this ever happen?"

"I don't know Susan, it's a long story. My fault. All my fault. Trying to make things right. I'm sorry."

This time Susan offered her hand. And James took it. And tried not to cry. It was hard, so hard, but it was a busy restaurant. He got back his control. "Susan, I'll tell Charlie everything, give him the chance to call it off. I don't think he will, and I promise you it can work. I don't want to tell you what's planned. It'll compromise you. If your boss is on the case, you could be at risk. Best if you don't know any more. But I'll look after Charlie – and his friends – I promise. I believe in their cause, and in them."

"OK Dad. You do what you think is right."

"I will. And it will be for Charlie before anything else. I promise."

"We haven't even spoken about Mum. She's sitting at home fretting. About Charlie, about Will in Ukraine. When did you last speak?"

"A long time…"

"You've got to break the ice one day, Dad. With everything such a mess."

"I know. I will. Just let me work out how. Take one thing at a time." Something close to anger flashed across James's face. Susan got it.

"Sorry, Dad. I didn't mean to… If I can help."

"Oh, my girl… let's talk more when we can. When this is all over."

"When it's over – in a good way, please let it be in a good way."

"I will make sure it is. I promise, I promise."

"Dad, I love you, still love you."

James blinked back more tears. "Suze, I love you more than you could ever imagine. Please trust me right now."

"I will, Dad."

***

The afternoon was hard. She had her report to finish, but her team needed her help on all sorts of things. They were, at least, a welcome distraction. It always helped to be able to concentrate on something immediate, something that mattered to someone else. But every time she sat down to write, the discussion with James came back into her mind. She had to trust him. Trust him to look after Charlie and his friends. But how was he going to do that? How had he, her Dad, got in so deep with that bunch of idealists and attention-seekers? Guilt. He said it himself. Making up for the lost years. But the best thing he could have done was get Charlie a proper job and keep him on the right track. Away from HOPE and those impossible dreams. How were they ever going to fight the Authority? Especially when the English people had voted for it in overwhelming numbers so recently? People wanted a respite from upheaval, and were prepared to sacrifice a bit of liberty for that. People just wanted a decent life. Enough money to live and protection from all the threats around them: terrorists, refugees, Russians, the environment. Everyone accepted now that things had to be done to minimise further global warming – the Fenlands had been flooded, for God's sake. They didn't need HOPE telling them there was a problem. And kidnapping footballers? How was that going to endear them to the public, even if they did succeed? How could Charlie get himself involved in that? He loved his sport. Yeah, but he loved his drama even more – wanted to put on a show, with him at the centre. The dramatist, the egotist. *H5* – Henry V of course, striding towards his Agincourt. Of course. Death or glory. Charlie couldn't just do things the quiet way, the boring way. The way that worked.

Susan's thoughts were interrupted by an unwelcome sight, hovering over her desk. Yorkminster was back from his Cabinet Office jaunt. He looked tired, not his usual smug, nauseating self. "Can we talk, Susan?" They found a meeting room. Susan waited for him to start – it was his conversation.

"You OK?" he asked, seemingly genuine. A change of tack? Susan was wary.

"Yeah, I guess so."

"You must be worried about Saturday."

"Depends."

"Depends on what?"

"On what the real story is. Whether there's even a story."

"So you don't believe what I've told you?"

"I don't know what to believe."

"Look, Susan, I can protect your brother, if we can only stop him from trying this crazy stunt on Saturday."

"How would you do that?"

"If I could just speak to him."

"Believe me, I would love to speak to him, but I don't know where he is and I can't talk to him. He won't talk to me. I'm the Authority."

"You really sure about that?"

"Really sure."

"How's the report?"

"You'll have it tomorrow, like I said."

"Look forward to it. I'll be around tomorrow afternoon. Cabinet Office again in the morning."

Planning my brother's murder, thought Susan. But she held her tongue.

"Nothing you can tell me?"

Susan just stared at him.

"OK, I believe you. It's just some of my colleagues find it hard to believe."

"Believe what?"

"That you know nothing."

"What have you told them?"

"That you know nothing."

"Really?"

"Yes, really. I'm on your side Susan. I know you have your doubts about me, but there's more to me than you realise."

Oh no, here comes the confession, thought Susan. *Or another way to get me to say something?*

"I'm sure. Maybe you can tell me sometime. Not now though. There's work to do."

"Yes, of course. Sorry for distracting you."

"That's OK. Just I'd really like to get back to it now."

"Sure, go ahead."

Yorkminster looked lost. Crestfallen. Susan experienced an unusual feeling. Sympathy for him. He was probably out of his depth over at the Cabinet Office. With all the security and military types. And No 10, no doubt. All wanting answers. And he didn't have any.

"Look Chris, if I could help I would. But there's nothing to say."

"Yeah, thanks. Well if you hear anything…" He got up and walked away, not looking back. Susan stared up at the ceiling and sighed. She'd let him down. She had to let him down. It was her family she had to protect. Her family… a shiver went through her, a cold bolt of realisation. Her family. What were they going to do to her family? What about Mum? Surely they wouldn't…

This is just getting worse…

Chapter Seven. Dark Night of the Soul
(13-05-27)

Will struggled to get to sleep after he took the call from Susan. The occasional burst of machine gun fire and misfiring missiles was bad enough, and the drip, drip, drip from a leak in the roof into a tin bucket conjured nagging images of a slowly ticking time bomb; but the real problem was that he felt like an utter shit. *What have I become? That was my sister, she was in distress, and I just said, not my problem. What am I doing? What have I become? What has this place done to me? Or is it just me? A selfish, cynical twat who can't even be bothered to hear out his sister. She obviously needed me, and that's all I could do. Nothing. Precisely fuck all. For my own sister.*

Will mulled over the call and the situation. Charlie was in some kind of trouble. It was happening on Saturday. If Susan knew that, it must be something to do with the Authority. She was probably taking a risk telling him. Another thing he didn't think about at the time. Add another lash to the sentence. How could he help? Calling Charlie really wasn't an option. That could put everyone in danger. *Dad... yes Dad!* He called Dad regularly, mainly to talk football. Helped keep him sane. He didn't even need to hide that: it would be OK on the regular network. *Slip in something about them knowing about Saturday, while we are talking about Saturday, about the EEL final. Come on Barca, beat Tottenham-in-disguise.* Would Dad know what it meant? Not sure, but if he got the message to Charlie, Charlie would. Yeah, he'd do that – call Dad at 12.00. Routine stuff, normal time of day. Before he went to the press briefing. Yeah, that was the best he could do... *Wish that fucking rain would stop.*

The morning dragged. Will went out with a local photographer, Serhiy, to check out the frontline. Nothing much, nothing different. Grey skies, mud: everywhere mud, damaged shelters, rebuilt shelters, an overturned truck beginning to rust, a machine gun protruding from a battlement, some weary troops, soaked to the skin, marching half in step. One lad - he looked Middle Eastern -

with a smile on his face, amid a sea of dreariness. Not quite gloom, not suffering, just boredom. Grinding boredom. Serhiy snapped the smiling boy, gave him a thumbs up. He got a middle finger back, and an even bigger grin. Will wondered what was making him so happy. Maybe just not being in a refugee camp. Everything was relative.

"Could make a nice shot, that one, Serhiy. I'll take it for the FT. The *Mystery Smile*. Hey, Oleh, turn it round now will you? I need to make a call home."

***

James' wristpad buzzed, just as he got ready to go the office. He called up the holo. An unexpected image, especially at this time of the day. "Hello Will, what's up?"

"Just thought I'd call, Dad. Been a while. Susan called last night. Reminded me."

"Well, we're all busy."

"Hmmm, I wouldn't describe myself as busy. It's pretty quiet here. Deadly dull in fact, as long as the odd rocket buzzing overhead doesn't excite you."

"Well, you wouldn't want to be hit by one."

"No, but you've got more chance of being blown up on the Underground."

"I'd rather not think about that, thanks."

"Sorry, you lose a sense of proportion out here."

"Any chance of a move?"

"Still waiting for Kiev, but no news."

"Well, fingers crossed. Looking forward to the Final on Saturday?"

"Sunday's more important. If we win and Forest don't, we're champions – again."

"Glad you stayed out of the Elite then?"

"Well, yeah. Better football."

"And you win all the time, without Chelsea, the Mancs, Liverpool and they-who-shall-not be-named around."

81

"Well, it's revived a few of the old giants. Back to the seventies."

"Thirties more like."

"Well, whatever. Good to be battling it out with dirty Leeds again. Listen Dad, check every other sentence."

"You what?"

"And Sheffield Wednesday. I remember you telling me about those epic replays. *Every other sentence.* Get it?"

"Er yes. Will you watch the game on Saturday?"

"Yeah. Lots of Gooners here. *Susan said they know about Saturday.* We'll all be supporting Barca. *Something to do with Charlie.* The foreign journos will be baffled, as usual. *Did you get that?* Anyone but Tottenham-in-disguise".

"Stratford Olympians you mean? *Yes. Who's they?* West Ham fans wouldn't call themselves that. Be fair."

"Total sell-out. *Susan's lot I guess.* They hated each other until they saw all that money. *She thinks Charlie needs to know.*"

"You could have joined us. *I'll tell him.* We'd have been the best."

"And sold our souls? No way. *Thanks, Dad.* Say hi to Suze for me too. *Do you know anything about Charlie?* Say I'm thinking of her."

"Will do. *I know a bit.*"

"Gotta go now. Press brief. *Tell me.* Never know, something interesting might have happened."

"OK. Take care of yourself, boy. *Charlie's planning something at Wembley.* And enjoy the game. Vive les Blaugranas."

"Mixing languages there Dad. *Bloody hell!* Have a good day yourself. *Keep me posted.* Bye."

Duty done. Couldn't do any more. Will could only hope – and watch. *Jesus, Wembley!*

James knew what he had to do. The first thing was to call Susan…

***

On Wednesday night, Fran had just got home from the Lyttleton. It was nearly 11.30. She was tired, but elated. The play was going so well. Her wristpad buzzed. Who would that be at this time of night? She called up the holo, but it was audio only. Couldn't be a friend or family then. She felt nervous, but she couldn't think why. Unless it was something to do with Charlie. She never knew where he was or what he was doing these days, except that it probably wasn't a great idea.

"Hello, who is this?"

"Yes, is that Francesca Willoughby?"

"Yeah, and you are?"

"I'm trying to get in touch with Charlie Mowbray. I believe you know him."

"Who are you, please?"

"I'm afraid I can't say, but I have some important information for him."

"What sort of information?"

"I'm afraid I'm not at liberty to share it with anyone else."

"Well, fuck off then, and don't bother me again."

The holo shut down. Fran felt scared, really scared. Scared for herself, scared for her parents, asleep in the house upstairs, scared for Charlie. What had he done now? Why couldn't he just come back to her, settle down? His Dad could get him a good job. He wouldn't have failed. Why was he always looking for the big moment? That voice on the phone. It was well-educated, public school. Not just one of his drug friends. Not one of Jack's gang. It sounded like a spook. And if it was a spook, then what was Charlie getting himself into? *Oh Charlie, my love, come back to me. Please! I love you; I wish we could communicate by telepathy. I wish I could just get him back and cure his restlessness. I wish love and art were enough for him. Oh, I hope he's OK. What shall I do now? I can't wake up Mum and Dad. Just have a glass of wine, try and focus on tomorrow's performance. I need to get that fall right. Let myself go. Think about that. Not Charlie. Not now. But I'll have to talk to someone. James, yes James. He's still talking to Charlie. I need to talk to James. He'll know what to do.*

***

Olivia had felt uneasy ever since she'd spoken to Susan. Something felt wrong, really wrong. Susan was not her normal self. She'd been evasive, but her body language, even on the holo, couldn't disguise the strain. Charlie had gone missing, up to what she didn't know. Meanwhile, Jack Oldfield was spreading rumours around Glastonbury. You could usually take what he said with a pinch of salt, but what if there was something in it? She felt helpless. And that was before she even began to think about Will, stuck in the war that had no end in Ukraine. She didn't feel she could share these feelings with Michael, not fully. He knew she was anxious, comforted her. But there was something holding her back. He knew that and gave her space. If she wanted to talk more he'd be there for her. Olivia appreciated that, but knew who she really needed to talk to. Except she hadn't for so long. How could she now?

There was just one glimmer. Emma was in Glastonbury that day. They'd agreed to have coffee in the Marquee Moon that afternoon. Their relationship had been awkward – more than awkward – when Emma and James first upped sticks and moved to Bristol. But Susan staying friends with Emma had slowly brought Olivia round, and when she heard that Emma and James were having difficulties she felt an instinctive sympathy. When James moved back to London during the week, Olivia reached out to Emma and found that they had a lot in common, besides having both been let down by James. It centred on a love of the arts – all the arts. Emma was keen to learn more about painting, Olivia was fascinated by Emma's ventures into the Bristol music scene. She loved Emma's young lad, Archie, too. There were distinct traces of Charlie in him. And Emma worried about him just as much as Olivia had worried about Charlie, when his Dad was no longer there for him.

They settled in Olivia's favourite spot in the corner of the café and Michael brought them coffees. They talked for a while about Archie: his love of the guitar, how he'd just formed a band at school, how he wasn't focused enough on his exams, which started soon. He needed a grade 1 in coding to get into holo design, but preferred to practise his scales. And he'd just got a new girlfriend. "Terrible timing! Same attitude as me, I guess," said Emma. "A drifter, a dreamer. Beware your dreams…"

"Follow your dreams," said Olivia. "Only one life. James will be there to help, won't he? Financially, anyway."

"Yeah, finance won't ever be a problem. Or maybe that's part of the problem. Too easy for Archie to try a bit of this and that. Too easy for James to think that money, security, is enough. Too easy. Archie needs the role model right now."

"He's got you."

"Exactly. Still drifting, dreaming. And it's easy. Because James will always be there with the money."

"I know how it is!"

"Sorry Livvy, I know you've got bigger worries. Any news about Charlie?"

"Nothing. Off the radar. Susan's worried about something now. More than just her work, I can tell. She won't say though. I'm sitting here and no-one will tell me anything! All I'm hearing is rumours cast about by Jack Oldfield."

"God, is that twat back? Why Charlie ever let him think he was worth something, God only knows."

"Apparently Charlie has dumped him."

"Well that explains the rumours. Probably all made up. Just getting his own back. He always was a lying bastard."

"You really think so?"

"If he's true to form. Look, Livvy, I can't really see what Charlie sees in the HOPE movement – just a bunch of rehashed ideas from Marx and Greenpeace with a bit of circus added – but I'm sure he won't do anything really stupid, or dangerous."

"He's already been brought in by the Authority a couple of times."

"Yeah, but they let him go, didn't they? A bit of harmless dissent does their image with the Europeans good. Means they'll still trade with us."

"I suppose so. I'd just like to know where he is and what he is doing. I was wondering if James might know something. They're still in touch."

"Funding him, I should think."

"Not his politics, I don't think. The Authority suits James down to the ground. Much easier to make money in a stable economy, and with all that building in the Wash."

"Us next, you know? The Levels."

"I heard. Surely they wouldn't just…"

"The Authority can do anything. Glastonbury would be OK – you've got the Tor! You might be an island though. Back to King Arthur."

"Oh God, I hope not. But Emma, I hate to ask, but…"

"Will I speak to James? Of course I will."

"Oh thank you so much, Emma!" Olivia's wristpad buzzed. "Oh let me take this." Audio only.

"Hello, is that Olivia Mowbray?"

"Yes, who is this?"

"Just a friend of Charlie's. I've got some news for him, but don't seem to be able to find him."

The caller spoke with an educated voice, very clipped. Didn't feel like the sort of person Charlie would be friends with.

"I can't help you I'm afraid. He's away at the moment."

"Would you know where?"

"No, no I don't."

"It's important I contact him."

"No, sorry, I just don't. Tell me who you are."

The audio cut out. Olivia trembled.

"Who was that, Livvy?" said Emma, frowning, putting her hand on Olivia's forearm.

"I don't know. A strange man. Posh. Said he had important news for Charlie. Wanted to know where he was. Cut me off when I couldn't say. Oh my God, Emma, that wasn't good. Charlie must be in trouble."

"I'll call James right now. Is there anywhere we can go?"

*No-one makes a fool outta Jack Oldfield. No-one. Not even fuckin'
Henry the Fifth Charlie fuckin' Mowbray. 'Specially not Charlie
Mowbray. After all I done for him. Got his fuckin' drugs for him and
his mates ever since we were at school. Yeah, alright, he didn't
touch them much himself – he was a boozer, Charlie. Phenomenal
boozer. Maaan, we had some sessions. Me and Charlie. And the
girls, who got him the girls? For all those school parties. Jack
Oldfield, that's who. All the contacts. All the girls, all the drugs.
Helped make Charlie Mowbray what he is today. Yeah, what is he
today? Some cunt who thinks he's Henry the Fifth or whatever. I
have to lose you, he said. I gotta stop seeing you, he said. I'm sorry
mate, he said. I know we've had good times, but things are moving
on. I've got new responsibilities. I've got to shake off the old ways,
the old people. People need me to be different now. I've got to lead
this group to a new level. They need me Jack, he said. They need
me, but they don't need you. I'm sorry, but they don't want you
around. This is more important than us, he said. I won't forget you,
I'll never forget you, he said. You've been a big part of my life – my
old life. I've got a new life now. People need me. They need me
100%. The Cause needs me. They need a leader. A leader who can
speak for them. Articulate the vision. Know what that means, Jack?
Know what that means? Of course I fuckin' know what that means. I
got my A levels. Didn't go to no poncey-arse university. Why would
I wanna do that? I know how to make money. Always have known
how to make money. Like Charlie's Dad – he knows how to make
money. Good job, cos Charlie hasn't got a fuckin' clue. Not a clue.
Always needed people like me and his Dad to keep him. And now he
says he doesn't need me, doesn't want me. That his friends don't
want me. Who're they? Those HOPE nutters? That serious girl, the
one who never smiles? Whatsername? Rosa. Rosa fuckin' Voreky or
somethin'. She's been a right bad influence on Charlie. Gave him
ideas. Went to his head. Didn't like it though when he got off with
the other one. Hah! Hilarious. Yeah, the one with the grey eyes.
Burned through you. Like ice. She was nice. Spoke to me. I could of*

given her one. Definitely. Wouldn't of tried though, cos she was Charlie's. Yeah, she was the nicest. The only one I could stand, really. Gabs. That's what Charlie called her when Rosa wasn't around. Bossy Rosa. She's the one that gave Charlie ideas. Told him he should be the leader. Of the whole thing, not just the political wing. That was OK, the political wing – they just went round talking bollocks. Just like all the others. No, she said, you should lead the action wing. We need to be bolder, we need someone to lead that to new heights. Someone with charisma. You Charlie. Charlie liked that. Suited his ego. Henry the Fifth. Always fancied himself as Henry the Fifth. Ever since he did it at school. Used to call me Sir John when he was doing that. I didn't mind. Better than factotum, though I wasn't bothered about that neither. I liked being around Charlie. He was a laugh. The girls liked him. I found them, but they really liked him. Yeah, so they were friends with me too. Might have been anyway, but Charlie guaranteed it. We made a good partnership, me and Charlie. A good partnership. And then he goes and says I don't need you, I can't know you. I mean, he said, read Henry the Fourth Part 2, act five, scene five. So I did. I know thee not, it said. Fall to your prayers… fool and jester. Fool and fuckin' jester – is that what he thought I was? I have turned away from my former self, so will I those that kept me company. I memorised that. It's good that. I'll have to use it on someone one day. Some twat I don't wanna know anymore. But he used that on me. His best mate from a long time. Turned away. Thrown me away. Like a piece of shit. Flushed me down the bog. Yeah that's what he done. Down the fuckin' bog. Like a piece of shit. A fool and jester. But no-one makes a fool outta Jack Oldfield. No-one. Not even Charlie Mowbray. That nice man at the Met who sells us the drugs – quality stuff, discount prices – he was really pleased to hear from me. Gave me a free bag in return. Yeah he was pleased. You sure about this, Jack? he said. Really sure? Yeah I said. I heard him and Rosa Voreky talking about it in the pub. They told you? he said. Not exactly, I said. They didn't know I was there. I was watching him after he dumped me. No one fools with me. I'm sure they don't, said the man from the Met. Is there anything more?

No, just that, I said. Like, I didn't wanna really land Charlie in it, just make him look stupid – and stop that stupid prank. I mean, kidnapping footballers at Wembley. Who put that stupid fuckin' idea in his head? Must of been Rosa – she hasn't got a clue, not a fuckin' clue. Neither of them have got a fuckin' clue. I'm doing them a favour, I really am. A few months in prison won't do them any harm. Might straighten their heads out. Better than dying in a barrage of fuckin' lasers at Wembley. And ruining the match for everyone. I mean, if they are for the people, why are they disrupting a fuckin' football match, the most important one of the season? To bang on about the weather! I mean, we all know it's bad. We only have to watch the weather reports. There's shit happening everywhere. And someone told me the Levels are gonna be flooded. No doubt so those fuckers in Bristol don't get their arses wet. Look after the cities first. Always the fuckin' same. All those university ponces taking the decisions. Looking after themselves. Nothing fuckin' changes. The Authority has made sod all difference. Same as ever. Still get my drugs from the Met and the cops down here – exactly the same. Just different gangsters making the money. Yeah, nothing changes. You should realise that Charlie. Nothing changes. Don't worry your pretty arse about it. Just get your Dad to give you a nice easy job. And get back with Fran. She was the best. Yeah, I know I annoyed her sometimes, but she put up with me. I liked her. She could act too. Saw her in London recently. She didn't know I was there, but yeah I was. She was fuckin' brilliant. I loved Fran. Get her back Charlie, man. I love her… and you mate. I love you too. Not like a poof, obviously, but you're my best mate. I need you man. You need me. Your factotum. That's me. I don't mind that. Just not a fool, or a jester. No, no-one calls Jack Oldfield a fool, or a jester, and doesn't regret it. You'll regret it Charlie. But I'll forgive you, if you forgive me. Go back to Fran, come back to me. Just don't say you don't know me. Never ever say that to me again Charlie. Never again. Don't make a fool of me Charlie. No-one makes a fool of Jack Oldfield. No-one…

***

James walked back to his office in Mayfair after meeting Susan. He needed to clear his head before getting on to his contacts. What Susan had told him shouldn't have been happening. He'd had assurances that no-one important in the Authority knew what HOPE were planning. But now, it seemed like there'd been a leak from somewhere. Some double-dealing. Which meant no-one could be trusted. And that called into question the arrangements at Wembley. He couldn't allow Charlie and his gang to walk into an ambush. Susan's bluntness had shaken him, really shaken him. Her belief that Charlie was going to die; the assertion that it was all about his paternal guilt trip; the concern for Olivia... and ultimately her trust. In him. She had given him her trust. Could he repay it? Could he ensure that Saturday would work? Had he thought all the implications through? He thought he had, but now the doubt crept in. The Authority, other than its dark reaches, shouldn't have known. But what did it know? That there might be a kidnap attempt at some point on Saturday? At which point? Susan didn't know that. Did the Authority?

He sat on a bench in Green Park. It was warm for May. Since the wind had dropped the air had become thick with London heat. A lot of people were stretched out on the grass, shoes cast off, soaking in the hazy, smog-laden sun. *Way past lunch time*, James thought, *don't people work anymore? Can't all be tourists. Still, that's not a bad thing. Why are people still doing seven hours a day in offices, when AIs can do most of the hard graft? The Authority is too scared to encourage the investment – doesn't know what it would do with all the people with time on their hands. Well, if you pay them the same for doing less they'll be happy enough. And the money will find its way into the right places and create new jobs, as long as they control my world properly. That's the obstacle. They're too scared. Labour thought about the basic income, but didn't have a chance with the forces ranged against it. Has to be done by the establishment party for the sake of self-preservation. They'll come round to it. Must do. Or there'll be more HOPEs than they can imagine. Think long term, you idiots... C'mon, enough of that, need*

90

to focus. What do I tell Charlie? Can't keep it from him any longer. He needs to make the choice. He and Rosa. She's hard core. She'd be happy to escalate, risk a few lives. I still don't think Charlie would. He was adamant that this could only go ahead if no-one died. I have to keep that promise to him. Shit, I'm making a lot of promises to people. Can I keep them? Surely yes. Susan didn't actually say they knew anything other than the fact that something was planned. Better try to find out if there's more. Better get back...

Back in the office, James retired to the personal space he hardly ever used. He preferred to be out on the floor with everyone else, catching the market movements, the latest news, on the big screens. But he had a place that he could retreat to when he needed to do some serious thinking. And this needed serious thinking. Could he let his son and his five companions carry out their plan on Saturday? Had the risks, so finely calculated, changed? Or changed materially? That was the point. He now knew that the Authority – the mainstream Authority – knew. But he didn't know what they knew. He would have to activate the code only to be used in the case of a potential show stopper. That had been agreed. No contact before Saturday, unless the risk had escalated. He readied himself to make contact.

Then his wristpad buzzed. It was Emma. What did she want at this time of day? He called up the holo.

"Emma, how are you doing?"

"OK thanks. James, I've been over at Olivia's today. Something really weird happened, really frightening."

"What? Tell me."

"We were talking about Charlie and Susan. Olivia's really worried about both of them. She can't get hold of Charlie and Susan's holding something back from her, she knows. Then she got this call. Audio. Some posh guy asking after Charlie. Saying he had something important to tell him. When Olivia asked him who he was he cut off. Spooky. It's like all this is related, James. Olivia is sitting there feeling scared and powerless. I said I'd call and find out if you knew anything."

"No, no I don't. I've not heard from Charlie or Susan recently. Had a chat with Will about the football last night. He seems fine, but frustrated sitting there in Kremenchuk. But OK. So no, nothing. But that call is worrying. He gave no indication of what it was about?"

"No. It was the way he just cut off. And the voice. The voice really freaked Olivia. You need to call her."

"It's been a long time."

"Yeah, but this is serious. It's about your kids, James. They're still your kids."

"I know. I'm in touch with them all. Just not in the last few weeks. I'll see what I can find out. Archie OK?"

"Guitars and girls coming before his exams. Otherwise, yeah. He needs you, James."

"I know. I'll be down soon. After the next week. We're sponsoring the EEL final on Saturday. Taking up a lot of time."

"Archie's exams start in two weeks."

"I know. I'll be there for him. I really will."

"Please be, James. He needs you. I need you… Olivia needs you."

"I'll do my best, I promise."

"I trust you, James. Take care. Call if you hear anything."

"I will. I honestly will."

More promises, more trust. How did this happen, how did the whole family suddenly need him? When there wasn't much he could do. But they were his family. He couldn't walk away. Not anymore. Never again.

The wristpad buzzed again. And now it was Fran! *What the…?*

"Fran, nice to see you. How's it been? What can I do for you?"

"Oh James, I'm so glad I could get hold of you. I got this creepy call last night. Audio only. From someone looking for Charlie. He cut off when I tried to find out who he was."

"Posh voice?"

"Yeah, why?"

"He called me as well."

"About Charlie?"

"Yes."

"What's happening, James? Do you know what Charlie is up to? No-one seems to know where he is. He's disappeared with the HOPE gang. Rosa, all that lot. Gabi O'Leary no doubt."

"I know Rosa, not Gabi. Who's she?"

"Ask Charlie, next time you speak to him."

"Oh, OK. Sorry if…"

"No, it's alright. I don't care about that right now. I'm more worried about Charlie and what he's up to if mysterious people are after him. I'd say Authority people, from weirdo last night. And how did they know my number? Stupid question. They know everyone's number. That's why it must be the Authority. What did he say to you?"

"Pretty much the same as to you by the sound of things. Didn't cut me off, but politely declined to tell me anything."

"So what are we going to do, James? I'm scared. What if they are stalking us? I felt really nervous just going out to the shops this morning. I'm worried about Mum and Dad. What if they get approached? I've got a performance tonight, and all this shit happens."

"Don't worry Fran, you'll be OK. I'll get on the case. I know people in the Authority. Don't say anything to anyone. I'll see what I can find out. Stay calm."

"I'll try. You're all I've got here, James."

"It's OK, I'm here for you."

"Thanks so much, James…"

She started to cry. But before James could say anything else she cut off. *Oh shit*! James ran his fingers through his hair and just stared at his desk. Examined the grain of the dark wood, the indent where someone had dropped a speaker on it when they set up his music station. *Focus. The code…*

***

James wasn't sure how reassured he was about what he was able to establish. His contact in the Authority said that the mainstream didn't know much. It was unhelpful that Charlie's old sidekick had blurted to the Met in a fit of pique, but he didn't seem to know that much. Nonetheless, it was now known that a kidnap attempt was possible on Saturday, at Wembley, even if no-one outside the sympathetic core knew any more than that. Security would now be even more intense. The PM had considered whether to call off the game, but had decided that it wasn't an option. This was England's first opportunity to host a major sporting event since the Authority had taken over. Part of the journey back to full acceptance in Europe. It had to be a success. And there were always threats to any big event. The information they had didn't really distinguish this threat from any other credible threat – if it was that credible. Enquiries were underway. No-one seemed to know anything. She apologised for Intelligence contacting Olivia and Fran, but it had to be done – they were obvious people to question. Had to put on a show for the mainstream. They hadn't pressed too hard. And no-one knew where the key members of HOPE had gone. They hadn't had a cell structure in the past – far too amateurish for that – but they did seem to have dispersed effectively this time. As far as the contact knew, there was no good reason to call off the project. But the element of surprise about where and when was even more important now. It had to be perfect.

Thanks a million, thought James. *Spooked my wife, my ex-wife and possible future daughter-in-law – or at least she was until Charlie got really serious about HOPE. And really, I'm none the wiser. Just hoping the mainstream doesn't know any more than she was letting on. I'll just have to give Charlie the full picture as I know it. He – and Rosa – will have to decide.*

***

After his rejection by Charlie, Jack stayed in London for a few days. Just trying to figure out what had happened. And what Charlie was up to. He watched Charlie's house for hours from a café on the opposite side of the road. Charlie had moved further north in Notting Hill after moving out of Fran's place. Not that far from the canal. When Jack got bored in the café he walked up to the canal and walked westwards. Past the derelict gasworks, the disused factories, the secret fishermen, the drug dealers. This wasn't his patch, so he stayed well clear of them. He marvelled at the way the canal crossed the North Circular road, above rather than below it, and the views of the Wembley arch. One day he got as far as Alperton, where the strange green buildings made him think he was in some kind of sci-fi set. He got off the canal there and took the tube back to his home turf. He was going to go back to Glastonbury soon, but he wanted to get something on Charlie first, something he might be able to use. No-one made a fool of Jack Oldfield.

He got lucky the next day. He'd been sitting on a bench by a bus stop within viewing distance of Charlie's place when he came out. It was six o'clock. He had his favourite black leather jacket on and still wore his shades, even though the light was weak under the clouds. *Looks like fuckin' George Michael*, thought Jack, remembering someone his Mum liked when he was a kid. *Bloody hell, where did that come from? Both posers, that's what. Same gear. Same attitude – look at me, ain't I the best? Wankers.* He kept his distance. Charlie followed a familiar route. He was going to the pub, Jack was sure. The Revolution Rock. They'd been there loads of times, him and Charlie. Just him and Charlie. *Mates. Yeah, the unlikely lads maybe. But opposites attract. Well not like that. Just mates. Good mates. Where did it all go wrong? It was that Rosa. Must have been. But no-one makes a fool...*

Jack was right. Charlie went into the Revolution Rock. Jack waited for a while. See if anyone else he knew turned up. Maybe they were already in there. *Give it ten.*

After five minutes, bullseye! Rosa Voreky, or whatever she was called, came along. *Looking shifty*, Jack thought. Carrying a plastic bag. *What's in there?* Jack said to himself. *HOPE's plans for world domination? Yeah, no fuckin' chance of that. Not a fuckin' clue. Load of dreamers. How Charlie got himself in with this lot I really don't know. Well, I do. He likes the birds. And they love him. Yeah,*

Charlie Farley. Eating out of his hand. Except Rosa of course. She takes no shit, that one. Reckon Charlie's under her thumb. That's how he got into this. Well, yeah, that and his ego. Chance to make a splash. Make a name for himself. Always wanted that, Charlie. I didn't mind. He was my mate. Yeah, and I admit, I got some girls first because they were after Charlie. I organised it, Charlie made it happen. A great partnership. Until Rosa came along and fucked it up. Don't know what he saw in her. Just not like him. He had Fran. Why would you leave Fran? Gorgeous. Lovely person. For all this bollocks... I'm going in. Now.

The Revolution Rock still had its snugs. It used to be an Irish pub when Irish pubs were all the rage. Now it traced itself back to the heart of Notting Hill. Reggae music. Always reggae music. The crowd was diverse: age, colour, gender, no-one cared. The vibe was everything. Charlie loved it, Fran loved it, Rosa loved it. Even Jack loved it, though he thought the toffs had taken over. But he did a few deals, and he always loved to be chilling with Charlie. His mate. This time though, he wasn't chilling. He was hiding.

He saw that Charlie and Rosa had settled into one of the snugs. It was still early and the one next to them was empty. Hood up, Jack went to the bar and ordered a lager. He walked back towards the door and around some tables, approaching the empty snug at an angle where there was no way Rosa or Charlie would spot him. Anyway, they already looked engrossed, in their own world. Jack settled in, his back to where Charlie was sitting. So near and yet so far! His hand shook as he took a glug of his lager. This was weird. Spying on his mate. *Gotta be done though.* He sat back and listened...

"Rosa, you know, I'm still not sure I'm the right person to be leading this."

"Charlie, you have the charisma; everyone follows you. Your every word."

"But I was happy doing the political stuff. You know, being the actor. That's what I am. An actor."

"You are more than that Charlie. You are the inspiration. Our Trotsky. Our Henry the Fifth."

"Well, I'll take the latter. Don't want an icepick through my head. And I've certainly done the Hal bit. I've even ditched my Falstaff. So I guess I'd better finish the story. Agincourt. The odds are stacked against us, just like then, that's for sure."

Me, that's fuckin' me he's talking about, mumbled Jack into his lager.

"Charlie, we have planned this to the finest detail. Your Dad has given us the money, acquired the equipment, worked the security, lined up our escape. We have everything for the perfect mission."

"And you can work with Gabi?"

"Of course I can work with Gabi. The Cause is greater than any individual feelings."

"How do you feel?"

"How I feel doesn't matter. We never took our relationship all the way, so why should I feel possessive? I don't own you, or anyone else. We believe in common ownership: that must apply to our own lives too."

"Yeah, you see, I'm not sure about that. The political and the personal. They're not the same."

"They have to be the same if we are to change things."

"Isn't that just going back a hundred years? To Communism, Naziism?"

"Never Naziism. Never. Communism, well, there are lessons…"

"Huge lessons. Millions died. I don't want anyone to die. Not a single person. No political cause is worth a person's life."

"Charlie, if we are to succeed, there may need to be sacrifices. We have a duty to the wider world. Things have to change."

"I know; but not by killing people. Oh man! I know this was all my idea. Wembley, football, massive audience all around the world. Perfect chance to address the people. Let them know what HOPE is about. Rally the people to the Cause. Let the hostages go with no harm done. People see we're peaceful, that ours is a cause worth supporting. I know it was my idea. But is it real, Rosa? Is there any chance of all my goals being achieved? Especially no-one getting hurt?"

Fuck me, a Wembley heist. Charlie Mowbray, you are pulling the big one. Or you think you are mate…

"Charlie, have faith. In the Cause, in the project, in our team. In us."

"Yeah, I do. Honest I do. But I have to ask the questions. This is the step up, Rosa. This is higher risk than anything we've ever done. Exponentially higher."

"And the rewards are higher."

"Yeah, I guess so. Can't say it's what I ever envisaged when I came on board."

"Remember why you came on board, Charlie. Remember how angry you were about the coup. The democratically-elected Labour government overthrown by an establishment coup. Constantly undermined until they were so weak that the establishment didn't even need to use force. Just a corrupt parliament. And enemies within the party. Enemies of socialism. Just like the 1920s and 30s. History repeats itself. Always. Because power and control is everything. The interests of the people, of the planet, are secondary to those who seek power."

"But we're seeking power, aren't we?"

"In time."

"And will we be any different? Won't we just be corrupted like everyone else before us?"

"We cannot believe that, Charlie. We must have belief that there is a better way. But we need the people behind us to achieve that. Saturday is just the beginning."

"The long march begins."

Yeah mate, the long march to fuckin' prison…

***

The team had separated after the meeting in Wiltshire. No further contact with each other until arrival at Wembley, except in an emergency. Charlie was holed up in an apartment in a luxury block overlooking Paddington Basin. Courtesy of James. He looked out towards the Westway, sparkling with traffic as the sunset went

98

through its last throes. In the far distance the Wembley Arch glowed in the faint purple light. Still a day and a half to wait and wonder. Everyone knew what they had to do; everyone knew the risks. It was going ahead, unless they got a message from Charlie. One word: *Dunkirk*. They had a safe haven in the south east of Ireland, courtesy of the INSF. Afterwards they would make their way there. It had all been organised. Could they be confident about it? Well, they had no choice but to be. Charlie had assured them that there were people inside government who supported their cause, who believed that the coup was wrong, that much stronger measures had to be taken to prevent environmental catastrophe. That proper democracy needed to be restored. He trusted James. His Dad, who'd promised never to let him down again.

One word, *Dunkirk*. That's all it would take. And the whole thing would be over. Except it wouldn't. If the Authority knew what they'd planned, then they'd be after them. If they managed to get to Ireland that wouldn't be the end either. People would be searching for them, though the Irish government and the Authority weren't the best of friends. That would help.

But no! *Mustn't be thinking like this*, thought Charlie. He lay on the sofa as the light in the room grew dim, a copy of "King Henry V" open at Act 4, Scene 1, pages face down on the floor. He stared at the ceiling and muttered the lines he'd always loved, ever since that starring role…

> *Oh hard condition, twin-born with greatness,*
> *Subject to the breath of every fool, whose sense*
> *No more can feel but his own wringing.*
> *What infinite heart's ease must kings neglect*
> *That private men enjoy?*

He wasn't a king, but it was all down to him now. The team were ready, wherever they were. Ready to go, unless he sent them that one word. The word of noble retreat. But chaos too. Near defeat. The end of HOPE probably. The end of the Cause. It would be for him, anyway. Rosa would keep it going, but it would never be the same. It all rested on him, and his power to use that one word. How had he ended up with such responsibility? He was just an actor. A charlatan. Better off pissing around with Jack Oldfield than leading a serious cause. But he was the leader. Maybe the Cause had chosen him. Rosa had chosen him, believing in what he could do for the Cause. People followed him. They always had. He didn't know why - they just did. He owed it to all of them now. The Cause depended on him. How could he walk away?

He called up some music that took him back to when he and his Dad had got back together. It was one of his Dad's favourites – he'd heard the band round at his Dad's place and had gone with him to see them play in London. The Apollo in Hammersmith. He remembered going for an Indian down on King Street beforehand and feeling a bit tired and hot, until Adam Granduciel started to play his guitar. And then he felt transfixed, as that guitar sang. As it cried and then erupted. Sitting there with his Dad, who was surreptitiously wiping away his tears in the dark. The album he'd heard was "Lost in a Dream" by The War on Drugs. Charlie was vaguely aware of it when it came out in 2014 – Will had been banging on about it – but it wasn't really his kind of thing. Until he saw the effect the songs had on his Dad, and began to realise why, as they sat there in the circle, at the Apollo.

"Start with *Suffering* and shuffle," he whispered. He closed his eyes as the music came on. Thinking about the pain, the loss, the melancholy in that melody, in Adam's voice; thinking about Henry V, thinking about responsibility… and death. Just one word, *Dunkirk*.

It was the call from James that had rekindled all his doubts, despite James's reassurances that the Authority didn't know much and that everything was still in place. After the talk with Rosa in the Revolution Rock, he'd resolved to be steadfast. He'd felt good about Wiltshire, though a little worried about whether Rosa and Gabi would stick together when the going got tough. He had to believe in both of them. Believe that they would not let the Cause down, not let him down. He knew Rosa loved him, but would never put her feelings before the Cause. He loved her too, but worried that it was for *what* she was, not *who* she was. Gabi he adored, but he knew it wouldn't last, and he'd had to put their relationship to one side as preparations intensified. God, life was complicated!

Why couldn't I just stick with Fran, my only...? Why did I put all this before her? I wonder what she's doing now? Maybe she's on stage; maybe she's sitting at home, just down the road. I could go and see her, just in case it's the last time... No, can't think like that. It's going to work, still going to work. And can't take any risks with anyone. Fran, the family. I'm on my own now. Just me and the power of that one word.

And how did Susan get involved in this? No wonder she sounded so weird when she called me. All that stuff about loving me. And what did I do? Cut her off. My big sister, the one who kept me together when Dad left. And I cut her off before she could tell me herself. What risk was she taking to do that? Massive. For me. Even when she doesn't believe in what I'm doing. And I cut her off. What kind of brother am I?

"Suffering" was coming to its peak, when the piano and saxophone drifted in and took the feelings to another level. Gently; no grand gestures. Just truth in simple beauty. Charlie clenched his fist tight and brought it to his mouth. He gnawed at his knuckles, feeling the hard bone beneath the skin. Eyes closed again, he immersed himself in the music and felt the warm tears work their way out and trickle down past his ears. He let them fall, lost in a dream.

***

Mark came back with Susan after work. They walked down to the Thames and had a drink at the Old Ship, just by where the river bent westwards. They stood outside and leant against the river wall. The sun was beginning to set. The clouds were streaky and there was a haze from the pollution. The jetties and old boats started to form silhouettes against the reddening sky.

"It's so beautiful here, Mark, when the sun goes down. One of my favourite places on earth. So serene, even with the A4 a few minutes away."

"Helped by the smog. Have you ever stood at the top of the Arc de Triomphe at sunset, on a smoggy Parisian evening? Spectacular."

"No, I haven't. But I'd love to. It will have to be with you now, as you brought it up."

"That would be a pleasure and privilege."

Susan smiled and rested her head on Mark's shoulder. He put his arm round her shoulder and they stood there for a while, silent, just gazing at the increasingly spectacular skyscape of pinks, yellows, blues, purples. "Our own impressionist painting," said Mark; "But better than any painting."

"So true," said Susan, feeling secure for the first time that day. "Oh Mark, what a day. And it finished with me feeling sorry for Yorkminster. What is happening?"

"Crazy times, Susan."

"You can call me Suze if you want. Like my family does. Not *Siouxsie*, like Yorkminster does."

"How do you tell the difference?"

"Depends on who's saying it. You're allowed. If you want to."

"I'd love to… Suze." He blinked, and blinked again.

"That's Suze without an 'i'. Not sure why. I think it's just the way Charlie spelt it when he was little."

"You didn't hear from Charlie?"

"No, I don't suppose I will. Just hope Dad talked to him. I assume he'll let me know if anything changes. He just promised that it was all still OK. And asked me to trust him."

"And what did you say?"

"I said I would. I want to. And what else can I do?"

"Not much I guess. What about your Mum?"

"I don't know, Mark. I'm not sure what I can tell her. I'm worried they might be listening in. And it's probably best if she doesn't know what's planned. Might make her vulnerable if anyone starts asking. Oh, I don't know, it's so difficult."

"Is she on the lo-fi?"

"No, which is ironic, because she was so lo-fi until recently. Said she didn't like looking at people in thin air while she spoke to them. Felt so unreal."

"I guess it is when you think about it. Someone is there, but not there."

"Yeah, but it's normal now. For our generation, anyway. I mean, even DELE has it."

"Justice hasn't apparently. Except for directors and above, and private office."

"That's no surprise. It's always been in the dark ages, and it's got no money at all."

"True. Anyway, shall I tell you what I think you should do about your Mum?"

"Please."

"Call her when we get back. Just so she knows you're OK. Don't say too much. Don't tell her you spoke to your Dad."

"Just on the standard network?"

"You haven't got much choice."

***

Back at the flat, Mark offered to cook some pasta while Susan called home. She showed him round the cupboards. It felt good, felt like this was something real. It buoyed her up, as she thought about how to start the conversation with her Mum. She didn't need to call up the number, because her wristpad buzzed.

Olivia.

"Mum, I was just about to call you - really."

"Really? Telepathy. Both worried about the same things, I should think."

"Like what, Mum?"

"Well, I was worried about you after our last call. You didn't look right."

"I told you, Mum, it was just going to the Base. Little Amie."

"Nothing about Charlie?"

"Except I don't know where he is or what he's doing. But I'm used to that."

"You haven't heard anything on the grapevine about any plots?"

"I don't have a grapevine, Mum."

"Alright, but I had a strange phone call yesterday."

Olivia's words froze Susan rigid. "What kind of call, Mum?"

"You alright Susan? It was short. A well-educated accent. A man who wanted to find Charlie. Said he had some important information for him. Cut off as soon as I tried to find out who he was."

"You didn't tell him anything?"

"No, why? Is something wrong? Is Jack Oldfield right?"

"I don't know, Mum." This call was getting dangerous. What if someone was listening in? "Look Mum, just don't get drawn into any conversations with strangers."

"Susan, you sound like me talking to you when you were a teenager."

"Sorry, Mum. You know what I mean. None of us know what Charlie is doing. It might be better if it stays that way. And let's just hope he doesn't do anything stupid."

"Oh Susan, let's hope so. Are you sure you are alright? I was so worried. I sit here and worry about all three of you."

"We're grown-ups, Mum. We can deal with things. They don't always go well: that's just the way things are."

"You will tell me if you hear anything?"

"Of course I will."

"Emma was with me when I got that call. She was going to speak to James. He must know something about Charlie. Have you spoken to him recently?"

"Not recently, no." Susan hated herself for saying this.

"I haven't heard back from Emma. I expect she's busy with Archie. He has his exams soon."

A chance to change the subject! "How's he doing? I heard he's in a band and got a new girlfriend too."

"Yes, Emma's really worried about his priorities. You can guess where his exams come."

"He's a teenager. And with his Mum and Dad…"

"Don't judge, Susan. They've done well for him."

"How does Dad manage that? He's in London."

"Well, we don't know how other families work."

"We know his Dad pretty well."

"He did his best for you."

"From a distance."

"He cared. It was just…"

"OK, let's not go down that road now. It was wrong of me to say that. I care about Dad still. I'll speak to him soon."

"And let me know…"

"Of course I will."

"Love you, Suze."

"Love you, Mum." The holo vanished. Susan slumped in the chair. *What a fucking mess.* She was blowing hard as Mark came in with a glass of wine.

"Done? How was it?"

"A mess, Mark, just a mess. A disastrous fucking mess." And she sobbed. "I'm so sorry Mark, I'm just crying all the time. I hardly ever cry."

"You don't normally have all this stuff to deal with." He sat on the arm of the chair and stroked her hair, tracing the line of the dark waves. She reached out to his hand and grasped it tight. He kissed her forehead and she looked up, the glaze of tears still shining in her hazel eyes. "Dinner's ready in five minutes. Come and tell me everything."

Chapter Eight. The Decision
(14-05-27)

Charlie hadn't slept well overnight. A strange bed, even stranger circumstances. He was dreaming crazily, like he'd had a couple of bottles of Malbec and a large chunk of Gorgonzola. He couldn't remember much, except the last dream. It was horrible, what he could recall. Fran, Rosa and Gabi were the last three contestants in the *Hunger Games*. Except it was in the middle of Oxford. Everyone on the streets was walking around normally while the contestants hid and watched out for each other. They all had guns. Gabi had her left arm in a sling. Rosa had a trouser leg missing and a large gash across her thigh. Fran's face was black with soot, except where a tear had run across her cheek. The bubble was closing in and they were all being forced into the New Bodleian. They were knocking shelves of books over, all running to the far corners of the library. And in the middle was Jack, surrounded by a bunch of knights in mediaeval armour and white tunics, with the cross of Saint George, giving them orders to find them and kill them, until just one was left. He would take her for his wife.

The knights found Gabi first. Her movements were inhibited by her broken arm. She cried as she ran. Two of the knights caught up with her and she fell to the ground. One of them pulled his sword from the sheath. He raised it and brought it down.

Aaaagh! He woke up, before the sword hit Gabi. *Where is she, where's my Gabi? Where's Rosa, Fran? What have I done to them? It must be my fault. I need to get back in there.* He was sweating; his back felt like it had been arched all night. His heart was racing. He needed to get back to the dream. Needed to find out what happened. But he couldn't. You never can. He tried to reimagine the scenario, but every time it went somewhere else. He couldn't find Gabi, or Rosa, or Fran. Only Jack, laughing, swearing. Promising vengeance. He sat up. Rubbed his hair for a few seconds, wiped his eyes. Tried to slow his breathing. It was seven o'clock. *Need more sleep. Need to rest today. Need to be right for tomorrow.* He lay down again, shut his eyes.

It was ten when he woke up again. *What the fuck was that? Oh God, it must mean something. But does it? It's just a dream. They take you to some strange places. Doesn't mean they have any significance. But all my women. The ones I love. But I can't love three. Is that what it's saying? No, I just said it doesn't mean anything. But who did I want to win? Please, I don't want to answer that. But shit, who would I want to win? Who was I most worried about? I can't remember. I must remember. There must have been someone I tried to save. When they all got trapped in the New Bod. Why there? Crazy. What did I try to do? Wasn't I one of the sponsors? I don't remember. I must have been. Who did I sponsor? I think it was Fran. I was so worried about her. Yes, I remember now. That streak across her face. I wanted to kiss it. Clean the dirt away. I wanted to send her a bottle and some cotton wool. But they said it wasn't the time. I cried, and tried to do it. But Jack wouldn't let me. What did he have to do with it? Wasn't he with the knights? Couldn't be both places. Yeah, but in a dream, you can do anything. I don't know. Just forget it. Just a dream. Just restless. Of course I'll be restless. Probably be worse tonight. Just got to live with it.*

He got up and had a shower and went for some breakfast in the one of the waterside cafés.

He had a bike, in the basement of the block. An old mountain bike: nothing flash, nothing too conspicuous. It was a dead day, the calm before the storm. A lot of time to think. They'd built that in to allow for last minute changes to their plans, but it was all done and dusted. So a day of nothing. No contact. Just remembering where you had to be, who you had to be, what you had to bring, what time, on Saturday. All going to plan, perfect. Except for the fact that the Authority knew about it!

Yeah, except for the fact that the Authority knew about it. That was a pretty big fucking exception. Charlie thought back to that moment the previous night when he'd lost himself in the music and been at peace with himself and his decision. There was no turning back. Not now. Not unless he heard something from his Dad that made things even worse.

He was glad to have the bike. Cycle the canal, the river, and just think. Kill some of those hours. He wondered what the others were doing. Rosa would probably be reading - something inspirational. Or writing poetry, her favourite way of expressing her feelings. Gabi – she'd probably still be in bed, headphones on. She'd go for a run, if she could. Or to a gym. She'd be somewhere east, probably. She'd catch a film in the afternoon; maybe another one in the evening. She loved the movies, Gabi. Especially those old, obscure, European ones, all subtitles and existential angst. Charlie wished he could be with her in the cinema, feeling a bit bored, but just feeling her warmth beside him.

He sighed, and got back to business. Helmet, dark glasses. Didn't normally wear either, but best to do so today. Eliminate the risk of a chance recognition. No, minimise. You couldn't eliminate all risk. What if the Authority knew more than Dad thought, or was letting on? Someone might be lurking around the Basin. There was nothing obvious at breakfast, but he might be followed when he went out. What was the alternative? Sit in the room all day, going out of his mind? Fuck that. He had to get out, clear his head, get some exercise. Take the risk.

He headed west along the Paddington branch of the Grand Union canal. He loved this stretch. It wasn't pretty, except around Little Venice, but it was interesting. Hidden London. A place for drifters, lost souls, out by the Scrubs. It was important for tomorrow too. No harm in taking one last look around. As he progressed he could see it there, not so far away, on the other side of the canal, beyond the unkempt hedges and the derelict land, interspersed by soulless prefab warehouses, scrapyards and railway lines. The Arch. The destination; the moment of destiny. Rising above all the mediocrity surrounding it. Calling him: *this is your mission. Under this great monument, your moment.*

He continued, mulling over what he would say when he had that moment. He'd discussed it with Rosa, but he wouldn't be reading from a script, or be able to stick to one. It would be spontaneous, heat of the moment, whatever that moment was going to be like. Just three messages – he wouldn't have long. Democracy – the planet – the war in Ukraine. Come with us, have hope, support HOPE. Rosa wanted something about socialism, but Charlie vetoed that. Too theoretical, dull. Had to be things that people could grasp instantly. Henry V understood that. Shakespeare understood that. *Follow your spirit, and upon this charge cry 'God for Harry, England and Saint George!'* Bumping along the canal, alone, Charlie raised his fist and cried out those words. It could be done!

He took the canal all the way to Southall and then turned onto the main branch, heading down to Brentford and the Thames. He saw barely a soul: a few fishermen, a few kids bunking off school, some hardy walkers. But mostly it was just him, and the silence. A lone heron perched on the thick branch of a submerged tree: still, composed, ready for action. Two swans glided over the water's surface: elegant, silent, inscrutable. Charlie took inspiration from them. Whatever he felt, whatever his doubts, his fears, tomorrow he had to have that poise, to stay in control, lead by example. He could do it, he knew he could.

He felt better, assured.

He crossed Kew Bridge with the river at low tide, and descended to the towpath. Familiar territory, bringing back memories. Walks and rides with Fran. Family trips to Kew when they were young and still living in London. He headed downstream towards Hammersmith. Under the grey immensity of Chiswick Bridge, down to Barnes, where the railway bridge stood out from its surroundings, like a bit of Newcastle transported to the plush suburbs of London. He crossed on the pedestrian path over the bridge and continued alongside Dukes Meadows, where some families picnicked with their young children, carefree. As he came to the grandeur of Chiswick Mall, he remembered wading through the flooded street at high tide, with Dad carrying his shoes and socks for him. And how Dad always used to say that if he could ever afford it, this is where he would live. He probably could afford it now; *if only he was still with Mum...* He came to the Old Ship, just down from where the river bent sharply. One of Susan's favourites. She loved the sunsets there. He thought about his sister. Stuck in her office, worried. Cut off by her own brother. He chained his bike and rested it against a tree. He went into the pub and bought a beer. He came out and leant against the river wall. He'd been here many times – with Susan, with Fran, who loved the sunsets too. Holding her tight in an autumn glow. He gazed out at the water, and watched the rowers on what remained of the river at low tide. Another heron, perched on one leg on the dry river bed. The gulls swooped on scraps. And he thought about all the things, the people, he cared about.

And he thought about *Dunkirk*.

He tapped on his wristpad and whispered the numerical code. The first step. He stared down towards Hammersmith Bridge, laden with traffic, as usual. Daily life…

H5 – D – U – N – K – I – R …

He paused. *The heron…swans…poise…my family…my comrades…Fran…love…fear…the Arch…the moment…cry God for Harry…the mission…duty…hope.*
HOPE.

Cancel.

***

Will was just finishing shaving when there was a knock on his door. "Who is it?" he shouted. "Serhiy," came the reply.

What did he want at this hour?

He let Serhiy in. He was breathing heavily. "You OK?" asked Will. "Looks like you've been running."

"We gotta get you outta here, man. Asap."

"Why?"

"We heard some ISPs are coming down from Kiev. Interested in you. Working for the British. Your Authority wants to speak to you. You don't want to do it via ISP."

110

"ISP? What would they want with me? Fuck, must be something to do with Charlie. What do I do?"

"Quick, pack essentials. All evidence of identity, address, etc. Van outside in ten minutes. *Kiev Charcuterie*. Take you to Kiev. Get in touch with your office when you get there. Not before. We tell them what's happening. Suggest you get train to Warsaw or Berlin. Friendlier countries. Get over to Sweden or Netherlands. They the safest."

"OK, but won't I get stopped at the border?"

"Driver will have something for you. Hurry. I gotta go. Before it gets too busy." He stepped towards the door.

"Serhiy."

"Yeah, Will, what?"

"Thanks for what you're doing."

"No problem. Don't wanna see you tortured by ISP." And he was gone.

Will gaped at the door. *Fuck. Charlie, you have landed me in some big shit.* He gathered his most important things, shoved them into a sports bag and went out into the street.

***

He was in Kiev by early afternoon. There had been a couple of checkpoints, but nothing rigorous. It was a bit frightening in the refrigeration unit – it was only as they approached the checkpoints that he had to go in, but it was bloody cold, and what if he had to stay in there for a long time? What if they searched it? The driver assured him they wouldn't be interested. He gave Will a thin chip to insert into his wristpad. New identity. Still a journo, but Irish. The photo was cropped and enhanced from one of Serhiy's efforts that Will used for his byline. That boy had done him proud. The ISP – International Security Police – were notorious. Ostensibly there to work for the NATO forces, they were recruited from some of the old Ukrainian paramilitary forces, and happily did a job for those countries who affected a concern for human rights. Deniability. Will knew all about that. But he never expected to have to confront the reality himself. Thank God for Serhiy. Who was he working for?

Once in central Kiev, he contacted the FT office. They knew he was coming. They had train tickets for him for the journey to Berlin, via Warsaw. He'd have to make his own arrangements to get across to one of the Scandinavian countries from there, or maybe Amsterdam. It made sense to try. Sooner or later he'd have to hand himself in, but best to get somewhere that definitely took people's rights seriously.

The controls on the train as it crossed into Poland were non-existent. At Warsaw he had to wait nearly two hours before he could get a train to Berlin. He sat in a café, paranoid about everyone who glanced at him. He had a couple of beers to relax – best to look normal. He bought an English language magazine which featured a preview of the EEL final at Wembley. *England's return to respectability*, it said. *Not after tomorrow afternoon*, thought Will. *Where will I be then*?

***

Yorkminster was having a terrible time at the Cabinet Office. Back at DELE, he felt like he was something. A Director, a big cheese. Made it up from the ranks. Joined the Home Office as an executive officer twenty years previously. Showed promise and got himself into the fast stream. Made steady progress up the ladder. Knew how to network. Knew the value of taking credit for the things that ministers liked. Knew this would make him unpopular with some people, but *c'est la vie, gotta look after number one*. He was doing alright: there was still a chance he could go further, maybe not right to the top of the department, but pretty close. He felt good about himself, even when he knew that the likes of Susan and Mark held him in contempt. Who were they? *Been to University, so what? Lefty liberals, what do you expect? Civil Service is full of them. Never going to like someone like me. No point worrying about it. Though I wish Siouxsie would. Nice girl. Intelligent. Bit up herself.*

Too emotional about the Bases. But I like her. Wish she could take that at face value. I'm on her side.

But the *Bolingbroke* meetings were in a different league. He couldn't quite admit it to himself, but he felt intimidated. Down in the basement, surrounded by paintings of politicians from Britain's glory days, room full of stern-looking men from the Home Office and security services. Only two women. One the chair, from the Home Office. Ferociously intelligent, frightening. Never smiled. The other a junior official from No 10, but full of herself, being from No 10. Talked bullshit, but with extreme confidence. The only person he felt comfortable with was a guy from the Treasury. Why he was there, Yorkminster had no idea – except there was always someone from the Treasury at any important meeting. They liked to keep their fingers in every pie. There was always money attached somewhere.

But the biggest problem of all for Yorkminster was that he had nothing useful to say. He gave his update of arrangements, his liaison with the FA and the EEL executive; but what the Bolingbroke group wanted to know was whether he had obtained any information from Susan. Intelligence hadn't made much headway with its calls, and the potential perpetrators seemed to have vanished. No-one knew where H5 was. And no-one had any idea how or when any kidnap might be attempted. Some members of the group suggested that the threat needed to be downgraded to just another possible attack. The only evidence was from a drug dealer who'd overheard something in a pub. Not the sort of intelligence they would usually act on, without verification.

Yorkminster told them about the discussions he'd had with Susan. He said he felt she was telling the truth, that she was a good civil servant who didn't approve of what her brother was doing. She really didn't know anything. Of course she had family loyalties, but he knew her well, and could see that she wasn't covering anything up. He was challenged by the chair. Didn't he have a handle on anything that he could use to put a bit of pressure on her? He thought about it. No, there was nothing obvious… except, maybe, her work with the refugees on the bases in the Wash. Yeah, she'd

113

got pretty emotionally attached to some of the kids there. Might be a lever…

Oh my God, why did I say that?

It didn't get a lot of traction with the group, but the chair suggested he explored that avenue further just in case it might yield something. And then the killer blow. *We'll be getting into the details of security arrangements after tea. Don't feel you need to stay unless your departmental interests are directly impacted by those arrangements. We can update you all afterwards.*

In other words, *fuck off, you're no use to us.*

He stayed for tea. A face saver. The chair was very nice to him. DELE did an excellent job. The final was obviously organised superbly. It was important for England to be welcomed back to the highest levels of football. The people needed that affirmation. The Authority welcomed it. The man from the Treasury whispered conspiratorially that they were superfluous now and might as well go and do something useful. The woman from No 10 spent all her time talking into her wristpad. But she would stay.

Yeah, thought Yorkminster, *no point in sticking around. Not wanted. Fuck 'em. I've got stuff to do back at the office. Susan's report for a start…*

***

He'd just finished reading Susan's report about the visit to Base One when she came up to his desk.

"Can we talk, Chris?"

"Of course. About your report? Very good, by the way."

"Well yeah, that too. But there's something else."

They found a room. Susan wasted no time.

"Why have you brought my Mum into this?"

"What do you mean?"

"You know what I mean. Some spook called up my Mum yesterday. In the middle of the day. Trying to get information on my brother. She doesn't know anything. You said you were on my side."

"I am Susan, I am. But I can't do anything about Intelligence."

"You must have heard something at all these Cabinet Office meetings."

"Nothing, Susan. Honestly nothing. They don't know anything."

"Really? You probably shouldn't have told me that. Just in case I'm in cahoots with Charlie."

Oh shit, I shouldn't have.

"But I believed what you told me, Siouxsie."

"Susan."

"Oh, sorry. Susan."

"Really?"

"Really what?"

"You didn't shop me or my Mum."

"No, I promise. I'm not trying to hurt you, Susan."

"OK, I believe you. What happens next?"

"I don't know. I got kicked out early because I had nothing useful to say."

"Oh, really?"

"Yeah. In the nicest possible way of course. It's the Civil Service."

"I'm sorry about that. We aren't big players in this. Best to stay out of it."

"I guess you're right."

They looked at each other. A kind of relief. They weren't enemies. The enemy was somewhere else.

"You read my report?"

"Yeah, very good, like I said. It's helpful."

"Enough on security?"

"Just about."

Susan waited for him to mention Amie, or her brother. He didn't. He seemed subdued, broken even. *Let it lie. Maybe he is on my side.*

Maybe.

***

Olivia was helping to clear the tables after lunch at the Marquee Moon when, to her surprise, Emma walked in. She'd been very supportive the day before, but Olivia didn't expect to see her again for a while. Emma looked upbeat, suspiciously so after yesterday's strange call.

"Hi, Livvy, sorry to surprise you like this, but I've got something for you in the car. Have you got a moment? It's just outside."

"Oh, this is… a bit of shock. Something? I can't imagine what."

"It's OK, Livvy. Really OK. Something you've needed for a while."

"Oh. OK. Let me just get my bag." Her heart raced. Emma said it was OK, but something felt odd. Wasn't that awful man on the phone was it? Or…

She followed Emma out. The car – not Emma's, but something much more expensive – was parked in a side street a few minutes' walk from the café. The windows were tinted.

"Look inside," said Emma. Olivia gingerly opened the front door of the car. Her heart seemed to stop for a moment. Everything seemed to stop.

"Hi Livvy, how are you?"

James.

Olivia burst into tears. Emma put her arm around her. She whispered, "It's alright, Livvy I'll be here for you. But you two need to talk."

"I know, I know." She wiped her eyes and got into the car, shaking. James held out his hand to her and she took it. She closed her eyes and felt the warmth of his hand around hers. A thousand memories flashed by and the rewind came to a halt on that first night in Kennington. The self-effacing guy who liked the same music and seemed so interesting, even though he was one of the bankers talking football in the corner. And then fast forward: Charlie, that summer after his finals. So full of life, so handsome, with his beautiful girlfriend, so ready to take on the world.

Her reverie was broken by Emma. "Look, I'll leave you two to it and go back to the café. I'll let everyone know you're fine. I'll wait there for you." She closed the door, gently, and turned back toward the High Street. Olivia and James gazed at each other and James's grip on her hand tightened. She didn't resist. He motioned to speak, but Olivia got there first.

"Oh James, please tell me, what is happening to our children? Do you know?"

"Livvy, I'm so sorry, it's been so long. I've been meaning to…"

"It's OK, I'm not angry. I'm just worried. Really worried. And yesterday a man…"

"Yes, I know. Emma told me. That's why I'm here, now. I want to help."

"How?"

"Aaaah, by just telling you what I know. It's going to be alright."

"Really? I've been hearing all sorts of things about Charlie. Bloody Jack Oldfield spreading rumours around town. Susan's stressed, I know, but she won't tell me why. And Will, well, I never stop worrying about him out there on the battlefront."

"He's OK; I spoke to him on Wednesday. Nothing much happening out there. He's frustrated; needs to get to Kiev. But look, Livvy, I need to tell you about Charlie."

Olivia gulped and took her hand away. "Charlie?"

"Yes." James leant back and stared out of the front window of the car as he spoke. "Livvy, Charlie is fine, but he is involved in something big, for HOPE. This is the moment of truth for them, and Charlie has become their leader." He sighed and went on. "There's something happening tomorrow. The intention is to grab some airtime at the football final at Wembley."

"How?" Olivia fixed her stare on James, although he continued to address the car window.

"I don't know how much I should tell you, Livvy. It may be dangerous for you."

"He's my son. I need to know."

"OK, OK… he and some of his colleagues plan to take hold of a couple of footballers tomorrow, and demand the cameras give them some coverage so that they can address the watching millions. Get across the message about what's wrong and what needs to be done."

"Oh my God. That's madness. How can they do that? They'll be caught, surely. Who knows what will happen to them? Will they have guns?"

"They'll be armed, but not to kill. Charlie has always been insistent. No-one dies."

"But how can he guarantee that? How can he be sure that he and his friends won't be killed?"

"He can't be sure, but arrangements are in place."

"What sort of arrangements?"

"That, I better not say. Honestly."

Olivia grimaced. For the first time she felt anger. "But you know…?"

"Yes, I know."

"How?"

"I'm supporting him, supporting HOPE."

"You're what? How? What do you mean? You're helping him to perpetrate this mad scheme?"

"It's not mad. It can work. It will work."

"How on earth can you say that? Oh yes, you can't tell me. Too much information for poor ol' Mum to take in."

"Don't say that Livvy, it's not like that. It's just…"

"Alright, I don't need an explanation. Not about that. But I do need to know why you are supporting HOPE. I don't disagree with what they are saying, but I don't like the way they are saying it. They are making themselves enemies of the Authority. That's very dangerous. Charlie is putting himself in danger. For what? Is it that woman Rosa? He's left Fran again. Why? She's always been there for him."

"It's not Rosa. It's the Cause. It was the coup that turned him. Before that it was a bit of a game."

"But why are you helping them? That just gives them ideas. And look at what that has led to. This madness!"

"I promised I'd never let him down… again." The tears welled in his eyes. And Olivia understood. She leant over and hugged him. He sobbed into her shoulder. And they swayed gently in each other's arms, clinging on to their reawakened memories.

Eventually, Olivia gathered herself. She breathed hard and whispered into James's ear. "Let's go back to the café. Emma's waiting. I expect everybody's waiting."

And they walked back to the Marquee Moon, arm in arm, oblivious to the world.

Chapter Nine. Wembley
(15-05-27)

Charlie woke early. He'd slept surprisingly well – must have exhausted his supply of crazy dreams the night before. There was no going back now. It was going to happen. He showered and had some coffee. He didn't feel hungry. Just slightly sick. The nerves kicking in – of course they would. His biggest ever show. He went through all the routines in his head one more time. The night before he'd deleted all references to the plan from his system. Triple-deleted. He hoped all the others remembered to do the same. He went through his speech again. Keep it focused. High impact. Won't have much time. He called up the TV holo. Amazon Elite Soccer channel. The build up to the final was already on. Security forces outside the stadium, though no mention of any specific threat. Jet copter views from above the arch. *This'll be Dan's view*, thought Charlie. *We are totally reliant on him. Without him we don't get out. He'll be at the King's Cross copter dock now, fine-tuning things. Readying himself to take Dad's clients to the game. In their box by midday. Utterly pissed by the time the game starts. Hope they haven't fallen asleep by the time the action begins. The real action…*

He went down to the café at nine and forced himself to eat something. Needed a reserve of energy before setting off. On all the screens, it was about the game. The café had a few fans kitted out in Barcelona's distinctive colours. The tension built inside Charlie. These next few hours were going to be hard. Just needed to get on with it. Back in the apartment, Charlie started to regret his choice of breakfast. *Should have just stuck with the yoghurt and fruit. Good sugars. Not all that fucking bacon. God it was nice, but…* he rushed to the bathroom and threw up. *Oh fuck, what an idiot. But, it's alright. Out the system. Best way.* He tried to slow down his breathing. He filled a glass with water and went to lie on the sofa. "Henry V" was still on the floor from the Thursday night. He picked it up and started to flip through the pages. *Harfleur, Agincourt… St*

Crispian's day, we happy few, we band of brothers. He stopped there and studied the speech with the same intensity as he had when he'd been learning it at school. And felt the same burning desire for something, something that would mark him out, make him different, special. What was it? Henry knew…

> *But if it be a sin to covet honour,*
> *I am the most offending soul alive…*

Yes, thought Charlie, *this will be the most honourable thing I have done, we have done. If we fail, if we die even, at least we have tried to do something to change this world for the better. We will have given people a lead. And maybe we will succeed, and one day lead people to a better place. The odds may be against us, but we have to try. We – I – owe it to my country, my people. We cannot go on as we are. Accepting the worst, sliding towards more catastrophe, unable to express ourselves. The Authority has to be defeated.*

Yes, fucking yes! Defeated. Charlie got up. Raised his fist. *Let's go for it!*

***

He left the apartment at eleven, with his rucksack empty apart from a bottle of water. They weren't meeting until one, so he decided to start the journey to Wembley on foot. Could get on the tube later. A good chance to clear his head. He felt buoyed up now. The day was bright, just a few clouds scattered around the blue sky, moving rapidly in a stiff breeze, which was keeping the air fresh, if a little dusty. His stomach was in knots, but at least he'd cleaned it out. He took a glug of water and set off towards the Edgware Road, which was a few minutes to the east. The pavements were busy: people waiting for buses, heading into the Arabic grocery stores, dawdling outside the cafés. A few men studied their holo-maps and pointed east. *Heading to Lords for the cricket,* thought Charlie. *Not where the action is today.* He smiled. This was beginning to feel good. He headed straight up the Edgware Road, through the smarter environs of Maida Vale and onward to Kilburn, where the buildings got shabbier and the people looked harder. A young couple hanging out by a bus stop with cans of super strength lager looked at him suspiciously. *Don't get paranoid now*, Charlie told himself. *They can't suspect me of anything – except being a toff who's got lost on his way to Hampstead.*

He picked up his pace until he reached Kilburn tube station. Time to take the train to Wembley Park. Mingle with the crowds. Put on the Olympians beanie and the shades. He'd thought about shaving his hair or dying it, as his picture - and Rosa's - would be in the police records and might have been issued to staff in the ground. But Dad had assured him that nothing like that would happen. He hadn't said how he could guarantee that, but Charlie had to take that all on trust. He was taking everything on trust. The Authority knew they were coming and there'd be no welcome party. That was a lot of trust. But Dad had said he would never let him down.

Never.

The Jubilee line train was already pretty crowded. There was a festive atmosphere. A group of Barca fans sang the *Cant del Barca*. The Olympians fans smiled and looked a little bewildered. They didn't really have a song anymore. A few shaven headed middle-aged men attempted a rendition of *I'm forever blowing bubbles*, but it fizzled out before the dreams could fade and die. *The Tottenham fans were hardly going to sing that*, thought Charlie wrily. *Or that execrable attempt at a new anthem.*

The crowd edged its way out of Wembley Park station past the armed guards, and flowed onto Wembley Way. Charlie's heart stirred. It was always an impressive sight: the mass of people oozing over the bridge, the stadium looming large beyond them. The Arch: simple, majestic. At its best when lit up, but still awe-inspiring when a glowing white, as it seemed today. *And how can we beat that*, Charlie asked himself, *how can we inspire people today? When we are about to mess up their football match. They won't see a match today. All they'll remember is us. And how will they remember us? The people who ruined their day out, or the people who gave them hope?* He felt sick again, even sicker. Would people care about their message? Could he rouse them to hope for a different way? Or were most people just happy with what they had? As long as they were safe and had money to live the way they wanted? Charlie's heart sank. Had they really thought about this? Had they imagined what it would be like as they walked up Wembley Way and really thought about it at the moment it was about to become reality?

No! Can't think this way. Remember HOPE. The Cause. Remember Henry. Remember what he said at this moment:

O God of battles, steel my soldiers' hearts.
Possess them not with fear.

Possess me not with fear, God. Or doubt. We are on the threshold of something great. No time to doubt the Cause. This is our fate. This is my fate and I will happily go to it…

***

They didn't meet until they were at the table in one of the hospitality rooms, courtesy of Elevation Funding, James's company. All using different identities, which James had helpfully transferred onto their wristpads. Just another privileged group amongst the company clients, the wealthy tourists and the well-heeled supporters of the two clubs. They were younger than most, but didn't stand out in any way. The same smart casual clothes, the same haircuts. The same ease when faced with a huge wine list, or ten kinds of seafood for starters. They chose some wine, but hardly touched it. The same went for the food. No-one was hungry. But they ate and drank something to avoid suspicion. The next hour was tortuous. Making conversation, talking about football, business, mutual friends. No politics. Waiting for the call.

14.20. Forty minutes to kick off. They got the signal. They took turns to go out to the toilets, taking their rucksacks with them. They walked past the toilets until they came to another corridor on their right. That took them out of sight of the guests. At a door marked *Private*, they knocked four times and were greeted by a man dressed in the black and maroon of the security staff. He took their rucksacks and fitted them inside with the hover packs they needed for their mission. "Remember, keep the flap open when you put your bags on." He handed them a hover control, which looked like an old fashioned computer mouse, and reminded them how it worked. They had practised the manoeuvres enough times, but the reminder felt reassuring. Finally, a small laser pistol. "It will only stun, but no-one will know that, if you point it at them. Good luck."

With fifteen minutes to go, they went out to their seats. Prime viewing: front row, mid-tier, about twenty metres to the left of the halfway line. A lot of the seats around them were still empty, as the hospitality guests were slow to take up their places. Always time for another glass of something. Charlie remembered something his Dad used to go on about while watching the football in the old days. *The prawn sandwich brigade.* He was never sure what it meant, as a young boy. It just sounded funny and nothing to do with football. He smiled, and thought of everything that James had done to make this mission possible. It couldn't have happened without him. Charlie just hoped that he had his own tracks covered. James assured him that he had, that there were people on the inside who shared their aims. Charlie looked along the row at his comrades. They seemed calm. Gabi was next to him. He took her hand and squeezed it gently. She leant across and kissed his cheek. "It's happening," she whispered.

"Yeah," Charlie replied. "You ready for the magic?"
Gabi nodded and smiled, her pale blue eyes burning bright. "Can't wait."

The crowd began to buzz, as the video screens showed the teams entering the tunnel. The music started up: the anthem of the European Elite League. Charlie could feel his heart racing. *Not long now, not long.* The teams came out as the anthem reached its climax and fire cannons and confetti machines blasted into action. Massive psychedelic holograms seemed to explode out of the floodlights, and swirled over the pitch. The crowd roared, stood up and waved their flags: the dark red and blue of Barcelona, the white, navy and claret of the Stratford Olympians. The two teams lined up amid a melee of TV cameras, dignitaries, match officials and royal minders. Charlie fixed his gaze on King Charles, waiting impatiently to greet the teams. Barcelona's song began, their followers raucous in their rendition of the *Cant del Barca,* the anthem of the *Blaugrana.* Olympians fans struggled through their own, as Charlie and his comrades put their rucksacks on their backs and fastened the belts. And then, with pop superstar Stellar Hey - glittering in the afternoon sun - poised to belt out the verses, the military band struck up the National Anthem. *Wait for glorious, wait for glorious…*

Agincourt!

Charlie, Gabi, Mike, Rosa and Luke climbed onto the ledge in front of them, activated their hover packs, and jumped.

***

It took the crowd a while to register what had happened. The National Anthem continued to its conclusion before a hush descended over the stadium and everyone stared up at the big screens. There, amid the chaos, stood Charlie and his comrades with two Stratford players separated from their team mates. Rosa and Gabi had their pistols pressed against the spines of the two players, while Mike and Luke stood guard, guns pointed in the direction of the players and officials, who were now surrounded by guards. Gabi's left arm hung limp by her side. She'd fallen awkwardly on it as they landed on the Wembley turf. She was looking through a haze of tears, grimacing with the pain. But she had a job to do. She stood firm. Charlie hadn't noticed Gabi's plight, as he screamed at the TV camera crews to come over to him. *"I wanna see and hear what I say on those big screens. No cut outs. Got it?!!"* They nodded. This was great for them – much better than filming the dignitaries shaking hands with the players.

It was time for the speech of Charlie's life.

"All of you in this stadium today, all of you watching around the world, please listen to what I have to say. I'm sorry to interrupt your football, but we have a crisis in this country, a crisis across the world, and we need to act. We are HOPE, we want to lead you against the oppressors to a better world. I have three things to say. ONE, England is ruled by a dictatorship with no democratic basis. They gained power with a coup; the elections of 2025 were fixed, opposition was suppressed. We must overthrow the oppressors and restore the rights of you, the people. TWO, there is a criminal war going on in Ukraine. The two sides are colluding. Surplus young men from all over Europe, refugees escaping from danger in Africa, Asia, the Middle East, have all been rounded up and put in the trenches. Disposable. Out of the way. Sacrificed to hide unemployment, the plight of the homeless. It must end. WE must end it, with a democratic uprising. THREE, our planet is in danger, but it is fighting back. Around the world, extreme weather events destroy communities, usually the poorest. Whole cities face the threat of being submerged. In England, already the Fens in the East of England have been flooded. The Somerset Levels in the West are next. It is a disaster. And our government does nothing, except build roads and refugee camps above the water. It remains in thrall to the big corporations and the banks. Profit comes before the planet, before the people. We need action. We need hope, we are HOPE, we..."

As Charlie moved towards his conclusion, from above the arch came a blur of silver in the sunlight, growing larger. Dan's jet copter swooped out of the sky and landed thirty metres from the action. No shots fired, as the guards became confused about where to aim their guns. "Run, NOW!" shouted Luke. Mike took the player that Gabi had been minding, as he saw she was struggling. "It's alright mate," he shouted at the footballer. "You ain't gonna be hurt unless they start firing - so now, run!" Charlie didn't complete his oration, but ran with them, towards the open door of the jet copter. Gabi was lagging behind as the pain seared through her arm with every stride. A laser shot out from the guards and struck her on the leg. She stumbled. Another hit her in the shoulder, and she fell

126

onto the turf, screaming with the agony. She tried to drag herself over the grass, but could hardly move.

The others reached the entrance to the copter and climbed in, the players needing little encouragement. Charlie heard the screams and turned around to look. "Gabi! My Gabi!" He motioned to go back to her, but Rosa pulled him back into the copter. "No, Charlie, we can't, we have to go, now!" He relented and the door closed as the copter took off. Still no more shots. Only those two, which had downed Gabi. The copter shot skyward, out of the stadium, past the glistening arch, and was soon a speck in the distance.

The crowd, hitherto transfixed by the events on the ground, erupted into a confused roar. It was almost a cheer, maybe a gasp. On the field, just confusion. The players and officials were urged to leave the field, but many of the players didn't want to go. They were jostled by the guards and punches were thrown. The crowd began to roar its disapproval; the *Cant del Barca* rang out from the Barca areas. The Olympian fans chanted the team's name, and those of the two captured players. People began to leap out of their seats and run towards the pitch. The dazed stewards made no attempt to stop them. Encouraged by the early invaders, more people did the same, and the pitch was engulfed by the crowd. The security forces were powerless. The crowd headed toward the remaining players and lifted them up, passing them over their heads like they would a singer crowd-surfing at a concert. The players raised their fists, snarled and pointed at the authorities, the dignitaries in the official boxes. King Charles was long gone, spirited away from the turmoil. The crowd's chants were still football-based, but they were angry. People were angry. They weren't quite sure what about. But the authorities were getting the blame. The cameras were still filming. The big screens were still going. The authorities seemed to have given up the ghost.

Charlie and his friends did not see any of this, but they would have been amazed at the reaction they had provoked. A boil of frustration, suppression, had been lanced, and the authorities, the Authority, didn't know what to do about it.

***

"Gabi, my Gabi, we fucking left Gabi!"

Charlie was distraught, shaking. Rosa had her arm around his shoulders. "Charlie, it's OK, she is alive. Our mission succeeded. You must stay calm. You are our leader, we need you."

"But they got her. They'll torture her, to find out what she knows."

"Don't think about that Charlie. Stay strong. Think about the Cause, you must think about the Cause."

"I know, I must. I will. But Gabi…"

Rosa leant into him and whispered, "Be careful Charlie, the players must not hear, but surely your father will find a way to protect her."

"Oh God, I hope so, I really hope so." He breathed hard and slow and tried to regain his composure.

"Your speech was amazing, Charlie. So powerful, so passionate. So clear. The people, people around the world will have heard your message. The battle has begun."

"But where will it lead. What power do we have?"

"We have the power of words, Charlie. The power in people's minds. In their memories. We have hope. You have given them hope."

"I don't know, I've just ruined their fucking football match. And I've lost Gabi."

"We can pray for Gabi. We must believe in our Cause. Believe that today you gave that Cause to thousands, maybe millions of others. You did it, Charlie."

"We did it. We all did it, Gabi did it. She fell for us, for the Cause."

"Yes she did, Charlie. And I hope the Cause, and her love for you, will keep her strong. You must believe."

"I do, yes I do."

They clung on to each other, swaying with the swoops and lurches of the jet copter. And Rosa kissed Charlie's forehead, as he sobbed into her shoulder, for one last moment. For now.

***

The players had been blindfolded as soon as they were settled inside the copter. Luke and Mike assured them that they wouldn't be hurt and that they'd be left somewhere soon, from where it would be easy to get back to their team. They were given fleeces, as both were shivering – with shock, fear. Luke told them a bit about the Cause, why they'd disrupted the final. Talked about how he supported the Olympians even though, as a Spurs fan, he'd thought it was a step down in class joining up with West Ham. The English player smiled and joined in the discussion. The young Brazilian just looked bewildered.

They quickly arrived at the northern reaches of Wormwood Scrubs. Dan brought the copter to a hovering position a few feet above the ground. "OK boys," shouted Luke above the noise of the hover blast, "It's not too far down. Time to jump. Just head towards civilisation. You'll be OK. Sorry to detain you, but we just needed to get out alive. Good luck – sure they'll play the game in a couple of days. I'll be watching from somewhere. Come on you Olympians!" The players jumped, and Dan took the copter upwards. The players stood there, gazing at the silver machine, as it shot away. The Englishman even managed a wave, before he looked around, realised where they were, and pointed towards the buildings in the distance.

It wasn't far to the Grand Union canal. Dan took a short diversion first, so the footballers didn't get any sense of where they were heading, and then doubled back to the canal. He brought the copter to a hover position again, this time by the disused gas works: the frames of the tanks skeletal, but still there decades after they served any useful purpose. This time Charlie, Rosa, Mike and Luke jumped out and scrambled towards the canal towpath. The jet copter soared away, Dan taking it to its final resting place. The place was deserted, desolate, as it usually was. An old, decaying barge remained moored to a post; otherwise, nothing.

"Where is it?" said Charlie.

"Any moment," Rosa replied.

The four of them looked around, wary. A jogger appeared in the distance; they scurried back to the bushes by the gasworks, and waited until she had passed. Mike ventured out on his own to check. The others stayed where they were. "Should have done this first time," said Rosa. "My fault."

This time Charlie reassured her. "It's no big deal Rosa. You've been brilliant. Everything has been planned perfectly. And thanks for helping me back there. And for saying what you said."

"I meant it, Charlie."

A couple of minutes passed before Mike signalled at them to come over. They dashed over to the towpath as the barge came into view, gliding almost silently over the murky water. It stopped at the bank and the driver threw a rope over to Mike to hold onto as the others clambered onto the small deck and filed into the cabin. Mike leapt on and the barge went on its way, unobtrusively, along the waters of hidden London.

Inside the cabin, the four friends relaxed for the first time in hours, maybe days. "We did it," said Luke. "We fucking did it!"

"A long way to go yet," cautioned Rosa.

"Yeah, but immediate mission accomplished," said Mike. Charlie went over to the small fridge and found a four pack of lagers. He brought them over to the table and handed them out. Rosa wasn't sure, but opened her top with the others.

"Cheers," said Charlie. "To HOPE. The journey begins." They rapped their cans against each other's. "A long journey ahead, but this is our first big step. We stay together, we stay true. We can win."

"To Gabi," said Luke. We love you, we are with you. If you falter, we will not blame you. You are one of us, always."

Charlie choked for a moment, and then raised his can to Luke. Falteringly, he said, "You said it like I just couldn't have done right then, Luke, man. I love you, man, I really do."

Rosa raised her can, and smiled. "Gabi, my love is with you, wherever you are. May you be strong. May there be people who will protect you. May we be together soon. At liberty. Marching in

130

triumph. Marching for our Cause, for our people, for our planet. All our hope is with you, for you."

She looked towards Charlie and they hugged. Rosa was trembling now, and Charlie soothed her, running his fingers through the waves of her hair. He gently raised her chin so that it brought her eyes up towards his and he kissed her on the lips. Once, twice, then slowly, deliberately. Lost in time, lost in memories. They looked up at Luke and Mike, who looked sheepish. "Sorry guys, emotional times," said Charlie. "No problem, man," said Luke. "I know where you're at." He raised his can to Charlie.

And the barge cruised serenely on.

***

They made their way past the scrubland, the factories, the tower blocks, the non-descript housing estates, a tree-lined golf course, until they reached a bridge at Perivale, on the lower reaches of Horsenden Hill. They jumped off the barge and climbed up to the narrow road, where they walked briskly south until they came to a side road. A car was waiting for them. From there they took the short journey down to the A40 and headed west, to Oxfordshire. There were a few more jet copters in the skies than usual, but no road blocks or even a visible police presence. Mike drove and took care not to exceed the speed limit, just in case. Not far from Banbury they took a turning off the motorway and onto the country roads, through the rolling hills and picturesque villages of middle England. Wealthy England, the England whose privileges the Authority was there to preserve. Charlie gazed out of the window and thought of home, Glastonbury, and of the cottage they'd taken in Wiltshire to go over their plans. He recalled the moment when Rosa had looked daggers at Gabi – poor Gabi! – and then of those beautiful words she'd spoken on the barge. He loved Rosa for that. Love. He loved and feared for Gabi: injured, vulnerable, bound for interrogation. He shivered again at the thought of that. *Please don't hurt her any more.* And he thought of Fran. What would she have been thinking when she heard about the events at Wembley? Would she have been mid-rehearsal, or getting ready for a performance? Could she go on tonight? What state would she be in? He thought of Susan – what would they do to her? Would they pick her up, or wait till Monday when she got into work?

God, I've made life difficult – no, made it dangerous, really dangerous – for a lot of the people I love, he thought. *I hope it's worth it. It has to be. Remember those words, my words, at Wembley. It has to be worth it.*

Eventually they turned onto a narrow track that took them to the English stables of Marcus O'Toole, a wealthy Irish horse breeder. A friend of James, who invested some of his millions for him in places that allowed deniability, and made fantastic profits. A long range jet copter was waiting for them. And already in it, smiling with a beer in his hand, was Dan. "Hi guys, you took your time. And don't worry, I'm not the pilot this time. Done enough of that today!" Charlie rushed up and hugged him. And so did all the others. Sheer relief that they'd all got this far. All except Gabi. Dan knew about that already, and told them about the protests at Wembley after they'd made their escape. One security guard had lost control and started firing at the crowd. No-one badly hurt, except the guard, who'd been grabbed and kicked to pieces by the angry fans before his colleagues had managed to get him away. All on TV until the Authority had got a grip and imposed a blackout. "We sure benefited from their incompetence today. I was expecting to be pursued by police copters. I was ready to bail out and crash the thing, but there was nothing. Nothing – amazing."

Charlie smiled. "Not just incompetence. The Authority is not united. We know that. We exploited that. Money exploited that. My Dad's money."

"We have to exploit capitalism for our own ends until we can destroy it," said Rosa.

"I'll drink to that," grinned Luke.

"Yeah," said Charlie, "Maybe. Let's just concentrate on now. Enjoy the triumph and then work out what we do next. And how we get Gabi out of her fix."

"To Gabi," Luke shouted, as he took a beer from Dan.

"To Gabi – we fucking love you!" Charlie cried. Rosa managed a half smile, feeling rebuffed – and peripheral. Mike noticed and put his arm around her. "We love you too, Rosa." She looked up, and beamed at Charlie through watery eyes.

They took their seats as the familiar roar of the jet copter started up, and soon they were hovering above the tree line. "Sunshine coast here we come!" shouted Dan, as the copter pointed west. Jets on full and they were off, part of the regular racing traffic between England and Ireland.

Destination: County Wexford.

Chapter Ten. Watching, Waiting
(15-05-27)

Susan went over with Mark to his place on Saturday morning. They figured that if anything spectacular did happen at Wembley that afternoon she might receive some unwelcome visitors later on. Being at Mark's didn't eliminate all the risk, but as far as they knew, no-one in DELE was aware that they had been seeing each other. There had been no hints from Yorkminster, and they agreed that he would have found it impossible to resist letting them know he knew. Susan packed clothes for the weekend and for Monday morning. She had to go into work – doing otherwise would just have raised suspicions. She was braced for a day of interrogation, hopefully of the civilised kind.

But anyway, there was Saturday afternoon to get through first. Susan felt tense as they took the tube to Putney Bridge. What exactly was her brother going to do? When and where would they try to kidnap the footballers? *Don't let it be anything that leads to people dying,* she prayed. *Or getting hurt. It's just not worth it. And how can they hope to fight the Authority with stunts? People don't care much. They want stability. They've agreed to sacrifice a bit of political expression in exchange for that. It's not an unreasonable bargain in the circumstances. Things were a terrible mess, going back years. Ever since Brexit, really. Dad would say since the 2008 banking crash. We've just got to try and make the best of things. Take the small victories. Amie, for example. If we can give her and her family a new life, that's progress. One thing can lead to another. Charlie winding up the Authority could just set things back. Oh my brother, my baby brother! Don't hurt yourself. Don't hurt anyone…*

After they'd left Susan's gear at Mark's flat, they crossed over Putney Bridge and walked along the river in the direction of Wandsworth. Gleaming towers of empty apartments rose over the river. Built in the 2010s, they'd always been mainly for the foreign investors to hide their money. Not much had changed in ten years.

The Labour government had attempted to force the owners to rent them out at reasonable prices if they didn't occupy them for at least eight months of the year; but the initiative had floundered in the face of numerous lawsuits, and then the coup had put an end to such nonsense. The oligarchs were back in control and stronger than ever. Mark remarked that the architecture was pretty spectacular nonetheless, and that he loved to walk along the urban riverscape, seeing new patterns and shapes every time. There were a few nice and fairly quiet pubs dotted around too, and they settled in one of them for lunch. They thought about staying there to watch the game, but Susan was worried about getting too emotional if something did happen; so they ambled back to Mark's place and readied themselves for the ordeal. Susan cuddled up to Mark on the sofa and briefly dozed off. As she stirred, Mark was caressing her with his fingertips - so tenderly - and she felt like she was in the safest place in the world.

"Oh Mark, be strong for me. I'm so scared. And I don't even know what of."

"I will. And try not to think about it. There's ten minutes to kick off and nothing's happened. You'd have thought the chance for any sort of kidnap was going to take place inside. But look, there's the players about to come out. Maybe Charlie called it off. Maybe it didn't work and..."

"He's been arrested? Oh please, no."

"Sorry Suze, shouldn't have said that. Thinking out loud. Lived on my own for too long."

"Oh no Mark, it's OK, really. I just don't know what to think."

The players ran out, and the ground became filled with blazing light and smoke, from the fireworks and the holos. As the air cleared and the teams lined up, there was still nothing unusual happening. Surely that would have been the last opportunity?

And then the anthems began...

Susan and Mark gazed at the screen, silent, transfixed. Susan realised she was grasping Mark's hand so tightly that his blood might stop circulating, and tried to relax. But she couldn't. There were Charlie and his fellow warriors: the blonde girl, Gabi, who she knew about from Fran, with her arm hanging limp, looking in pain. Rosa looking fierce. The two men, calm… and then her brother. Beginning his speech. The cameras homing in for the close up. His hair gleaming bronze in the sunlight, emerald eyes sparkling as he declaimed. Susan hardly caught the words, just snippets. *Oppressors, the people, the planet, hope, HOPE.* The passion in Charlie's words was what mattered, a blazing passion blistering the airwaves. And those eyes. Challenging you to believe. *My brother, my little brother. A man. A leader of his people. Our people. My people. I believe him. I believe in him.*

My brother, he's Henry V again.

***

It was half past ten before Will got into Berlin. He took the U-Bahn to Rosenthaler Platz in Mitte and found himself a room in a hostel he remembered from trips with his parents. They'd had a nice apartment in an adjacent building, which shared the café with the hostel. Dad had been a big fan of Berlin – always said it was somewhere he could live. And now Will was here, living off memory, wondering what would happen to him next. He was tired from the escape and the train journey, but buzzing. There was no point in trying to sleep, so he wandered down towards the river, where he knew there'd be some nightlife and plenty of places to eat. He settled in one of the big Irish pubs the Berliners seemed to like and ordered himself a large Weissbier and some Bratwurst. He watched the locals and the tourists, out on a Friday night, knocking back the beers with seemingly not a care in the world. The screen around the walls beamed mainly German football, but a couple of screens were previewing the EEL Final. *More of the hated Olympians*, he thought. *Come on Barca. Wonder what my little brother is going to do. Can't see it working. Security will be on clampdown, surely. Unless there's a conspiracy of some sort. No chance - thinking like a journalist all the time*, he admonished himself. *No way they are going to let this one go off when they already know something's planned. No way. Shame to miss it though. Could stay here to watch the game – or the HOPE special. I'll know then how hard they are going to be looking for me. Could contact Hanna – Kiev will probably have alerted them that I'm on my way. They won't have been efficient enough to bug every FT communication. Would they?*

Four beers later Will stumbled out of the bar feeling a lot more confident about what lay ahead. He'd got talking to some Irishmen who were in Berlin on business and with some German women who worked for one of their clients. Amazingly, one of the women, called Sofia, knew Hanna and offered to pass on the message that Will was in town. That was helpful. He explained that he was on a trip that he didn't want his bosses back in Frankfurt to know about just yet, but was keen to talk to Hanna. So it was best to keep it off the network. Hanna would understand. Sofia seemed eager to help, and by the time he'd left he'd got a coffee with Hanna organised for the morning and a date with Sofia in the evening. If he was still in Berlin.

The rain had started to fall as he made his way back to the hostel. The city was quieter now. The lights still shone from a few bars. The neon signs of the Vietnamese restaurants still glowed and illuminated the soft rain drifting through the night air. But it felt eerie. For a while Will felt like he was being followed. He thought about taking a diversion, but worried that might cause suspicion, if he was being followed. Eventually the figure turned into a nightclub, and Will relaxed. But this wasn't good. The euphoria from the encounter in the bar, especially with Sofia, began to wear off. Will even wondered whether Sofia was a plant, an agent of the Authority, or the ISP. *Don't be fucking ridiculous,* Will told himself, as the rain started to come down harder. *I met some random people. Talked football, shared a beer. Got on with Sofia and found we had a mutual acquaintance. It happens. She was out with those guys. How could she be a plant? How? Just not possible. Just not. Cool it, man. Cannot be a set up. All the others in that group knew her. She was one of them. No way it could be a set up. No way. I might stay tomorrow. I liked her. And I'm seeing Hanna. And I've got to see the football. Just fucking think clearly, man.*

But he couldn't shake off the worry. He got back to his room, damp and shivering, and took a hot shower. As he came out of the cubicle, he leant over the sink for a moment and thought he was going to throw up, but nothing came. Staring in the steamed up mirror he exhorted himself to stay strong, to accept he would, at some point, have to hand himself in - but preferably at a time of his own choosing. Get far enough away from Ukraine that they'd most likely send him back to London, not Kremenchuk, or Kiev. He could get a decent lawyer then. Contact Dad, get him to use his contacts. And what did they have on him anyway? That Susan said *they know about Saturday*. And Dad thought it was something to do with Wembley. Big deal. That was the sum of his knowledge.

Oh God, what will they do to Susan? Bloody hell, I've not even thought about that. Too busy obsessing about myself. Jesus, I hope she's OK. Shit, and what about Serhiy? That boy did me a massive favour. What if they found out he tipped me off, arranged the escape? He's fucked. All for me. And what can I do here? Fuck all. Maybe Hanna will know something. Maybe she can make sure Serhiy gets help. Maybe they've already done that. Surely they wouldn't have just let him go hang in that arsehole place. No, the FT wouldn't do that. But what if the Authority...

Will got dressed again and went down to the bar. It was shut. He cursed. *Need some JD just to settle the nerves. Won't sleep otherwise.* He went to reception, where a man watched the news on a small old-fashioned TV. Will introduced himself. The man smiled – his name was Mesut. "Ah yeah, Mesut, nice to meet you, Mesut. Just like my man Ozil."

Mesut kept smiling – inebriated Englishmen were nothing new, especially since the Ukranian war had begun. "Arsenal," Will slurred, "played for Arsenal."

"Yes," said Mesut, "what can I do for you, Sir?"

Will asked if there was any chance of getting some whisky – had a hard day, just trying to wind down. Yeah, had a few beers, but still a bit hyped. *Stop making excuses*, he told himself, *Mesut won't give a shit whether I'm an alcho or not. Depends on whether he can be arsed to help.* Mesut disappeared through a door at the back of the reception, and returned with a large wine glass full of whisky, and a plastic cup full of ice cubes. "Oh my God, that's so brilliant," Will exclaimed. Mesut smiled, and just said, "No problem." Will shook Mesut's hand and went back up to his room, feeling guilty that he'd even doubted the man's interest in helping him. "Brilliant service, brilliant service," he whispered to himself, as he struggled to open the door to his room while holding the glass and the cup. Some of the ice cubes fell out. "Fuck," he muttered, and stooped down to put them back in the cup. He banged his head against the door and almost dropped the glass of whisky. He felt a bit out of breath. He sat down with his back to the door and popped some of the cubes into the glass. He took a slug of the whisky. It *was* Jack Daniels, or some other bourbon. It burned his throat, but in the nicest way. He sighed and closed his eyes.

About half an hour later he felt his shoulder being shaken. He thought it was a dream for a moment, but it was Mesut. He helped Will up, opened the door and brought in his whisky. The ice cubes in the cup had melted. Will apologised and thanked him profusely. Mesut looked at him like he'd seen the same thing a thousand times before and offered to go and get more ice. Will said no, he didn't need it, but five minutes later Mesut returned with a fresh supply. "Magnificent service," Will declared, and Mesut smiled knowingly, before nodding and disappearing down the corridor.

"Yeah, good fuckin' service," Will slurred, as he staggered towards his bed. He propped up the pillows, settled down and called up the TV screen. He put some fresh ice into the glass...

***

"You need to get out of Berlin soon," said Hanna, leaning over the table towards Will, who was nursing a coffee, but wishing he had a Bloody Mary in front of him. He'd woken up still in his clothes at six in the morning. He'd undressed and dived under the covers for a few more hours, but still felt like a dry fishbone when he got up. He had a reviving orange juice and a bowl of yoghurt, fruit and granola down in the hostel café. Mesut was helping to serve. He smiled a wry smile at Will, but said nothing.

Hanna lived in West Berlin and Sofia had suggested they meet in one of the big places on the Kurfurstendamm. Easy to find, and less chance of being spotted if you didn't want anyone to know you were there. Not a cool place for the journos to hang out. Hanna was already there when he arrived. She looked pleased to see him – that was nice after the traumas of yesterday. They'd been on training courses together in their early days on the paper. Hanna was now number two in Berlin, and spent most of her time reporting the latest diplomatic developments in the war. Berlin was where everyone headed for the big picture. Kiev was too close to the action for that. As for Kremenchuk – it was Will's biggest regret. No coups, just an accumulation of evidence about the pointlessness and hellishness of the whole affair.

"This place is crawling with agents," said Hanna. "Kiev let us know you might make your way here, but didn't say much more. I didn't know how we'd hear from you. You really got lucky meeting Sofia last night."

"Yeah, and she was really nice."

"Thought you might like her. Definitely your type."

"Not like you?"

Hanna blushed. "Well, you know about me and Mikel."

"Yeah, I know."

"That OK with you?"

"Of course." Which meant *no*. Will had really liked Hanna when they trained together. They'd been out a few times, but they'd never worked together in the same place, and nothing came of their relationship. Will had always regretted it, but had never figured out how to tell Hanna what he really thought of her. And she'd never invited him out to Frankfurt, where she started, or Berlin. And he didn't think she'd ever want to come and see him in London. So nothing happened. And he regretted it like hell. Now she was together with Mikel, who was some kind of film director; and, until yesterday, he'd been stuck in Kremenchuk with no interesting stories to tell. And now he was on the run. From whom, he wasn't sure. If not the ISP, then surely the Authority. All because his little brother planned to mess up everyone's entertainment that day. Will did not feel in a good place, although sitting with Hanna in the bar was making him feel better. It was sweet misery, if nothing else.

"Do you know anything about Serhiy?" Will continued. "He got me out of there, and I don't know what risks he took to do so."

"No, we've heard nothing. Good or bad."

"Surely they'll suspect him."

"Sure, but he has good connections with the opposition. I think he'll be out of there. Somewhere safe in the right part of Kiev."

"I hope you're right."

"So do I."

Hanna gazed at him, and held out a hand. Will took it. "Look Will, I really care about you, and that's why I think you need to get out of here. Soon."

"I said I'd see Sofia tonight."

"I'll explain for you."

"Will you?"

"Of course I will. And when things get better, maybe we can see each other sometime."

"I'd love that."

"So would I. Really. But you have to get out of here."

"I will. Might just stay for the football final. I won't explain right now, but it could affect how interested they are in me here."

"Will, I'm a journalist. You've just intrigued me. I need to know now."

Shit, thought Will, *shouldn't have opened my mouth.* "I don't want to put you at risk, Hanna."

"Oh Will, everything you say makes me want to know more!"

So he told her - about Charlie, about his Dad, about Susan, about how Serhiy got him out - and then urged her to keep it to herself. He knew it was madness, but just couldn't hold back. Once he started, he just needed to tell the whole story. He looked down at his empty coffee cup and wanted to cry, but held back the tears. Hanna brushed her leg against his and they kept them touching, feeling the electricity of the contact. An affirmation. Will felt a new

141

optimism, which he knew had no real foundation. Not now, anyway. But it gave him hope. About now and about the future.

Hanna offered to book his rail ticket to Amsterdam and transfer it to his wristpad. That way he'd have no direct trace on the station records. It all helped. First he had the football though. He couldn't miss that. Not with his brother about to change all their lives.

He went back to the bar where he'd met the Irishmen and Sofia, about an hour before the match was due to begin - just in case the action took place before the match. The preliminaries were uneventful. Will bought a second beer and got back to his seat just as the teams came out. The anthems and the fireworks began. The crowd in the bar ignored what was on the screen and continued talking, until suddenly it became clear that something had happened. Silence descended as Charlie moved into close-up.

Will felt a huge shiver down his spine and began to tremble. He wasn't sure what he was feeling. Astonishment, bewilderment, fear, pride… yes pride. *Go for it Charlie boy! My brother*. He wanted to shout to the people around him, *that's my fucking brother!* As the jet copter appeared out of the sky and the gang ran for it with the two players, the bar erupted into a roar. It was incredible! Will couldn't figure what was going on. Was it support or rage? The guy sitting next to him put his arm round his shoulder, punched the air and hollered something completely incoherent. The only word Will could discern was *HOPE!* The cameras panned onto the people running for the copter. The girl with the blonde hair stumbled and fell. They couldn't hear the sounds of the laser fire but they saw her feel the back of her leg as she fell. Will felt a surge of sympathy and anger. The poor girl! She looked to be in agony. There was something wrong with her arm. A close up showed her crying. And then it panned out to Charlie, turning round, seeing her there, prone on the turf. He looked desperate. He started to shout, but a dark haired woman pulled him away and they all scrambled onto the copter. It shot away. And the cameras moved back onto the remaining players. They looked angry and started to remonstrate, as the guards tried to move them away. The crowd started to spill onto the pitch. The bar was in uproar now. Chants of *We want HOPE!*

echoed through the place. Will felt completely dazed as the man next to him tried to hug him and chanted the refrain into his face. He pulled away, feigned an apology and just stared at the screen. The Wembley turf was full of chanting fans, players held high. Fingers pointing at the elite boxes. Faces contorted with anger.

It's a fucking people's revolution! Will felt the tears stream down his face this time. His brother Charlie Mowbray had sparked something extraordinary. Will felt so proud of him. Someone was taking on the Authority. The whole world had seen it. The whole fucking world!

He made his way to the Hauptbahnhof, elated, drained, confused. He wanted to fight now, but knew he had to run. And that girl, the blonde girl. He wanted to reach out and help her, rescue her. And now she'd be in the hands of the Authority. Poor girl! What would happen to her now? They had her. The bargaining chip. Interrogated. Maybe tortured. Always denied, but how did they get all of their information? *I so want to help her. But I can't. No-one can. She's fucked. Please, let her be alright. Charlie looked distraught. Was she his girl? He left Fran for someone. Was it her? Oh my God. Poor Charlie. That will matter more to him than anything. Take the edge off his triumph. Please let her be OK. Please...*

Hanna was waiting for him at the station. She didn't need to be there - the ticket was already registered on his wristpad - but she wanted to say goodbye. It felt so good to Will to see her standing there. Just waiting for him. He rushed up to her and held her tight. They stood there, just holding on to each other, saying nothing, eyes shut, lost in the moment. Hanna broke the silence, looking up and whispering, "Take care, my darling. I will be thinking of you."

"Hanna, this is such a special moment. Thank you so much for coming back into my life. If only for this moment."

"It won't be for just this moment. I promise."

"You do?"

"Yes, Will. I always remembered you. Maybe you didn't think so, but I did. We made different lives, but I never forgot the times when we trained together."

143

"Nor did I, but I never imagined…"

"Will, you don't believe in yourself. You are intelligent, witty, a great journalist, but you don't believe."

"Oh God, I know, Hanna. How could you tell?"

"Just the way you were. It felt like there was something you wanted to say, but you couldn't."

"Could things have been different?"

"I don't know. Life just goes on, doesn't it? We never know what happens next."

"You're telling me."

"So, you never know, Will."

"But you're…"

"Not necessarily forever."

"Really?"

"I don't know. But hey, you mustn't miss your train."

"I'd miss it for you."

"You can't. Not now. Just get home first. Safely. What will you do in Amsterdam?"

"Go to the British Embassy, I guess. I don't want to go into hiding. I've not done anything. I don't even know anything. I'm just related."

"He was awesome."

"Yeah, amazing. I couldn't believe it."

"You must be proud. And worried too, I'm sure. But remember how great he was."

"I will. Always will."

They stared into each other's eyes and embraced again. Will wanted to declare his love, but was still too scared to. Not now. Maybe another time. If things worked out. If she was free to say yes.

"You must go now, Will. There's only five minutes."

"Yeah. See you. Thanks for everything."

"My pleasure." She smiled the most beautiful smile Will had ever seen. That was it. He pulled her towards him. There was no resistance. They kissed - slowly, deliberately.

But he had to go. They lingered, their fingers still entwined, reluctant to make that last break. He took a deep breath, let her hands fall from his and turned for the platform. "I'll be in touch, as soon as I can."

"I'll be waiting. Be strong."

"Yeah, I'll be strong. You take care too…"

He clambered onto the train at the first door, just before it pulled away. He imagined Hanna watching the train as it disappeared, a tear in her eye. Maybe more than just a tear. Maybe.

He could always dream.

***

The Bolingbroke group was convened for eight on Saturday evening. Before that Yorkminster was on the holo pulling together what information he could about the events at Wembley. He tried to organise a DASO virtual conference, but most of his team weren't answering - not least Susan. *Damn her!* The Bolingbroke group was bound to ask about her and he was going to look a real chump if he had nothing to offer. Mark was nowhere to be found either. Those two were always in cahoots, so no surprises there. *You'd think there was something going on between them. Come to think of it, maybe there is. That would explain a lot.*

Peter Edmondson played a blinder though. On to all his EEL and FA contacts and both clubs. No one had a clue how HOPE could have pulled the kidnap off. A lot of worry about the reaction of the players and the fans. Angry with the Authority for failing to prevent the kidnap, but fearful of its reaction to events. For a start, EEL and the clubs wanted the game to be rearranged for Wednesday evening. Too much money hanging on it, and the Spanish regular season wasn't yet over. But the FA feared that the Authority and the Met wouldn't want to risk any further unrest. Playing behind closed doors was mentioned as an option.

Pete was brilliant with the private offices too. They were going frantic, trying to make sure the Secretary of State was properly briefed before he went to COBRA on Sunday morning. They

145

jumped at the closed doors option as a face saver, and instructed Yorkminster to put that forward at Bolingbroke. He thought it was a terrible idea - it would be a farce and just remind people of HOPE's success. But he didn't say so. He could tell they wouldn't be taking no for an answer. They wanted to know where Susan was too. They weren't at all happy with Yorkminster's ignorance. "Go round to her fucking house," a young woman, maybe half his age, snarled at him over the holo. He didn't want to do that, knew how Susan would react. She was probably as traumatised as the rest of them – most likely more so. After all, her brother had just masterminded the stunt of the century and made a speech to millions across the world which, he had to admit, had been quite brilliant. He didn't say that to the private office girl either.

He thought about asking Pete to go over to Susan's, but he was best employed on gathering information from the sports people. Reluctantly, he took the tube across London to Hammersmith himself. Just enough time to have a word with Susan if she was there, before heading back to Westminster for Bolingbroke. He was filled with gloom as the tube heaved its way through central London, laden with tourists. How he envied them, jabbering away, with apparently not a care in the world. Heading for a restaurant, or a show, or just Buckingham Palace. Not on a mission to snoop and snitch on a valued colleague, a young woman he admired, and was fond of, even if he struggled to express that properly. And what would she think of him now? The pits. Just another rat in the sewer.

God, I hate this job sometimes, he thought.

He got out at Hammersmith and made his way down Kings Street for about ten minutes. He turned left, towards the A4 and the river, and then right, onto a quiet street full of pleasant terraced houses. Number 19 it was. There was a small paved garden out front, with a few potted plants and two large bins. He went in and pressed the buzzer by the side of the door. He could hear the whirr of a camera on the other side of the door, but there was no answer. He tried again. Still no answer. He rapped the door with his knuckles, with the same result. But he felt it shift as he did so. He pushed it and it clicked open. He felt a shiver of fear. Someone else had been round, broken in. Whoever it was hadn't bothered to conceal the damage to the lock. Had Susan been there? Maybe she was still inside. Hurt, tied up, worse... surely Intelligence wouldn't do that. They'd just haul her in for questioning, surely.

He stepped cautiously into the landing. The kitchen was to one side. No-one in there, but some drawers had been left open. He went forward into the living room. Pictures of what he assumed were Susan's family adorned one wall. And there was Charlie Mowbray, the hero/villain of the hour. The shock of wavy blonde hair, the confident smile, the adoring face of a woman he took to be Charlie's mother. Another featured Susan, Charlie and a second boy, a little older and more serious-looking, standing triumphantly at the top of Glastonbury Tor. Next to it was a rather low quality shot of Charlie standing under the stage lights, crown on blonde mane, sword in hand, declaiming something dramatic. Henry V perhaps. *H5 - of course.* He looked around: the draws of a desk were open, some papers and knick knacks lay on the rug. Cabinet doors were open; a glass lay shattered on the wooden floor boards. The holo device on the desk had been tampered with. On closer inspection, it looked like the control wafer had been removed.

He touched nothing – didn't want his fingerprints on anything. But there was still upstairs. If he went up there, he'd be trapped if someone came in. But he had to. What if Susan was up there, hurt, or worse? He tiptoed up the stairs. He checked all the rooms. Similar to downstairs. No major wreckage, but items tipped out of draws. Whoever had been here was sending a message, a calling card. Almost certainly Intelligence – a burglar would have caused more damage, and stolen more. He moved downstairs and went to the door. He needed to exit without anyone seeing him. He opened it slightly. No sign of anyone, but he couldn't see much, because of the hedges. He'd just have to go, and brazen it out if necessary. There was no-one around. He got out of the street before he decided what to do next. There was a pub on the other side of the road. *No harm to have a pint,* he thought. *No-one is going to know me. Got a bit of time before Bolingbroke.* He had a decision to make. Would he try to contact Susan and tell her what had happened?

He went into the pub and bought a pint of London Pride. He found a seat and pondered what to do. If he didn't tell her, she'd know no different, but at some point she'd come back to her burgled home. In the meantime, anyone who tried her door could just come in and help themselves. A limited possibility, maybe, but if it did happen, it would just make her life even more confused and hurt. He didn't want that. On the other hand, if he did tell her, what would she think? Why was he round her house in the first place? And who would pick up on the conversation? Surely Intelligence would be monitoring any possible calls. He could be implicated in the HOPE conspiracy. End of career. No, just not worth the risk. He wanted to help Susan, but not at the expense of his own future. The do-nothing option was the only choice. Play it by ear. See what came out of Bolingbroke, and plan from there. He sort of hated himself for that decision, but came back to his guiding philosophy: *look after number one.*

***

The atmosphere at the Cabinet Office was tense, as they waited for the chair to arrive. Only the woman from No 10 was talking – to her holo. The head of security at Wembley was there. Ashen-faced. Five more minutes passed before the chair arrived, with two harassed-looking assistants. She took her seat at the centre of the long table and looked around the room, with an air of disapproval. Yorkminster felt about two feet tall and resented the fact. He'd known this woman in his Home Office days. She'd been a couple of years ahead of him. Nothing that special. Clever, yes – hardly unique in a big civil service department. Went into Private Office – the rest was history. And now she was here to admonish them. There was no upside for Yorkminster. All he could do would be to say how the clubs wanted the game back on as soon as possible. He knew what sort of reaction that would receive. *Oh well, life is shit sometimes. As long as I've got something to report back to the minister.*

"I hardly need to tell you how ministers view this debacle," the chair began. "COBRA meets at ten tomorrow, and they will want answers. And a plan. There are two immediate priorities: to prevent unrest from spreading and to find H5 and his gang. We will take these in turn – after we have sought to find an explanation for how HOPE were able to infiltrate Wembley, equip themselves with hover packs, launch themselves onto the field in the middle of the National Anthem with His Majesty nearby, secure captives, make a speech to millions without interruption and escape in a jet copter, unimpeded – apart from the girl. And then to disappear completely off our radar. Even though we had warning that a kidnap attempt was planned." An uneasy silence ensued, as everyone with any responsibility for the events stared down at the table, or their shoes. Yorkminster focused on the feint trace of his reflection in the polished wood, as the head of security at Wembley, Barry Wiggins, was invited to begin proceedings. *Whoa… rather him than me,* thought Yorkminster, as the abject official began his story.

Two hours later, they had just about established the facts. It appeared to be a sorry tale of incompetence and missed opportunities. Wiggins had insisted that the decision not to fire at the kidnappers was the right one – the safety of the players and guests, and later, the whole crowd, was paramount. In fact, Yorkminster thought, he gave a pretty good account of himself, although there was the still the mystery of how the gang smuggled the hover packs into the stadium. Attention turned to how the jet copter could get in and out of Wembley without any challenge, and how the police and then the RAF completely failed to follow the escaping copter. How could it disappear without trace? Wasn't every journey tracked? What emerged was that the Authority's system of surveillance wasn't as all-encompassing as everyone thought. *Fuck me,* thought Yorkminster, *if the public knew this, they wouldn't be half as cowed as they are.* Maybe the disturbances at Wembley would be the start of something. He thought back to Charlie's speech. Brilliant. Really resonated. He chastised himself for his disloyalty, *but yeah, this could be the beginning, when we look back.*

The plans for dealing with further disturbances were dealt with perfunctorily. They were a pretty routine response to any emergency. If the Authority couldn't handle that, then it really was on its way out. What everyone was waiting for was how they were going to find the gang.

"The girl," the chair began, "Gabriella O'Leary. English, Italian-Irish antecedents, Oxford-educated. Who knows how she got involved in this. Has she been questioned yet?"

"Not yet," said a man from Intelligence. "She is still under sedation. Doctors advise she won't be ready for any truth-extracting drugs until tomorrow. She broke her wrist landing on the pitch. She has severe muscle damage to her legs and shoulder from the laser fire."

The chair looked at him reproachfully. "Minsters will not be happy that there is no information from our only potential lead. Could questioning start early morning? Anything would be helpful. We need to show that there has been some action. And what about H5's family and friends? Have they been brought in yet?"

"Mother, Olivia Mowbray, yes. His girlfriend, Francesca Willoughby was questioned after she'd finished her matinee show at the National Theatre. Both appear genuinely ignorant of H5's whereabouts. And we hauled in our informant after a brawl in a Glastonbury pub. Too drunk to be of much use at the moment. There are two siblings. William Mowbray, an FT journalist on the front in Ukraine. Disappeared from Kremenchuk on Friday morning. Tipped off, we believe, by colleagues. They have been pulled in for questioning, although a photographer, Serhiy Pyatov, has also disappeared. We think Will, as he is known, has made his way to Berlin, via Kiev. Under a false Irish passport. He appears now to be on his way to Amsterdam. Whether he plans to make it back to the UK, we don't know, but if he uses public transport we will be able to track him."

"Let him get to Amsterdam. Then watch him. It's possible he'll know the whereabouts of H5. In fact Amsterdam is just the sort of place you could imagine them heading."

"That's exactly what we are doing. Shall I continue?" said the man from Intelligence, with a hint of irritation. The chair sensed that, and softened her tone. "The other sibling?"

"Susan Mowbray, a senior civil servant at DELE, wasn't present at her home when we visited. Our operative made sure that she would know someone had been round, and secured a read out from her holo. No obvious contact with H5 recently. Some anguished conversations with her mother. The two obviously worried about Charlie – that's H5 - but Susan, on the face of it, doesn't seem to know any more than what we fed her."

"What about the lo-fi?"

"We are looking at that. But breaking down the encryption is not always easy. The providers don't always cooperate. They may be unwilling in this case, given the impact H5's speech had on the public, especially outside this country. If we are able to make progress before ten tomorrow, we will obviously let you know."

"Chris, she's one of your colleagues. Have you been in touch?"

"I've tried. She's not contactable. I went round to her house before this meeting. No sign."

"Did you go in?" asked the man from Intelligence. "Yes," said Yorkminster, "Your man bust the lock – deliberately, I assume. Anyone could walk in."

"So your prints will be on things?"

"I didn't touch anything – except the doors, the banister, obviously." Yorkminster felt defiant, felt like saying, *what the fuck did you expect me to do*? He just stared.

"What about the girl on Base One? Her brother?"

"Well, they won't know anything," said the man from Intelligence.

"Obviously," hissed the chair. "But they may be a lever, if we want any answers from Miss Mowbray. Assuming we find her. We don't appear to be doing very well with anyone else."

"I'll action it," said the man from Intelligence. "We can arrest the brother." Yorkminster regretted mentioning Amie more than ever before.

"What about the father?" the woman from No 10 interjected. The chair delivered a withering stare in her direction, and said, "James Arnold, a partner at Elevation Funding, is away at present. He can be vouched for." And don't ask me any more questions about that, her look suggested. The woman from No 10 got the message. *Strange*, thought, Yorkminster. *Surely he'd be one of the biggest leads. He must be rolling in it... no wonder Susan can afford a house in Hammersmith.*

The question about James brought proceedings to an abrupt end. No thanks for attending, no summing up of what COBRA would be told the next morning. Yorkminster smiled at the man from the Treasury, who raised his eyebrows. They weren't hearing the whole story – that was for sure. He went back to his flat and reported back to private office. The young woman who'd screamed at him earlier was still there. She seemed grateful this time – he was able to give her a good account of the Bolingbroke meeting, and she even apologised for her behaviour earlier. *Stressful day*, she said. Yorkminster felt sympathetic. She was inexperienced, a bit out of her depth really. But doing her best. He left out any mention of the reluctance to discuss James Arnold. Best if the minister didn't wade into that one. And he didn't say anything about Amie and her brother. Didn't want the minister encouraging them on that front. Susan would hate him even more.

Yes, Susan. Where had she got to? Maybe she was with Mark. He knew where Mark lived. He could go there... *no, fuck that, I've interfered enough. I'm done with this. No, I'll keep my head down. No upside for me at all. I'm sure Susan will be in on Monday. She's too conscientious not to be.*

He poured himself a large glass of red wine and settled down with his holo, to see if he could find a broadcast of Charlie's speech on the web.

***

James had always planned to fly to Ireland on the Friday. All the arrangements had been made. He needed to keep a distance at the last. Elevation Holdings had a Dublin subsidiary – after Brexit, a lot of business had transferred there from London. The firm had bought an apartment in the city centre – it was a good investment, as well as being handy for James and others when they went over to meet colleagues and clients. Actually, they had bought a large part of the apartment block, and it was making the firm a fortune. All this pricked James's conscience, but it was what he was good at, and he was putting some of the money into a good cause. Saturday, if it went well, would show that.

After the impromptu visit to Glastonbury, he didn't feel like going back to London, and he took a jet copter from Bristol to Dublin. The encounter with Olivia had moved him deeply and had rekindled something. Walking along the streets of Glastonbury, arm in arm, it felt like the days when they first met. He felt a burning love, a desire to protect Olivia from all that was going on. He couldn't, but felt terrible at the suffering she was going through. He wanted to stay, to look after her. He knew that was an impossible dream; but it didn't make him feel any better that he had no choice but to continue with his plans. He met Michael at the Marquee Moon, for the first time. It was awkward, but James could see why he was the right sort of man for Olivia. There was something caring and respectful about him. You could see how the customers and staff warmed to him. He seemed genuinely interested in everybody. It was good to see that Olivia was in a good place at home, with a supportive partner. He felt guilty that he was no longer that man, but reminded himself he had a wife and son in Bristol. That just made him feel even more guilty! After all this was over, he said to himself, he was going to spend more time with them – and maybe Olivia too, if Michael and Emma were OK with that.

He spent a couple of hours with Emma in Bristol. After the discussion with Olivia, he didn't feel he could hold everything back from her. Her reaction was similar to everyone else who knew. Madness. Not because of the Cause. She totally supported that. People in Bristol would support that – her friends anyway. But how could it work if the Authority already knew? James hinted at arrangements again.

"I really hope you know what you are doing, James. Otherwise Charlie and his friends are doomed. They could even die. Your son, James."

"I know, but it will work. I'm certain. And Charlie really wants this. This could be the turning point."

"What turning point?"

"The moment the Authority loses control. And people start to believe there is an alternative."

"And that alternative is HOPE?"

"The alternative is their Cause. They could just be the catalysts, part of a movement."

"And Charlie's going to lead that?"

"Yeah, maybe. I don't know. But he is going to start the revolution."

"You believe this, James, don't you?"

"I do, I really do. I was sceptical at first, but Charlie and his followers have a passion, a belief. You have to have that to succeed."

"You need a lot more than that."

"That's where I come in."

"Oh." Emma paused, reflecting. "This wouldn't be happening without you?"

"No."

Emma hesitated again. Working things through in her mind. So many things. "I believe in you, James."

"Thank you, Emma, that means so much to me. And when we get past this, I'll come home, be there for Archie during his exams."

"Oh James, I still love you so much," Emma gasped. "Please come home. Or bring us to London. Let's be a proper family again."

"I will, Emma, I will. I really will."

"You promise?"

"I promise. I want to be a better husband and Dad. Look after you."

"It's not looking after I need James – it's love."

"I will love you, Emma, always."

"And Olivia?"

"Oh God, Emma, please. It was so hard today. And so good. And now…"

"James, I understand. I love Olivia. We've become such good friends. We can find a way, the three of us – and Michael. I know we can."

"Yeah, I would love that."

Emma glanced at her wristpad. "But you have to go now."

"I have to go now, you're right. But I'll be back soon. Tell Archie that. Give him my love."

They hugged. Emma's grip was tight and James could feel the warmth of the tears on her cheeks. His own eyes were glazed with a feeling that was love, guilt, regret… but also hope. He kissed her like he hadn't for some time. She responded, with a passion that outdid his. Renewal. Hope.

But first, HOPE.

***

James spent the evening at dinner with clients in Dublin. It was good cover. The clients were fine. The talk was all about the markets, and horses, and politics. *If only they knew*, thought James, as they sang their praises for the Authority and how it had brought England properly back into the fold. *If only they knew what my son is going to unleash tomorrow.* That made him feel good, at the same time as he pulled in more funds for Elevation Holdings. *What a fucking hypocrite I am*, he cursed himself. *But not for much longer. It's my family – my families – that are going to come first in the future. Whatever happens tomorrow.*

Back in the apartment he stood out on the balcony and looked over the city lights, the Liffey black but glimmering in the background. It had been a tumultuous day. A day in which he felt he had re-rooted himself. Realised – if he really needed to realise – what was most important in his life. Tomorrow was massive too. Charlie's moment – the fulfilment of James's promise to him. How he would always be there for him, never let him down. It was time to extend that to the rest of his family.

It had been agreed, with Charlie and his Authority contact, that they would only get in touch in an emergency. There were no messages when he got back after dinner, or during the rest of the night. There was nothing more he could do. It was just time to wait and see.

***

On Saturday morning, he took the DART out to Dun Laoghaire. He needed the fresh air. He walked out along the pier. There was something uplifting about just staring out at the waves, the ships, the distant hills, as he was buffeted by the stiff breeze. Something cleansing. It cleared his head, helped him to focus. He had made so many pledges, and he meant to keep to them all; but now was the time to think about Wembley. Had he ensured that all the necessary arrangements were in place? He thought so. The head of security was onside. A sympathiser. The stake in a Hong Kong property fund had helped. James was still worried about the team all getting their hover packs without anyone noticing. But they'd done the best they could. There was no way that Charlie and the gang could have got them through security outside. And he was worried that some of the security guards wouldn't be able to hold their discipline and not fire once they saw what was happening. And how Dan was going to get the copter out and all the way to the stables without someone in the Authority tracking him. But there was nothing he could do about any of that now.

He stopped at a pub near the station and had a sandwich and a Guinness. It slipped down beautifully. The first one always did. He didn't have a lot to do, so he had another. It soothed him. He felt more optimistic as he took the DART back into Dublin. He walked through the shopping streets, past the new developments that had sprung up as Dublin had grown as a financial centre after Brexit. The place was buzzing. How would the people of Dublin react to the events at Wembley that afternoon? He thought they'd be behind HOPE, unless they were more pissed off about the game being disrupted. That was something he and Charlie had worried about a lot. Football fans in England, en masse, weren't renowned for their liberal attitudes, although the Barca fans had a history rooted in the civil war experiences of their city. They were relying on that a bit. They had to make a judgement about whether people were frustrated and unhappy with life under the Authority and just staying quiet to stay safe, or pleased to have a stable economy and reasonable security and not much bothered about anything else. Surely the number of people being sent out to the Ukraine would be having an impact – especially in the poorer areas of the country. Always the first to be sacrificed. It was hard to know. But they had to take the risk and go for it. Now or never. James believed in Charlie. He was a late convert to the HOPE cause, but it had become his life. He'd sacrificed his relationship with Fran for it. His friends, especially Rosa, were totally committed. James sympathised. He'd benefited hugely from the Authority's rise to power. Making money had become so much easier. But he didn't feel good about it – just richer. Supporting HOPE was for the country, for Charlie, and yes, his conscience.

He went back to the apartment and called up the TV. Half an hour to go. No sign that anything had gone wrong yet. The festivities began. The players came out with fifteen minutes to go. The anthems began. The National Anthem… James's heart raced. He tried to spot Charlie and the gang. The cameras weren't ready for them. And then, there they were, swooping into camera shot. Gabi mistimed her landing, but got up and helped separate the two players. Her arm was hanging limp though. The first sign of something not going to plan. James shuddered. *Not now, don't let it go wrong now.* In the general chaos, the cameras panned to Charlie. He began his speech. *Astonishing. He's doing it! My boy. Amazing. So clear, so passionate, so true.* Then the blast of the landing jet copter. They turned and ran. The guards held back – that was crucial. Wiggins had done his job. But Gabi was struggling – she couldn't get into a rhythm with her injured arm hanging by her side. Laser shots were fired from somewhere – a rogue guard, maybe someone panicking – and they hit Gabi in the legs. She fell and writhed on the Wembley turf, like a footballer taken out in a heavy challenge. The cameras panned to Charlie by the copter, crying out to Gabi. Pulled back by Rosa. Climbing in – still crying out as the doors of the copter slid together. And then they were gone. The cameras switched attention to a melee amongst the players and security guards. The crowds started to come onto the pitch. This was surreal. James tried to see what had happened to Gabi, but the cameras had lost interest in her. More and more people invaded the pitch. *If the guards open fire now*, thought James, *we will have a full scale riot and massacre. Please don't let that happen. We never anticipated that. No-one dies, Charlie said. No-one dies. Wiggins knows that. But if the Authority overreacts…*

James was dazed, drained, by the tension, the emotion, the wonderment. And the pride. His boy, Charlie Mowbray, had done it. Made the speech of his life to millions, provoked a pitch invasion, with the crowds chanting anti-Authority slogans, and escaped. A turning point. What happened next, it was hard to say. The afternoon had shown how unpredictable events were. The moment the people said *Enough!* could never be forecast. Was this it? The Authority would clamp down, for sure. Charlie's speech would never appear again on English TV, but it would be on continuous loop everywhere else. Irish TV was already repeating it, as the crowd disturbance fizzled out. Wiggins had held fire, thank God. Now was the time to worry about Gabi – and the family. James had agreed to speak to his contact in the Authority at 4pm. Ten minutes to go. Ten wasted minutes – he needed to talk to her now. He paced the room, stared out over Dublin, glanced at the re-run of Charlie's speech, made a cup of tea.

Time.

Code entered. Holo activated. Audio only – easier, less detectable. James's contact began…

"Mission accomplished. Went almost perfectly. Just the girl."

"Yes, Gabi, Gabi O'Leary. Do you know anything about her?"

"Broken arm, leg injuries. In a lot of pain – under sedation. Not critical."

"Will be interrogated, presumably."

"Unavoidable. We'll ensure that it's only drugs, not physical. How much does she know?"

"Everything about the preparations, obviously. Less about the escape plans. Those were limited to Charlie, Rosa and Dan. Best not to know."

"Not necessarily. If she has nothing to give, they'll be tempted to try harder."

"She'll know it's Ireland, on the South East coast. Not the precise destination. She'd have known about the barge, but not where they were going, to get the copter to Ireland."

"We'll do what we can. You know your family – the ones we can find – are being brought in."

James shivered at the thought. Of course he knew it would have to happen, but now it was going to, he felt sick about it. Even if it was just a brief and physically harmless experience, it would be traumatic. How could he have accepted that? How could Charlie? What were they thinking?

"None of them know anything – except Susan, of course."

"You knew about that?"

"Yes, she told me. I was disappointed about that – didn't expect her to get involved."

"Sorry about that. Can't stop everything. Have to go through the motions."

"Sure, I understand the necessity. Just make sure they are unharmed, won't you?"

"We'll do our best. But events aren't totally in our control. Especially after the near riot at Wembley. And disturbances all over the country – mainly in pubs, where people were watching the game. Or expecting to."

"What sort of reaction?"

"Just like Wembley. Anti-Authority. Nothing very political – alcohol and football equals riot, given the chance. But the Authority is shaken – badly. This is the first time something like this has happened. It's headless chicken time. COBRA meets tomorrow, Bolingbroke group tonight. I'll be there."

"In the chair?"

"Of course."

"Good luck. Again, at midnight? Should have spoken to Charlie by then."

"I look forward to it. And give O'Toole my regards."

***

Jack and his mates settled in the Tor and Anvil early for the game. They were winding him up something rotten about his claims that Charlie Mowbray had a surprise up his sleeve. *What, him and that bunch of Oxford ponces?* was one of the kinder remarks. *Why aren't you with him then – thought you were normally up his arse?* stung Jack badly even if it was just one of his mates' jokes, and he nearly twatted someone after his third lager. But their attention turned to the screen as the fireworks went off and Stellar took to the stage. Some oaf shouted, *Get them out for the lads!* but the rest of the boys ignored him and joined in the National Anthem. *God save our gracious King!* Not for long though: *fuckin' hell, is that Charlie and his mates, comin' out of the fuckin' sky?! What're they doing?* And then silence fell abruptly upon the place, as the cameras focused on Charlie and he began his oration. The barman turned the sound up and they listened without a whisper. Not even a bad joke or a burp. Glued to the man they knew as the privileged charmer, who went to the posh school and university, and who always got the girls. Who they loved and hated. Who Jack worshipped. Who ditched Jack when it mattered. Who today was giving them hope.

Then, as Charlie and the gang turned and ran for the copter, the stunned silence turned to murmurs and the chanting began. *Char-lie, Char-lie, Char-lie! There's only one Charlie Mowbray, there's only one Charlie Mowbray!* As the copter rose and sped away, Jack scrambled onto a table.

We are the Mowbray barmy army!...We want HOPE!...Fuck the Authority!

The barman looked on bewildered – there wasn't much he could do. The landlord spoke into his wristpad, furtively. A teenage girl,

160

cleaning the glasses, looked petrified. Across the room four shaven-headed men, who weren't from the area, looked on. They didn't look happy, as Jack and his mates all bounced on the tables, falling off, spraying lager at each other, turning football chants into songs of praise for Charlie Mowbray and HOPE. Some of the lager headed the skinheads' way and soaked the bomber jacket of one of them. That was the trigger: a bottle spun through air towards Jack and hit him on the cheek, as he swayed on the table top. He plunged to the floor as the skinheads rushed towards him and his mates, roaring obscenities, brandishing empty glasses and bottles. There were more of Jack's mates than their assailants, but they were drunker. Fists flew, boots flailed, glasses smashed, chairs were hurled. A group of tourists cowered in a corner. The bar staff hid under the counter. Total mayhem.

Suddenly, the door to the pub flew open and a phalanx of armed police crashed in. Stun lasers were fired, taking down a couple of the skinheads, as they applied their boots to someone's head. A loudspeaker decried, *ALL OF YOU DESIST!* More lasers were aimed at feet, just to get the message across. The fighting ceased. *All of you, hands up in the air.* Jack was down on the floor; he tried to get up, but he couldn't balance. He felt his cheek - it was still bleeding. His blood was smeared across the floor. Sticky. Two of his mates were groaning on the ground. One of the skinheads looked unconscious. More police poured into the pub. The tourists and bar staff were escorted out, trembling, crying. Two policemen came up to Jack, and lifted him to his feet.

"Come on young Oldfield. There's someone back at the station who wants to talk to you."

Chapter Eleven. The Sunshine Coast
(16-05-27)

The jet copter approached the Irish coast as the sun was setting. The view to the West, past the gleaming towers of the new Dublin, was a canvas of pink and gold in every shade, streaked with cloudy shadows. Charlie was exhausted, but uplifted by nature's majesty. It dwarfed anything they could ever hope to achieve. He clasped Rosa's hand. They were one, for now. She had come good for him so many times today. She, not he, was HOPE. Always would be.

They landed at one of O'Toole's stables near Dublin, where a car was waiting for them. It took them down the coast, to a place on the cliffs not far from Gorey, in County Arklow. It was an INSF safe house. While HOPE had some connections with the INSF, which had formed to protect nationalist interests after the fallout from Brexit, this arrangement was all James's doing. His and O'Toole's. Charlie didn't know much more that. Probably best not to. The efficiency of the whole thing seemed frightening. This was a different league to HOPE's operations, way over their heads – until today, anyway. But who knew where today's success would lead. They hadn't planned it at all. That would be for the next few days. Lie low and think things through.

They ate together and talked through the day's events. It already seemed surreal that it had actually happened. They toasted each other with champagne, thoughtfully laid on by O'Toole, but it didn't feel right without Gabi there. They repeated their feelings for her, and vowed again that if she did crack under interrogation, they would never blame her, whatever happened as a result. They ran out of steam pretty quickly, exhausted by the intensity of the day. Dan was the exception. Manoeuvring a jet copter in and out of Wembley stadium, with the risk of being gunned down in the stadium, or shot down at any time afterwards by pursuing RAF fighter jets, didn't seem to have phased him at all. He persuaded Luke and Mike to go with him to the local pub to have a couple of beers and catch some music. The INSF contact had assured them that even if anyone did recognise Luke or Mike, they wouldn't inform on them. HOPE were heroes to the people of Ireland, offering the chance of a future in which the English government would not be as indifferent to the fate of all the people on their island as they had been since Brexit. Or was that since the first time the English had invaded Ireland?

That left Charlie and Rosa. They moved into the living room and activated the TV screen. The Wembley events were still on repeat on the news channels. They watched without comment. Rosa tucked up her legs on the sofa and rested her head against Charlie's shoulder. He put his arm around her, and slowly she eased down until her head was on his lap. He played gently with her hair as they watched his speech again. "So magnificent," she whispered. "So were you," he replied. She glanced upwards and he kissed her temple. He held her around her waist, gripping her tight and feeling a desire to protect her, even if she was the woman who had kept *him* from losing it that day. They stayed like that for some time, lost in a kind of bliss about the day's events and about the moment. It was interrupted by the buzz on Charlie's wrist pad. Not unexpected, but it broke the spell. It was James.

"Charlie."

"Dad."

"You did it."

"We did it."

"Yeah. How is everyone?"

"We're OK. Tired. Can't quite believe it happened. And the reaction... what's the Authority thinking?"

"Worried."

"Yeah ,I bet. Gabi, what about Gabi?"

"She's OK. In hospital. Hurt, but not critical."

"What are they going to do to her?"

"We can't prevent her being questioned when she's well enough, but we'll make sure she isn't badly treated."

"Thank God for that. But then what? They'll use her in some way to get to us, won't they? Can your people stop that?"

"I doubt it, Charlie. We're not in complete control."

163

"Yeah, I know that. We've humiliated the Authority, but that's all. They're going to be angry. Wounded animals. Could do anything. What do we do now, Dad?"

"Rest up - clear your heads. Remember what you want to achieve and think about what would be the next step without Gabi's situation."

"That's hard."

"I know, Charlie, but you and Rosa are the leaders of something important here, something that people could hang on to. Something to give them hope. You have to think like leaders."

Rosa murmured her approval, her head still resting on Charlie's lap.

"O hard born condition, twin-born with greatness," Charlie mumbled.

"What's that, Charlie?"

"Oh nothing, Dad, just Henry the Fifth. Just remembering. The responsibility of the leader. I'm not a leader, really. Maybe I just conned people."

James and Rosa protested in harmony: "No Charlie!" Rosa looked up, worried. James continued, "Don't think like that, Charlie. Think of today. Think of the impact you had. The whole world was watching. The whole world is still watching. It's the biggest show in every town. The Authority has blanked it on the official channels, but everyone's watching on the web. They can't stop that."

"But what can I – we – do now? We escaped, but we're now in hiding. If we poke our heads above the parapet they'll be shot off."

"For now you'll have to lie low, yes. But you can still put messages out. People will respond to them."

"Yeah, I guess so. I'll have to think about it tomorrow. I'm just done now. And, yeah, what about Mum, Fran, Suze and Will? Emma? What have I done to their lives?"

"As far as I know they're all OK. Your Mum and Fran got visits from Intelligence, but they went away happy they didn't know anything."

"Fuck! Even that…"

"C'mon, Charlie, you have to accept that was always going to happen. They're OK."

"Have you spoken to them?"

"No, but that's what my contacts tell me. They know."

"You promise?"

"I promise." More promises, always promises.

"And Suze and Will?"

"Susan is off the Authority's radar right now. They aren't looking too hard. She'll be questioned when she goes into work on Monday. If she doesn't go in then I guess they'll look harder."

"You heard from her?"

"No, she isn't answering calls. Not at home either."

"Good on her. Hope she's alright. Will?"

"Pulled out of Kremenchuk on Friday. Heading for Amsterdam, last I heard."

"Who from? Will?"

"No, my contacts."

"So they know? What's their game?"

"Not sure. Probably waiting to see if he leads them to you."

"That'll be difficult."

"Yeah, we'll just have to wait and see. But he should be safe now from the Ukrainian security forces. They're a bit less subtle in their methods."

"Dad, you aren't reassuring me. Emma OK?"

"Yeah, she's fine. I saw her on Friday."

"Man this is hard, really hard. Look Dad, I know it is for you too. Thanks so much for what you've done for us. It's just whenever I think about what we've set off, it scares the shit out of me."

"I can understand that, Charlie. Keep a clear head. You and Rosa talk. Work things out. We can talk again tomorrow."

"Good advice, Dad. Thanks again."

"I'm here for you, Charlie, you know that."

"Yeah, I do."

"Stay strong, my boy."

"I'll try, Dad."

"I believe in you…"

Fuck me… Charlie laid back into the sofa and took some deep breaths. Rosa sat up and put her arms around him. They held each other tight, eyes closed, as if in a slow dance. "Time for sleep," Rosa whispered.

"Yeah," said Charlie, "Stay with me, Rosa."

***

And so, after all the years of holding back, tempted but hesitant - other people, other priorities, afraid, maybe, of what it could lead to - they spent the night together. Their passion was silent, until it was over. And then, as they lay together, Rosa sobbed, and began to talk of her complex feelings for Charlie. The conflict of loyalties – to him, to their friends, to the Cause. And how she was scared of loving him, how she didn't want to hurt Fran, how Charlie's relationship with Gabi stung her to the core, but how she didn't want to do anything to harm their mission. How, right now, she felt for Gabi as strongly as he did. Charlie listened, reassured her, embraced her, comforted her. And thought about Gabi, about Fran. Especially Fran. He felt bad about it, but as he held Rosa and felt the pleasing warmth of her body next to his, he felt an urge to speak to Fran, to see her, to protect her from what he had unleashed.

He spent the night restless. Comforted by the presence of Rosa, but haunted by a feeling that he had wronged his true love, Fran; and, to make matters worse, had deserted Gabi in her moment of need. That dream came back to him. Gabi in the New Bodleian, arm broken, surrounded by the mediaeval knights. The sword coming down, as he woke. He shuddered at the memory. A premonition. Why did he ignore it? He was that close to signalling *Dunkirk*. Gabi could have been saved. Now anything could happen to her. Could his Dad really protect her? Who were these contacts that could wield such an influence? What had been the point? He got to make a speech at Wembley. It had nearly caused a riot, but what now? He couldn't do anything that would risk harming Gabi. And what had happened to Susan? Was her silence really so reassuring? What if they'd brought her in? What would they do to her? His imagination,

166

lying in the dark, with Rosa murmuring in her sleep beside him, ran riot. The sword falling on Gabi in the dream, the electric shocks in reality. Susan in a brightly lit room, tied to a chair, shaking as the door handle turned. Fran at home, weeping, as she surveyed the damage to her flat. And then Jack, what happened to Jack? Did they haul him in too? His Dad hadn't mentioned him.

He fell asleep as dawn broke. When he woke up Rosa was gone. Momentarily he panicked. *Not her too!* He called out, "Rosa!" He heard her footsteps on the stairs, and relaxed. She entered the bedroom, and smiled. "Are you alright, Charlie?"

"Oh yeah. I just… you weren't there. Maybe I was dreaming. Something bad…"

She sat down on the edge of bed and took his hand. "Don't worry, Charlie. It's natural. After all we went through yesterday. I had dreams like never before. Can hardly remember them now, but they were wild. I woke up gasping one time. My heart was beating so fast. You were dead to the world when I got up. I didn't want to disturb you. Come down when you're ready. There's breakfast on the table." She leant over and kissed him, and then went back downstairs. Charlie felt tears flooding his eyes. He wasn't sure why. But they felt good somehow. He let them trickle down onto the sheets and closed his eyes for a few more moments. Collecting his thoughts. Holding back the start of a new, unchartered journey.

∗∗∗

After breakfast and checking the latest news coverage, Charlie and Rosa went for a walk along the beach below the house, which sat a few metres back from the edge of a small, crumbling cliff, just a narrow road in between. Dan, Mike and Luke were still in bed, after a long night in the local bar. They walked arm in arm, close to the sea, into a stiff breeze, which made it feel chillier than they expected. They didn't say much to each other. Both of them strengthened by each other's company, but lost in their own thoughts. The brisk, salty air clearing their heads. After a while they sat down on the sand. It was littered by small stones and washed up shells. Charlie lobbed stones into the sea, took aim at a piece of wood on the shore, shaped like a giraffe. Rosa rested her head against his shoulder. It felt like a moment that should never end, but there was a discussion they needed to have. Charlie stopped his stone-throwing and stood up. Rosa followed his lead. Staring out at the waves, he began.

"What now, Rosa?"

"Us?"

"No… I mean, that matters too, but I mean what do we do now? We're here. In hiding – sort of. The boys spent the night in the pub – they could have said anything. We're probably safe for now. People here are on our side. But we can't do anything from here. What do we want to do next?"

"We have to get back to England."

"And get arrested - or worse?"

"We go underground. We change our strategy. And we find out what happened to the rest of our people. Your Dad didn't mention them."

"That's my fault, Rosa. I never asked. I wasn't focused on that. Gabi, my family…"

"Of course, I understand that. But HOPE is not just us, Charlie. We don't know whether our comrades have been rounded up. If they have, we need to help them. We can't do that from here."

"And how will we do that in England?"

"We have to judge the situation first. Then make the appropriate plans. We may need to change our approach."

"By which you mean…?"

"By all means necessary."

"I want no violence, Rosa. No-one dies – remember that."

"The game has changed now, Charlie. We have increased the stakes. The Authority will be after us, all of us. We have to fight that in whatever way it takes."

"We have to do this the right way."

"Which is?"

"Persuasion. Democracy. That's what I emphasised at Wembley. Democracy, the people."

"But we have to fight fire with fire."

"Us against the state? We're tiny, Rosa. We've made an impact well beyond our means – with words, gestures. We have to give the people hope, and let them force change. We're catalysts – we can't be the troops."

"Charlie, what you said was fantastic, inspiring. But it can only be the start. The Authority are bruised by that, but it won't change them. We need action by the people, yes, but we need to provoke that. We saw signs at Wembley, but how do we fan the flames?"

"Is it fanning the flames we want? That sounds like violence. People get hurt. We need a groundswell. Peaceful protest. So the Authority sees the need to change, lets the people vote for change."

"Charlie, that won't work. The Authority will only respect force. We have to marshall that. Foment unrest. Unsettle them. Start to hurt them."

"How?"

"I don't know yet. We need to find out what has happened in England. Get back there. Start organising. Start equipping ourselves."

"Equipping ourselves with what?"

"Guns, lasers, materiel."

"What materiel?"

"For bombs."

"No! I can't have that. No violence. I always said…"

"That was before Saturday, Charlie. We are in a different game now."

"I don't accept that. Yeah, we have profile now. But we can use that. Communication. Messages. Inspire people to make change themselves. The Authority is fragile. It must be. Look how Dad and his contacts infiltrated the security, how they are protecting Gabi."

"You hope."

"Yeah, I hope. You doubt it?"

"Well, what proof have we got?"

"My Dad's word."

"Yes, but…"

"But what?"

"Gabi's all they've got. They aren't going to give that away."

"And?"

"And… sorry Charlie, what do you want me to say?"

"You don't trust Gabi?"

"No, of course I do, but…"

"But what? Why is she there now? Because we didn't rescue her. You pulled me back."

"Charlie, don't say that. We had to go. We had to escape."

"We deserted Gabi."

"Your Gabi, yes I know."

"Yeah, my Gabi. So what? What's your problem?"

Rosa gasped. A look of fear on her face. "Charlie, no, don't overreact."

"I'm not overreacting. How am I overreacting?"

"Sorry Charlie, I didn't mean… please, let's focus on the issues."

"Gabi is the issue."

Rosa looked crestfallen. Charlie realised what he had done. She started to cry. He went to take her in his arms. She flinched, and he drew back. She looked up at him, her eyes still filled with tears, and relented. Like two magnets, they locked together.

"I'm so fucking sorry, Rosa."

She didn't reply, but just sobbed into his shoulder. They stood there, holding each other tight, oblivious to the dog that sauntered by, stopping for a sniff of their shoes. They didn't even notice the owner. Lost in their shared turmoil; both wondering where things were going to take them next.

***

In the afternoon, once Dan, Mike and Luke had got themselves together, they convened, to talk about next steps. They agreed that, for a while, Charlie needed to stay in Ireland. Put some messages out on the web, to build on what he had said at Wembley. There was nothing the Authority could do about that. The others should try to get back to England, make contact with other HOPE members. Start

170

building the resistance. O'Toole would be able to help with getting them back. The INSF could help Charlie set up some broadcasts. They felt good having had the discussion. What they had agreed felt achievable. The reaction to their escapade had been pretty unbelievable. The near-riot at the stadium; news of disturbances around the country, suppressed by the Authority, but reported in Ireland; the endless recycling of Charlie's speech. It had become the truth through repetition. They had to build on it.

They went up to the pub in the local village in the early evening. They sat around a table outside and gazed out at the rolling hills, with the mountain to the south, lost in a cloudy haze. The wind had dropped completely. The atmosphere was serene. The occasional car passed on the road in front of the pub; echoes of the voices from inside the bar provided a soothing background. Otherwise all was silence. Time stood still. They talked about their hopes, their fears, their friends. Gabi, of course, was a focus. Her heroism grew in stature with every statement. They wondered how James had managed to stay clear of trouble – if he had done. As the evening wore on, they reminisced about times past: university, school, childhood. Charlie mentioned the inspiration that he had taken from Henry V. They were fascinated. They asked Charlie to recite the key speeches, and after a few Guinnesses, he felt ready to do it. It felt good. It reminded him of his power to engage an audience. He had Wembley now, too. He felt stronger than at any time that day. *Keep the faith*, he told himself. *I can make people believe.*

Staring out at the beauty of the setting sun, in the middle of nowhere, tranquil and hopeful. It was the best feeling.

Charlie and Rosa shared the same bed again that night. The evening had given them a lift, but it still didn't feel right. They were going through the motions. They both knew that, although there was a love between them, there was too much to divide them. Charlie's split commitments, their different perspectives on what needed to happen in the long run, even if they'd agreed the next steps. They might be able to resolve their differences on HOPE, but Charlie's heart was a different matter. They both knew that. Rosa felt the weight of Gabi on her mind; Charlie had Fran too. His true love. Something about the last few days had brought that home to him, if it really needed to be. And yet even that felt wrong when Gabi was trapped in the Authority's net. Neither of them felt like discussing their feelings – not after what had happened on the beach, when just the slightest mention of her sparked a confrontation. They both felt lost, now it was just the two of them. They needed to cry out, seek the truth, but didn't dare. They held on to each other, silently acknowledging their shared predicament. Knowing they couldn't resolve it. It felt really strange, each taking comfort from the person they couldn't speak to honestly. It told them that they had a bond, but right then they didn't know how far it extended, or where it would lead. They couldn't open up. And there was nothing they could do to change that.

They both went to sleep feeling a kind of despair.

***

Fuck me, I feel like shit. My head is hammering like a fuckin' mallet. My throat's like someone rammed a sack of sawdust down it. My cheek feels twice the size where that bottle hit it. Woke up this morning in this cell. Been here before, back when Micky caused a bit of a ruck over at the cricket club. Had to stand up for him didn't I? Wasn't anything like this one though. Those skinhead geezers were fierce. Not sure what their problem was - we weren't doing no harm to anyone. I mean, our mate Charlie had just stormed Wembley and made that fuckin' speech. Of course we was a bit wound up. What a stunt that was - right in front of all those nobs, all those security goons. Amazing they didn't shoot - someone must of slipped them some big dosh for that. Charlie's Dad probably. He's gotta be behind this - can't see how Charlie and Rosa Voreky would have the gumption to line all that up. They haven't got a clue - heads are in the fuckin' clouds. But that speech, man - fuckin' inspirational. Made me wanna join HOPE, overthrow the Authority. About time someone did. Going nowhere. Nothing's changed, except you're scared of opening your mouth, unless you're just with your mates. Never know when someone's snooping. Yeah, Charlie Mowbray for Prime Minister. Rosa fuckin' Voreky could be his security minister. She'd like that, keeping us all in line. She's a stern bird, that one. No sense of humour. Never liked me. Dunno what I did to wind her up - except that Charlie and me was best mates. Jealous, I reckon. That's why Charlie dropped me. Nothing to do with fools and jesters - that was all bollocks. She just wanted him for herself. Except she had me in the way - and Gabi. Yeah Gabi, poor girl. Something was weird about her arm, and the one time someone fires a shot, it brings her down. Unlucky that. Charlie must be gutted - his girl. Can't really remember what happened after that - me and the boys was getting carried away. Then I get hit by that bottle, and voom! It all went off. We were doing them when the coppers turned up. Serious business those guys. Stun lasers, the lot. Not our local guys - they wouldn't have a clue. We know them all anyway. Know whose missuses they're tapping up on the side, what their favourite drugs are. Most they would have done was ask us to calm down, and take those skins in. Wonder who they were anyway. Fascists probably - that's what Charlie would have said. Authority plants I reckon - there to watch us. Watch me. Cos' I'm Charlie's mate. One of his gang. Always will be - no-one can take that away from me. Brilliant he was. Henry the fuckin' Fifth all over again. Our king. Wonder where he is now. I never heard anything about that. Mr Spooky wasn't too happy about that. Thought I was holding something back. But I wasn't - all I knew was what I heard in the Revolution Rock that time. And I told him that first time around. So much for being helpful to the Authority. It just means they won't let me out because Mr Spooky thinks I'm in the know and won't tell him. Ol' Barry's dead apologetic about it, but says it's out of his hands - I'm stuck in here 'til spooky-arse is finished with me. Weird guy that - dead posh, but looks like a Nazi, with his little glasses and greased back hair. Creepy geezer he is. Same one as the Met passed me onto before. Should've kept me gob shut. Shouldn't have blabbed. Feel gutted about that now. Charlie's my mate. Blood brothers, years together. And that speech - what an actor! Love him to death. I'd join HOPE now, I really would. But what could I do

173

after he ditched me like that? Just like that. Brutal. No respect. I can't know you, he said. Fool and jester. I ain't no fool, and I'm not a fuckin' jester neither. Charlie upset me and I wanted to hurt him. Get my own back. You dish it out you have to take it. I'm sorry I did it now, but who wouldn't of in my situation? Didn't do him any harm in the end - he pulled it off. Brilliant. Me and the lads loved what he did, even though it ruined the football. I dunno what the rest of the country thought, as I've been stuck in here ever since, but I bet there've been a few riots around the place. Especially up north - they hate the Authority up there. I went up to Manchester once, for some trade. Hard, they were. Scared the shit out of me. Yeah, bet HOPE have scared the shit out of the Authority too. That's why they sent Mr Spooky down to talk to me again. Went over all the stuff we spoke about before - to check I wasn't holding stuff back, I suppose. Then kept on asking what I knew about the escape plans. When he realised I knew nothing about that, he started asking for names of who might be in the know. How the fuck would I know about that? His guess was as good as mine. He got a bit ratty at one point, said there were other methods of getting information. I didn't like his smile when he said that, but what could I do? I don't know anything. Charlie blanked me just when things were getting interesting. I could of been one of the gang doing the stunt, but he blanked me. I didn't go to Oxford, so he cut me out. But at least that means I don't know anything. Yeah, maybe that's why Charlie cut me out! Never thought of that before. Maybe he was protecting me. I don't need protecting, but maybe he was. Shee-it! Never thought of that before. Maybe all that fools and jesters bollocks was just cover. Genius. Fuckin' genius. They don't make many like Charlie Mowbray. My man. And now he's disappeared off the face of the earth and the Authority's spooked. So Mr Spooky's on the case. Wants to see me again. What's he think I know? Fuck all, that what's I know. How many different ways can I say that? I didn't like that smile though. What's he planning? Fuck, hope I ain't gonna get electric wire attached to my bollocks. I don't know nothing, can't he see that? Gabi's the one they should be asking - she must know everything. I

174

ain't gonna say that though. I'm not grassing on Gabi, poor girl. Not even if I've got electrodes tied to my balls.

Surely Mr Spooky, you ain't gonna do that to me?

***

"COBRA was vile. The PM opened with a rant about everyone's incompetence, and it went downhill from there."

"Rattled then."

"More than rattled. Hysterical. I'm not sure even I had had realised quite how insecure the politicians are. They know they're sitting on a timebomb. Except they don't know when it's set to go off. That's why the disturbances at Wembley so unsettled them. They saw how little control you have over a crowd, unless you are prepared to shoot. And they don't want that. They still persuade themselves that the coup was entirely a parliamentary matter, and that the 2025 election legitimised them."

"Not unreasonable. It was a democratic vote."

"Up to a point. As your son so eloquently put it, the elections were fixed, the opposition suppressed."

A top official, at the heart of the Authority, quoting my son, without qualification. James tingled with pride.

"Yes, that's true. That's why we're talking. So what, if anything, actually came out of the meeting?"

"To start with, your first wife and son's girlfriend were taken in, but clearly didn't know anything. They were asked to come in to support Gabi when she was questioned this morning."

"I hope…"

"Don't worry, a mild dose of truth serum and the presence of the two women was enough for Gabi to lose what control she had."

Bastards, thought James.

The contact continued: "You were right that she knew little about the escape plan. Ireland was the best she could do. But that will be a start for them. Contact will be made with our Irish counterparts. How helpful they will be is a matter for conjecture."

"Not very, I imagine."

"At the political level, true. At Intelligence level, there are mutual dependencies, traditions of cooperation. They'll work with each other. I can't see that Charlie and his gang will be able to remain at their current location for long. They'll have to disperse. The Irish will turn a blind eye to that, I imagine. I'd aim for Spain or Portugal while the dust settles, if I were them."

"I was thinking along similar lines. My contacts are good there."

"I'm sure they are. Costa del Sol by any chance?"

"How did you guess?"

"There's one more thing."

"Yes?"

"A video. There's a video."

"Of what?"

"The three of them."

"What, Gabi, Livvy, Fr…"

"Yes. Live from Gabi's bedside. Goes out tomorrow, after the PM has approved it."

"Those bastards. You said they wouldn't…"

"No physical harm was done to any of them. They took little persuasion apparently. Gabi was out of her head on a cocktail of drugs. Only Francesca questioned it, but she turned out to be the star. She deployed her dramatic skills to full effect. There were tears…"

"That's outrageous! Who ordered that?"

"Our friend from No10. Not as vacuous as I thought."

"Do I warn them?"

"Depends how you think they'll react."

"Badly, that's what I think. Very badly. They're new to this."

"In which case, credit to our friend from No 10. I suggest you start booking those ferry tickets."

The holo faded. *Very fucking badly*, sighed James.

Chapter Twelve. Monday Morning Feelings (17-05-27)

As the jet copter passed over the watery expanse of the Wash, Will thought of Susan, passionate about the work she did in the Bases. He envied her - he didn't have a passion like that, or at least not until Hanna had come back into his life. Journalism had been his mission, but the experience in Kremenchuk, the way his fellow journalists sucked up to the authorities, to get their little scoops, to get a ride out with the generals to the front, nauseated him. His natural scepticism - vital for any good journalist - had become a dark cynicism. He'd accumulated enough material for an expose of sorts, but would anyone care? Would the FT even publish it if he couldn't verify all the facts? Taking on the Authority was a risky business. He wondered what had happened to Susan after the Wembley events. Would the Authority have picked her up for questioning? They must have suspected her of contacting Charlie after they'd fed her the information about his plans. And yet, if she had been able to tell him what she knew, Charlie surely would have called the mission off.

Will didn't know if James had been able to get a message to Charlie, but assuming some information had reached him, there was only one conclusion. Really, who'd attempt a stunt like that if they knew the Authority knew they were coming? It was madness. *Insanely risky, unless... yeah, there must have been an inside job. Why did the security guards hold their fire, except for the rogue laser that took down the blonde girl? How the hell did a copter get in and out of the stadium unchallenged?* Will's journalistic mind whirred. *Man, there has got to be one big fucking conspiracy going on here. I'd love to be working on this one. Except I couldn't - no-one would trust me. And I couldn't do anything that might expose Charlie... or Dad? Yeah, I wonder if he had anything to do with this? He's been helping Charlie, I know that. Always been coy about it, which immediately makes me suspicious. Seems to have his fingers in a lot of pies, Dad. Wouldn't be on this copter if it wasn't for his chums. Would probably be in someone's interrogation room by now - hopefully not back in Ukraine. Hope he knows what he's doing...*

He had spent Sunday wandering around Amsterdam, after arriving early in the morning. He checked into a small hotel near the station and found a café nearby for some breakfast. The city was shrouded in an unseasonal fog. It gave the labyrinth of canals an unsettling aura. Everywhere there were shadows that slowly became real, or faded before they could be revealed. People on their bikes wafted by almost silently, apart from the occasional tinkle of a bell, as the mist muffled all sound. Normally Will would have enjoyed this scene, got his camera out for some atmospheric shots. But all it did was heighten his sense of paranoia. Any one of those cyclists could be armed with a hypo-dart, or could just be tracking him, sending information back to Intelligence. A couple of times he jumped, as the lurking shadows materialised. One time it was a dog, out on its Sunday morning run; another time it was the splash of a motor boat, emerging from one of the tributary canals.

In the afternoon he joined the tourists queuing for the Riijksmuseum. He was conscious that a couple just ahead kept looking back at him. Or was it him? Maybe they were just looking out for some friends. Inside, Rembrandt's gloomy masterpieces just dampened his mood. There was no alternative: he headed for the Red Light district and went into one of the fabled coffeeshops. He wasn't a big drug user, but he bought a joint and a beer and settled at one of the tables. The combined effect of the spliff and the beer calmed his nerves. The dance music looping in the background was strangely soothing. He checked the news on his wristpad: the English sites were pathetically devoid of analysis about the events at Wembley. All they could report was that the final had been sabotaged by left wing extremists, led by Charles Mowbray. Some initial over-exuberance from the fans had quickly subsided. One of extremists - a woman called Gabriella O'Leary - had been detained. Rewards for any information on the miscreants were available. Will fumed at the censorship.

The rest of the world, of course, had gone to town. A near riot at Wembley; outbreaks of violence around the country, suppressed by armed police; the government in crisis after a series of catastrophic security blunders. And of course, endless tributes to Charlie and his address to the nation, to the world. Could it be the catalyst for change? What would HOPE do next - and where were they? A political spokesman for the group stressed their peaceful aims, and denied all knowledge of the operation, or Charlie's whereabouts. There was speculation that they were in hiding somewhere in the West Country. Another report suggested that they had been smuggled out to Amsterdam. That caused Will a moment of frisson - suddenly he imagined the possibility of bumping into the fugitives on some misty canal. What would he do then? Join them? He didn't fancy that. The media's favourite destination seemed to be Ireland. HOPE's alleged links with the INSF were cited. All denied, of course. Will wondered. Ireland sounded plausible. They'd been there as a family a few times, and he knew James had a lot of clients in Dublin and amongst the racing fraternity. That guy O'Toole was one. *Blimey*, thought Will, *it didn't take me long to work that one out. But how did they get them out of England? No, they've got to be in England somewhere. Wouldn't even be surprised if they were holed up somewhere in the capital still. Maybe one of those apartments down by the river that Dad buys for his clients which never get lived in. Fucking scandalous that. They were trying to clamp down on that when the coup took place. Cause and effect? Might have been the last straw.*

Feeling a lot more mellow, he went to the bar for another beer. A hippie type with long dreadlocks and a scruffy parka had just walked in and was ordering a Scotch. Nothing else. Seemed strange - he looked odds-on for the largest spliff on offer. He nodded and smiled at Will. He took out an envelope and put it on the bar. "For you mate," he whispered. His Scotch arrived. He downed it in one, said "Cheers," and turned to leave before Will could say anything. Will took the envelope, slipped it in his jacket pocket, paid for the beer and went back to his table. His hands trembled as he took the envelope out of his pocket and opened it. Inside was a single sheet of paper. It read, simply: *Be at Zandvoort station, outside, at nine tomorrow morning. You're going home. JA - no Gooner.*

Oh fuck, thought Will. *It is Dad, it has to be Dad. But what if it isn't?*

***

Susan slept in late on Sunday morning. She was exhausted. Mark had been to the supermarket and had brunch ready for her when she got up. They stayed in most of the day, simultaneously watching the uninformative English news channels and scouring the web for news on HOPE. Charlie and his gang seemed to have disappeared very effectively. There was a lot of speculation, but nothing of substance. Susan felt that Ireland was their most likely destination. They'd loved it as kids and she knew Dad spent a lot of time there. She suspected that he was pulling the strings, but didn't dare contact him so soon after Wembley. She wanted desperately to talk to her Mum too, but feared that any contact would lead to Intelligence paying too much attention to her. And yet, for all she knew, Olivia might already have had a visit, or been called in for questioning. The whole family was implicated. She admired Charlie for what he had done, but it affected them all. Mark advised that they lie low for the day. Let the dust settle and see what happened on Monday. She couldn't argue with the logic, but it hurt not to know how Mum was.

They watched some old movies in the evening, including the first two "Hunger Games" films. Susan had loved them, and the books, when they first came out. She could really relate to Katniss; and Jennifer Lawrence's portrayal of the young hero was just perfect. Her anger was authentic. The Authority had classified the films as subversive, but had done nothing to prevent people from watching them. Classic Authority - lots of bark, but not enough resources or competence to enforce its will. That was encouraging, if embarrassing when you were a civil servant. It meant the government was never going to end up like the Capitol in the "Hunger Games". Mark was less sure - he thought the Authority would learn from its mistakes, although he couldn't explain why the security at Wembley had been quite so useless. Had to be an inside job. But what did that mean for Charlie and HOPE? Where they just someone's puppets? Susan thought that was a bit far-fetched, but couldn't deny the insider theory. Which probably meant her Dad was embroiled in something that could easily spiral out of control. That really worried her.

The tube journey to work on Monday morning was tense. Susan knew that a confrontation with Yorkminster was inevitable. Then some kind of interrogation. Strangely, she felt less bothered about that. As far as they were concerned, she didn't know any more about the Wembley heist than she'd been told by the unsolicited message a week before. She still couldn't figure out how it had all gone off, inside job or not, when the Authority had known about it beforehand. Dad had said it was all going to be OK, and it had been, apart from Gabi's mishap. Susan knew about Gabi, although she had never met her. Fran had told her about a new woman, when she and Charlie had split. It wasn't clear whether it was Gabi, or Rosa, or both. Fran refused to accept that it was actually the Cause that had wrenched them apart. She had never believed that Charlie was that committed to HOPE. It was more the chance to show off - and the excitement of a new relationship. Susan wasn't so sure – she'd seen how angry Charlie was when the coup took place. She thought back to the massive argument they'd had about it, and about Susan's continued commitment to the civil service. They hadn't spoken for a while; but Mum's pleas for family unity had worked in the end. They made up, and agreed to differ - and not ask each other what the other was up to. It kind of worked.

She and Mark travelled in from Fulham at different times. Mark went first - he was always one of the earliest in the office. Susan arrived at DELE just after nine o'clock. She entered the lobby. The new security gates glistened under the fluorescent lights. She walked towards them and activated her wristpad. The gates opened, but as they did, two burly men in dark suits blocked her entrance.

"What do you...?" Susan gasped.

"Miss Mowbray?" The one with a grey-flecked red beard enquired. "If you'd please just come this way. There is someone who would very much like to speak to you."

They took a lift down to the basement. Susan's heart thudded. Grey, unpainted walls were lit by bare light bulbs. Along the walls were a succession of dark red doors. She had never been down here, but had always imagined this was where they did things like building maintenance. Now she wasn't so sure. Ahead, there was a single white door. She just knew that was where they were going. The palms of her hands felt sweaty; her mouth was dry. The bearded man opened the white door and beckoned at her to go in. The room was dimly lit and sparsely furnished. There was a dark wooden desk, with a high backed chair behind it, and two smaller seats at the front. There was an old anglepoise lamp on the desk, illuminating a portable holo. And in the high backed chair sat a gaunt man with slicked back greying hair and small, round spectacles. *The archetypal Intelligence type*, thought Susan. He smiled at her and indicated that she should take a seat. "Morrison, would you get us some water, old chap? I expect Susan's feeling a little nervous at this juncture. Are you, Susan?"

"Well, yeah. I was expecting to go into work, not be brought down here, with no idea what for."

"Now come, Susan, you must know what for. We've been worried about you. No sign of you all weekend."

"I was just staying with a friend." *Shit, shouldn't have said that. He'll want to know who now.*

"Oh yes, Mark Kingston. Very highly thought of, I believe."

"How do you...?"

"Know? Well, that I couldn't possibly tell you. Indeed, it was only speculation on our part, so thank you for confirming that."

Damn! I'm just no good at this, thought Susan. Morrison returned with a jug of water. The man in the high backed chair poured two glasses and pushed one towards Susan. She took the glass in her trembling hand and gulped most of it down.

"Susan, don't worry. It's normal to feel anxious in these situations. I've no ill intent. I'm just here to establish a few facts. Fill in the picture for our superiors."

"There's not much of a picture that I can fill, I'm afraid."

"Well, let's not despair. I have a few questions. I'd be most grateful if you could answer them to the best of your ability. I believe you were in touch with your brother on the lo-fi on Tuesday 11 May. Did you tell him about the message you'd received."

So they do monitor it, thought Susan. "If you know I spoke to him, then surely you know what I said."

"I'm afraid it doesn't quite work like that. Did you tell him?"

"No."

"So you had a conversation and you didn't tell him? This important piece of news, which could mean life or death? What did you talk about?"

"Very little. He cut me off."

"Oh dear. Why was that, Susan?"

"He doesn't trust me. I'm a civil servant, remember. I work for the Authority."

"Indeed. You had lunch with your father on 13 May?"

God, they know everything. "Yes. Is that OK? He's my Dad. We talk."

"Yes, yes, of course. So you'll be aware that he is HOPE's main benefactor."

"I didn't know that," Susan lied. "We don't go into the details of his business. He's in finance, remember. They keep things to themselves."

"Yes, of course. But you must have mentioned Wembley. Surely your brother's imminent capture, even death, would have been on your mind. As you said, you talk."

"Er, well... I didn't want to worry him."

"Ah, come now Susan. I think you've been telling me the truth up to that point. You must surely have told him."

183

Susan blushed. It was impossible to deny. "Well, OK, yeah, I did mention it. But all I knew was what that message said. There was no follow up."

"Thank you Susan. That's all I need to know for now."

For now? Oh my God, there might be more.

"Let's turn now to Amie."

"Amie?! What's she got to do with this? You can't bring her into it."

"I'm afraid her brother has been arrested for dangerous gang activity. A threat to the security of Base One. You know what that means Susan?"

"Yeah. Deportation proceedings. You're blackmailing me, Mr..."

"My name's not important, but you can call me Henry."

"OK, Henry. Let me tell you I don't know anything else, so if you forced anything else out of me it wouldn't be true. Don't use the future of a young girl as a bargaining chip. Have you no conscience?"

Henry - if that was his name - hesitated. "I'm afraid conscience is a bit of a luxury in Intelligence, Susan. Although I am a caring man, and I am a little worried about your mother."

"My Mum?! What have you done to her? How low do you go?"

"Don't worry Susan. No harm has been done to her. But I do know she is distraught about Charlie, and the danger he's in. In fact, she's worried about all of you. You haven't spoken to her since Friday; and as for your brother Will, last we heard of him, he was wandering around the foggy canals of Amsterdam."

"Amsterdam? He's in Ukraine, at the front."

"Not any longer, I'm afraid. He suddenly decamped last Friday. Made his way to Berlin. Got very drunk in the evening by all accounts. Took a train to Amsterdam on Saturday evening. Rather in love with a young lady from the FT, it would seem."

"This is all news to me. If you know so much, why are you questioning me?"

"A painting needs detail before its true meaning emerges, don't you find Susan? Anyway, thank you for being so helpful. I'll ask Morrison to see you back up to the lobby."

"I can just go?"

"Of course, Susan. What were you expecting?"

"Well..."

"I'd be delighted to talk at any time, Susan, if there's anything else you can tell me. And don't be too hard on Mr Yorkminster - he's only doing his job." He delved into his jacket pocket and pulled out a business card. He pushed it across the table to Susan. *Henry Devereux-Duchamps. Security Adviser, Home Office.* Susan took the card and smiled.

"In what century did your family rob their land from the native British?"

"From those well-known natives, the Saxons? 13th century, I believe. Long enough ago to be considered English, don't you think, Susan? Important we respect property, Susan. That's what your brother needs to learn. Respect Susan, respect."

"Well respect my mother - and Amie - then." She got up and followed Morrison out of the room.

***

Back on the fourth floor, Susan heard raised voices in one of the meeting rooms. The loudest was Mark's. She opened the door to find a furious-looking Mark and a red-faced, sweating Yorkminster.

"What's happening?" asked Susan.

"This man is a traitor to his own staff," sneered Mark. Susan had never seen him - or Yorkminster - like this before. "He knew you were going to be intercepted and questioned. He did nothing. Told no-one."

"I couldn't," said Yorkminster. "Those were my instructions. I've done a lot to protect you these last few days, but I can't go against orders."

"I was only obeying orders," said Mark. "Where have we heard that one before?"

185

"It's true," Yorkminster whimpered. "I don't like what's happening, but I'm a civil servant – like you. You can't just pick and choose which orders you like."

"Traitor," muttered Mark again.

Susan stared at Yorkminster. He looked pathetic, cowering at the table, while Mark stood over him. She felt an instinct to sympathise, hold off, but she had to confront him. "They've arrested Amie's brother. She and her mother could face deportation. That's you, isn't it? You told them about me and Amie."

"I had to give them something. I had nothing. DELE had nothing. They could have kicked us out of Bolingbroke altogether. As it was I got sent out early."

"Poor ol' Yorkminster. Humiliated at the Cabinet Office table. Sure that's never happened before, working for DELE. Worth sacrificing the lives of three helpless people to prevent any more of that," Mark rasped.

"It's OK, Mark," said Susan. She'd been intent on giving Yorkminster a roasting herself as she came up in the lift, but looking at him now, she didn't have the heart. "I guess we don't know what we would have done in the same situation. Maybe it just slipped out, under pressure."

"It did," said Yorkminster, looking up at her imploringly. "I hadn't intended to say anything. I just… it's not easy."

"That's what you're paid for," said Mark. "Staying calm under pressure."

"I know, I know, but…"

"Yes, I know, Chris," said Susan. "Don't humiliate yourself any more. Think clearly. Is there any way you can help? Amie's brother must have a lawyer."

"Shouldn't think he will," said Mark. "It's a refugee camp. The only authority is the Authority."

"They have legal advisers up there," said Susan. "I've met them. They are up against it, but they are committed. They care. I have some contacts, but the higher we can go, the better. Can you help, Chris?"

"I'll try. But while your brother's on the run…"

"He's right there," said Mark. "Amie and her family are bargaining chips."

Susan felt sick. Mark was right. This was all about her – and Charlie. They wanted her to make a choice. She sat down in a chair next to Yorkminster and put her head in her hands. She started to sob. Mark rushed to her side and knelt down by her. He put his arm round her shoulder. "I'm so sorry Suze, I was too blunt. We'll work this out."

"Oh, no, Mark, it's not you. It's just, it's just… so terrible. And I feel like somehow I could have stopped it if I'd been more forceful. Maybe with Dad…"

"Your father?" Yorkminster's ears pricked up.

"Don't you say a word," Mark threatened. "I will fucking kill you."

"Mark!" Susan looked shocked, and then laughed through her tears. Yorkminster looked dumbfounded.

"Sorry," said Mark, "But you know what I mean. We expect total cooperation from you. You have caused enough harm to Susan – and those poor people up in the Base. Have we got it?"

Yorkminster bristled. "I still have a job to do. So do you both."

"Ah, back to the real Yorkminster," laughed Mark. "We've missed you."

"Look Chris, can you at least find out a bit more about what's happening in the Base? At least make sure proper process is being followed. They can't deport them instantly. We haven't become that bad yet."

"I'll see," said Yorkminster. "And by the way, there's something else you should know."

Susan looked at him fearfully. "Not my Mum?"

"No, your house. It was broken into."

"How do you know? You did it?" said Mark.

"No," snapped Yorkminster. "I went by, to see if you were OK, after the Wembley events. The door was unlocked."

"You went in?" asked Susan.

"Yes. There wasn't a lot of damage – just papers and a few things scattered around, to show there'd been a visit. Your holo control wafer had been removed."

"That explains why Henry knew so much."

"Who's Henry?" asked Mark.

"My interrogator. Lovely man. Know him, Chris?" Yorkminster shook his head. "Didn't think you would. You're not really part of this, are you?" Yorkminster stared into space. "So my house has been burgled. Do you know if it's been secured?... No, you don't know anything. Fine – I'd better go and check the damage."

"I'll come with you, Suze," said Mark. "Yes, Chris, we are together. Why don't you tell them that too?"

Susan laughed. "They know that already, Mark."

***

When they got to Susan's street, it was almost noon. A cluster of school children were walking along the street ahead of them. They all stopped to look at what seemed like Susan's front garden, before being hurried away by their teachers. Susan clutched at Mark's hand. At the house police tape blocked the entrance. The door was open. They ducked under the tape and moved towards the door. A police officer noticed them and walked out, blocking them.

"Sorry, you can't come in here. What do you want?"

"I live here."

"Ah, let me just go and check with my commander."

The commander came out. "Hello, I believe you are the owners."

"I am," said Susan.

"Do you have ID? Holo proof preferably, Madam."

Susan summoned the ID holo from her wristpad. The commander took a small device from his pocket and scanned the image. "All looks in order, Madam. I'm afraid you've been burgled."

"I know."

"You know? How?"

"Because my boss in Westminster just told me."

"That's not possible. We were just alerted by a local resident that your door had been forced open and came straight down here."

"I'm afraid someone has been playing games with you, Commander. This isn't a local villain's doing."

"Oh… well, you'd better come in. But please don't touch while we take prints."

They looked around. Apart from the control wafer, nothing looked to be gone. There was some mess, but it was superficial, as Yorkminster had said. The police obviously had to do their job, and Susan respected that. There was really no point in staying. Susan gave the commander her contact details and suggested to Mark that they went down the road and had a drink while the police finished their job. The commander promised to call them once they had finished.

They sat outside in the street. There was a warming sun. They clinked glasses and sighed at each other. "What next?" asked Susan.

"You tell me," Mark smiled.

"I just don't know, Mark. My whole family appears to be tied up one way or another in Charlie's adventure. Will's wandering around Amsterdam – running from something, or someone. Mum's been visited by the spooks. Dad's deeply implicated in the whole business, but I don't know how. And Charlie…"

"He was extraordinary, remember. The reaction too…"

"Yes. I was so proud of him. It's quite hard to remember with all this other shit. But I guess I'm just going to have to get used to that. I don't think the Authority is quite in the business of arresting people because they are related to someone, but they are going to be watching me all the time. And you too, Mark. Are you sure you want to expose yourself to that?"

"If it's going to happen to you, Susan, then it's going to happen to me too. I'm with you every step of the way."

"Oh, Mark, are you sure?"

"I'm surer than I've ever been about anything in my life, Susan."

"Oh, Mark, I love you…"

And for a moment, all the craziness, all the stress and fear, seemed a million miles away.

Chapter Thirteen. The Decision (Reprise) (17-05-27)

It was a grey, overcast day. From time to time a light drizzle swept the beach, as Charlie walked alone, stopping occasionally to skim stones across the steely expanse of the sea. He needed to clear his head of all the conflicting emotions and work out what he wanted to do with HOPE. Rosa had been right to throw down the gauntlet. They couldn't just sit here in Ireland and let events take their course. They had to direct them, manipulate them. Otherwise Wembley would just be a flash in the pan. Written off as a stunt by a bunch of publicity seekers. A momentary loss of control by the Authority. But they had to be different – Rosa's proposals were too conventional for him, and too dangerous. He didn't want power at any cost, and not at the cost of people's lives. What would be the point of that? Did he even want power? Charlie wasn't sure. He wanted justice, he wanted liberty, democracy. Sure, he had felt a thrill like never before, as he addressed the cameras at Wembley, but at what cost? Gabi lying injured on the turf, trapped. Sacrificed. What had she been through since then? Charlie shuddered. The memory of crying out to her, but being held back by Rosa, merged with that dream again, the heavy swords descending. The horrible end.

He lashed out at a bit of driftwood on the shingle. As it flew through the air, an excited dog, a red setter, its fur straggly from splashing along the shoreline, rushed by. It picked up the driftwood in its mouth and brought it back to Charlie, tail wagging furiously. Charlie smiled and patted the dog on the head. He took the branch and hurled it down the beach with all the force he could muster. The dog yelped with delight and hurtled off in pursuit. Charlie turned to see the dog's owner, a sturdy man with thick grey hair and flat cap, a few paces behind him. The man came up to him with a smile, and offered his hand. Charlie reciprocated.

"Patrick Keenan, pleased to meet you. Lucy seems to have taken a liking to you. What'll be your name?"

The dog returned, panting, and dropped the branch in front of Charlie. He stooped to pick it up and threw it again. "She's a fine dog, Patrick. I'm Charlie M... er, Mortimer."

"What brings you here, Charlie? I saw you and your friends at Blackhills last night. If my memory serves me correctly, you were entertaining your friends with a speech as we went by. Would you be an actor, by any chance?"

"Yes, yes I am. Always acting! Yeah, my friends and I came over here to get a bit of fresh air and inspiration. We have a play starting in London in a few weeks' time, and it's not quite right yet."

"From London are you? Did you see the business at Wembley the other day?"

"Oh yeah. Amazing."

"You look a little like the young man, yourself. He was called Charlie too. Not Mortimer though."

Shit. What do I say now? "Mowbray he was. Charlie Mowbray. Yeah, people say I look a bit like him."

The man smiled again. "You needn't worry, Charlie. We all know who you are round here. Your secret's safe with us. INSF territory, this. You were magnificent. A true actor. A future politician, to be sure."

"Oh, er, thanks. Everyone knows who we are?"

"To be sure they do. Especially after the show your friends put on the other night. But like I said, we're with you. You're safe here."

Charlie breathed hard. "I appreciate that. But it does mean we can't spend long here, I guess."

"That'll be your decision, Charlie, but we'll be watching out for you. Now, c'mon Lucy, we've got some errands to do. Goodbye, Sir, and best of luck." They shook hands and Patrick Keenan strode on, Lucy looking back wistfully at her erstwhile playmate.

"See ya, Lucy," Charlie laughed and he chucked a stone in the dog's direction. She barked with delight, before turning to trot after her master. Charlie looked on, as man and dog slowly shrank into the distance. The whole village knew who they were. The whole of Ireland probably. Hiding wasn't an option.

***

Lunch back at the house was awkward. No-one really had anything to say. The boys were waiting for a lead from Charlie. Rosa's dark eyes were sullen, intimidating. Luke, Mike and Dan retreated as quickly as was decent to the back room, to catch up on the news. Charlie tapped the back of his spoon on the table. "People know who we are, Rosa."

"How do you know?"

"I met a man on the beach. Local man, saw us at the pub."

"Oh."

"What do you think we should do about it?"

"I don't know. You're in charge."

"C'mon Rosa, that's not..."

Suddenly there was a cry from the back room. "Fuck! Charlie, Rosa, come and look at this!"

They both rushed in. The screen had been paused by Luke, while they arrived. It was a picture of a hospital room. A young, blonde woman was sitting upright in bed, in a blue hospital gown. *Gabi.* Two other women were in the room. Another young woman sat on the side of the bed. *Fran.* On a chair, the other side of the bed, an older woman, probably in her sixties, with concern etched on her face. *Olivia.*

Rosa gasped. Charlie sank into an armchair. "Put it on Luke."

An invisible interviewer asked Gabi how she was, how it had been since the events at Wembley. She was woozy, disconnected. "It's been great," she said, looking straight ahead, expressionless. "All the doctors and nurses have been so kind."

"Man, this is sick!" Luke exclaimed. Dan shushed him.

"How are your injuries?"

"Not too bad. I broke my wrist." She pulled up the sleeve of her robe to reveal the plaster cast.

"I bet you wish Charlie could sign that."

"I so wish that. I wish he was here with me now."

"What message do you have for him?"

"Come back, Charlie. It was a mistake. The Authority understands."

"Thank you, Gabi. Now Fran, you were Charlie's girlfriend."

"I am Charlie's girlfriend."

"Yes, of course. And you're an actress in the West End?"

"National Theatre, yes."

"Can you tell me how Gabi's been treated since her arrest? "

"Pretty well, as far as I can tell."

"Does Charlie act?"

"Not at the moment. But he is good. You saw how good last Saturday."

"Indeed. Have you got a message for him?"

"Yes. Charlie, you were brilliant on Saturday. I was so proud of you."

"And?"

"You've made your point, Charlie. I think the Authority will listen. Don't make things worse." Fran was looking straight down at the bed. "We want you back, Charlie." She choked and wiped a tear from her cheek. The camera zoomed into close up for a moment, capturing the anguish in her eyes. Then it panned round to Olivia.

"Olivia, you are Charlie's mother. How does a mother feel at a time like this?"

"Worried, just worried."

"How do you feel about what Charlie did on Saturday?"

"It was so brave, but reckless. So many people could have died, and I know Charlie wouldn't want that."

"What do you think your son should do now?"

"Charlie, I know the cause of HOPE is very dear to you. I know how angry you are about the way things are. Many people are, especially young people. You're right to want things to be different. But they can be, Charlie. The Authority needed to stabilise things. When we are strong again, we can rebuild again. That is what they have said to me. That is their message to you, too. Maybe you can help in that rebuilding, in time. But is HOPE worth the risks you are taking, Charlie? Please think about it. Please take care. Please don't hurt yourself, or your friends, or anyone else. I know you aren't like that. Come home please, Charlie. We love, I love you. I miss you…"

"Thank you, Olivia." For the first time the camera switched to the interviewer. He intoned solemnly, "Charlie, if you are watching this, you can see that the women in your life are desperate to have you back. Please reflect on what they have said to you. They speak for our nation at this time. From St Mary's Hospital, Paddington, in West London, thank you."

The broadcast switched back to the studio. There was silence in the room. Luke whispered, "Fuck." They all cast furtive glances at Charlie. He sat in the armchair, his expression frozen. Motionless.

And then he exploded. A vase next to him went flying and smashed against the wall. He stood up and kicked the table aside.

"Fucking bastards! Fuck them! My fucking family, my fucking family, they did that to my family! Fuck those fuckers! Fuck all of this shit. It's all shit! All shit. I'm not having this shit. They aren't going to do that to my Mum. Fran. Gabi, what the fuck have they fucking done to Gabi? She was like a fucking zombie. They fucked her up. Fuck it man, I'm not having it man, I'm not fucking having…"

He lurched towards the cabinet, full of crystal glass and crafted crockery. Luke and Mike leaped up and pulled him back before he could inflict any damage. "C'mon man, calm down man! It's alright, it's alright!"

Charlie bent down and sobbed. "It's not fucking alright. They did that to my Mum, my Fran, my Gabi. It's all my fault. I should have said fucking *Dunkirk*. I nearly did. I had it on my wristpad. It was that fucking close. I could have called it off. None of this would have happened. I've fucked up everyone, everyone."

Rosa rushed up and took Charlie from the men. She hugged him and he wept into her shoulder. "Charlie, my love. Be calm now. Take some deep breaths, you're breathing so hard. Come on, you just need to relax. It'll be alright, it really will. No-one's been hurt."

"But they've been taken and made to do that. They would never have done that by themselves."

"I know, I know. But we have to think clearly. The Authority wants to provoke you, smoke you out. We can't fall into their trap. Come on. You need to lie down. Rest a bit. Clear your mind."

She took him upstairs and helped him onto the bed. "Close your eyes Charlie, and relax." She stroked his forehead. It was burning hot. "I'll get you some water." She walked through to the bathroom and returned with a cup. "Sit up and drink some of this." Charlie obeyed and gulped the water, coughing half of it out.

"Sorry," he spluttered.

"It's alright, Charlie, it's alright. Let's just sit here for a bit."

"Lie with me Rosa. I feel cold. I'm shivering. I need to feel you beside me."

"Anything Charlie. I'll make you warm again."

***

They had been lying on the bed together, under a duvet cover, holding each other tight - silent, eyes shut, but minds racing - for about half an hour, when Charlie's wristpad buzzed. It was James. Rosa groaned, and pulled away. "I'll get you some tea, and see how the boys are," she whispered. Charlie summoned the audio.

"Charlie, it's Dad. You've seen it?"

"Yeah, I've seen it."

"They are all OK. I have it on good authority."

"Oh yeah. How can they be OK, when they had to do that? How can Gabi be OK? She was a zombie."

"That will just be the painkillers, Charlie."

"And the truth serum?"

"Maybe. But it causes no lasting damage."

"Oh great, that's good to know."

"Charlie, stay calm. You need a clear head."

"Yeah, everyone's telling me that. You try having a clear head when your Mum and the two women you love have been abducted by the Authority and forced to go on TV to plead with me to come back. And no doubt they've been interrogated in between times."

"Questioned yes. Not hurt. I have assurances."

"That's nice for you."

"Charlie! We are in this together."

"Yeah, sorry Dad, but…"

"I know, Charlie, I know. It affects all of us. Look, it's pretty well known who you are, around your village."

"I know, I met a man on the beach who told me."

"You did?"

"Yeah, he had a nice dog. Called Lucy. Highlight of the day, chucking branches for her to fetch. Downhill from there, seriously downhill. Catastrophically downhill."

"There's no catastrophe, Charlie. Look, we need to get you out of Ireland. We've made arrangements. We can get you to Spain. You'll be safer, more anonymous, there. You can plan things from there. One of O'Toole's people will be round at 7pm tonight."

"Dad, I can't take this in. My head's spinning. You better talk to Rosa. Look, here she is, as if by magic. With a nice cup of tea. What would I do without her?"

Rosa looked bemused, then realised what was going on. Charlie transferred the call to Rosa's wristpad. She went downstairs to discuss the details with James. Charlie sipped the tea and called up the web on his wristpad. *Better see what they're saying about the interview…*

***

It was half past six. A car pulled up outside the house. "A bit early for O'Toole's people, said Rosa, peering through the window. "A bit small for all of us, too."

"It's not for you," said Charlie, coming down the stairs, with his bag. "It's for me. I'm going. Best thing for all of us."

"What? Where?" Luke spluttered.

"It's my taxi," said Charlie. I'm going down to Gorey. Police station. Give them a little surprise."

"What?!!"

"Hand myself in. Take it from there. Meanwhile, you can get away to Spain, unnoticed."

"Charlie, you can't," said Rosa.

"Why not?" said Charlie. "Best for all, like I said."

"No it's not, Charlie. We need you. HOPE needs you. The country…"

"I'm not giving up on HOPE, or the Cause. I'm making it easier for you to escape, and getting the Authority off everyone's backs. I don't even know what's happened to Susan or Will. But I doubt it's good."

Rosa slipped off into the kitchen.

"See you, guys. It's been a trip. Wouldn't have wanted to do it with anyone else. You're the best. Just remember what we did. Just the beginning." He hugged Luke, Mike and Dan in turn.

"You sure this is right?" asked Luke.

"Got to be," said Charlie. "Otherwise we're all fucked. And my family has a life of misery. I can't be doing that. No political cause is worth that. Should've thought it through better in the first place, I guess."

"Charlie man, you are a fucking hero," said Mike. "You did the right thing every step of the way. Don't have regrets."

"Appreciate that, man," said Charlie. "I'll try not to."

"Stay in there," said Dan. "You will always be HOPE."

"We are all HOPE, Dan, mate. We need a movement to be HOPE now. I'll try and work that out when I'm in the clink."

"I fucking love you, Charlie Mowbray," cried Luke, and they hugged again.

"Where's Rosa?"

"Here, Charlie," said Rosa, emerging from the kitchen. She was holding a gun. You can't go. It will be the end of HOPE."

"What the fuck?!" Luke exclaimed.

"It won't be the end," said Charlie, calmly. "It will be the start. Now, put that gun down and give me a farewell kiss."

"If you go out that door, I will shoot." Tears streamed down her face.

"Don't be crazy, Rosa," Charlie whispered.

"I'm not crazy. I'm doing this for the Cause. Boys, back off. This is between Charlie and me."

They retreated, stunned spectators.

"I'm going, Rosa. I have to." Charlie turned towards the door.

"I'll shoot, Charlie, I really will."

He opened the door and walked out. Rosa rushed to the doorway.

"Do what you like," Charlie shouted, his back still turned away from Rosa, as he walked towards the taxi.

Rosa took aim. Her hands trembled. She could hardly see through the tears. "This is it, Charlie."

"Goodbye then!" he shouted.

She tried to stiffen her arms. From behind her a man's arm gently eased them down. She yielded. It was Dan. He turned her round and took her in his arms. "Charlie, my Charlie," she wept. She was shaking violently.

Dan comforted her. "It's OK, Rosa. You're OK. It's all gonna be OK."

Charlie looked around as he got to the taxi. He saw the two people in the shadow of the doorway and whispered to himself, *love you all…*

He got into the taxi, and looked out at the sea as it pulled away. He thought of Lucy the dog, bounding up and down the beach below. Happy just chasing a stick.

***

As they travelled through the rolling countryside, the taxi driver played songs from an old Van Morrison collection. It brought back memories for Charlie. His Dad had played Van Morrison incessantly when they drove round this same spot so many years ago. "And It Stoned Me" came on. Charlie remembered all the words and sang them inside his head. Him, Susan and Will in the back. Susan always stuck in the middle, moaning about Charlie's wriggling. *And it stoned me, to my soul…* So beautiful, so uplifting as the horns joined the chorus, even if it was just about going fishing and getting caught in the rain. Charlie's eyes misted up. A tear trickled out. "You alright back there, Sir?" the driver inquired, catching Charlie's crumpled face in his front mirror. "Yeah, I'm fine, thanks," Charlie replied, regaining his composure. "I just love this song – reminds me of family holidays in Ireland, singing along in the back of the car."

"Ah, that's a lovely story, Sir," said the driver. "My father was a big Van Morrison man himself. Rubbed off on me, too."

"Yeah, we never forget," said Charlie. "Never forget those simple pleasures. Always treasure them. Precious memories."

"To be sure, that's right, Sir."

He got out at the bottom of Main Street in Gorey. He wanted a last moment of freedom, amongst people, people just going about their daily lives. The low cloud and shroud of fine drizzle cloaked the street in premature darkness. Most of the shops had shut for the day; lights shone from the pubs and restaurants along the street. Charlie stopped to peer into one of the pubs: a family tucked into burgers and chips, a group of lads downed their lagers, a couple of older men nursed their pints of Guinness. Charlie wished he was sitting in there with Rosa, planning the next steps for HOPE. Instead it had all fallen apart. Rosa… his saviour so many times in the last few days. And yet she'd held a gun in her hand and threatened to shoot him. For what? The Cause? Or because she so loved him that she couldn't let him go? That would take a long time to figure out. Maybe there was no answer.

So much to figure out… That video: he could hardly bear to think about it. Which bit was worst? The women who meant the most to him in the world sitting there, imploring him to return. Only Susan had been spared, and he didn't even know what had happened to her. His women, his *mother*, all humiliated in front of the world's public; all suffering because of him. He hadn't really thought about that when they dreamed up the plan. It was too exciting, too improbable, to think about the fallout for other people. They'd planned their own getaway perfectly, with Dad. But they'd forgotten about everyone else. He'd forgotten. *Too busy being Henry the*

Fifth, he cursed himself. Well, he'd done that; now it was time to protect the people he loved.

A young couple walked by, arm in arm, laughing about something. They kissed as they passed him. He felt a tingle of happiness and of longing. He wished he could be with Fran, doing the same. Fran, the woman who'd stuck by him, put up with his nonsense, for so many years. And what had he done? Left her. Twice. And even then, she'd spoken up for him in the video – that wouldn't have been in the script. What retribution had she risked doing that? So brave, so loving. *Please give me another chance one day*, he thought. *This time, nothing else, no-one else, will ever come between us. Please, one day…*

The Garda station was towards the other end of the long Main Street. It didn't look like a police station to Charlie – more a small hotel, or B&B. He knocked on the heavy wooden door and pushed it hesitantly. It opened: in the corner of a barely furnished room, a middle-aged man in shirtsleeves sat behind a desk. He looked up at Charlie, who cut a bedraggled figure, after lingering in the rain.

"Hello there. Anything I can do for you, Sir?"

"Er, yeah, thanks. This is going to sound weird, Officer. But, yeah, my name's Charlie Mowbray. You might have seen me on the news about Wembley at the weekend." The man smiled knowingly at him. "I'd like to hand myself in to the Irish authorities."

"You would, would you, Sir? Well take a seat if you will. I'd better contact headquarters. Would you like a cup of tea? You're looking a bit damp there."

"Thanks, yeah, I'd love one."

The guard disappeared into an adjacent room. Charlie sat alone in the reception, in the bright light. He was shivering, whether from the rain, or from nerves, he couldn't tell. This felt so strange. He could just change his mind and walk out. He looked around. There was a small camera attached to the ceiling, so maybe someone else was watching. Maybe not though, if there was something interesting on TV. After a few minutes, the guard came back and offered Charlie the tea. He had one for himself. "Just pull up your seat Mr Mowbray, and I'll take a few details."

They went through the formalities, before the guard sat back in his seat and smiled. "You'll be pleased to hear, Charlie Mowbray, that Dublin is very excited at the news. They'll be sending someone down straightaway. It'll be a couple of hours before they get here, so I'm afraid you'll have to entertain yourself in our local cell. There's no-one in there at the moment, though if any of the local lads get lively a bit too early, you might get some company."

"That's OK, whatever suits you, Officer. I'm at your disposal."

Another guard appeared, to take Charlie to the cell. He had a towel, which he handed to Charlie. "Dry yourself off, Sir. We won't be needing these handcuffs, will we, Sir?"

"I don't think so." Charlie smiled. He hadn't known what to expect, but this wasn't it.

As he got up to accompany the second guard to the cell, the first man stood up, and from behind his seat, offered Charlie his hand.

"Welcome to Gorey, Charlie Mowbray. Let me tell you, the whole of feckin' Ireland is right behind you."

Chapter Fourteen. Rays of Hope
(18-05-27)

Monday's events changed everything. The video plea had electrified people – either they abhorred the Authority's cynical decision to put pressure on HOPE by using Charlie's nearest and dearest as pawns in the game, or they just felt moved by the whole thing, the developing soap opera, and were desperate to know what would happen next. Charlie's decision to hand himself in, in a small town on the south east coast of Ireland, got both camps even more excited. The deplorers speculated about Charlie's motives, and whether, in some way, it was a clever double bluff. They were encouraged by the fact that, by the time the Dublin authorities arrived in Gorey, a group about a hundred strong had assembled outside the Garda station, with hastily created banners demanding *Justice for Charlie*, *Free Charlie Mowbray* and *Let there be HOPE*. The TV cameras were there to broadcast it all – the local Garda knew when they had a good story. The soap fans were beside themselves: what would it mean for Gabi, Fran and Olivia? Would there be more interviews? Would Charlie be re-united with Gabi? Or would ex-girlfriend Fran come back into the calculation? Or would he turn first to his mother? And what about Rosa, the mysterious *other woman* in the HOPE gang? Where did Charlie's loyalities lie? And where were the rest now? Were they still somewhere near Gorey? Or was that just a trick by Charlie to let them escape? The web, worldwide, was a hive of speculation, conspiracy theories, rumours.

After they had been forced to make the video, Fran was so shaken by the experience that Olivia suggested that she came back to Glastonbury with her. They needed to be talking, comforting each other, working together in the event of any other demands from the Authority. And figuring out how to help Gabi. After talking to her parents and the National Theatre, Fran agreed, and they made their way down to the West Country.

Susan caught the video at the pub she and Mark were sitting outside, after visiting her burgled home. Mark had just stepped inside to get another drink, and rushed out to call Susan in. Like everyone there, they watched transfixed. There was only one thing Susan wanted to do afterwards, and that was to get hold of her Mum. She managed after a while, and after they'd talked there was only one option for her. She was going down to Glastonbury too, and to hell with the consequences. For this one she insisted Mark shouldn't come along. She didn't want him to be put in any more danger. He needed to go back into work and make excuses for her. She reckoned Yorkminster was on their side now, after the last encounter, so he would go along with whatever story they came up with. Mark wasn't so sure, but went along with her judgement. They went back to the house, where the police were just finishing. She went through a few formalities, quickly packed a bag, and then made her way to Paddington station. Mark stayed behind to sort out an emergency locksmith.

Emma was freaked out by the whole thing. She'd believed James when he said he'd be back for Archie and his exams, but now he was completely off the radar. In hiding, she assumed. She couldn't get hold of him, not even on their usual network. She felt lost – and the only person she could turn to was Olivia. They spoke. Olivia seemed incredibly calm, given what she had just been through. She was taking control. Emma agreed to come over to the Marquee Moon the next day.

And then Charlie handed himself in. And the protests made their small beginning in Gorey. An extraordinary situation became even more unreal. But, at the same time, it reduced the tension for all of them. The Authority had got what it wanted, or at least some of it. It knew where Charlie was, even if he was in the hands of the Irish. Surely, now, it would get off their backs – unless he didn't cooperate. That didn't bear thinking about; but maybe, at least, they would have some time.

***

They sat around a corner table in the Marquee Moon after the lunch time rush had finished. Olivia, Susan, Fran and Emma. Michael brought them coffees and cake. Susan sat close to her Mum, with her arm around her shoulder. Her little girl again. Fran and Emma, too, looked to Olivia to set the agenda. She suggested they just tried to step back for a moment, and talk about other aspects of their lives, as if Charlie's adventure with HOPE had never happened. Emma talked about Archie – and the conversation with James, before apologising for bringing HOPE back into it. She got total support from the others. Fran talked about the success of her play, but couldn't resist saying how it wasn't the same without Charlie to share the feeling. And Susan talked about Mark, and how the last week had brought them together. Olivia shed a tear about that, before talking about the continuing success of the Marquee Moon and how important Michael had been in making that happen. And how that had helped her to continue her art, to the point where she felt it was time to have her own exhibition. He was her rock. A quiet man, happy in the shadows. But liked by everyone. It made them all feel better, concentrating on the positives for a moment, the things that gave them strength. They summoned more coffee and began the main business…

Olivia began. "It's so good to be here together, to share our feelings and try to work out what we can do now. To support each other, but also to help the men in our lives, or should I say the men in the Mowbray family? What's happened to them? I sometimes tell myself that I'm thinking too small, that I have to see the bigger, political picture to understand. But I still can't escape the feeling that they've taken leave of their senses. And then I ask myself, how could I have let this happen to my family?"

"It's not your fault, Mum," said Susan.

"No," Fran agreed, "You can't take the blame for any of this. It's all about Charlie. HOPE is all about Charlie. He'd deny it, but he's not ideological. He's impulsive, he's an actor. He needs a cause, a passion – and Rosa gave that to him."

"And the coup," said Susan.

"Yeah, the coup gave him the excuse. Don't get me wrong, I'm not questioning his sincerity. He believes in what he is doing – God, I saw that – but it's the limelight that drives him on. Like a moth to a flame."

"It's all because of me and James," said Olivia. "Charlie never got over that. Sorry Emma, I don't mean…"

"It's OK," said Emma. "I think I know what you went through. James is elusive. There's something going on his head that doesn't belong to anyone else. It's the thing that drives him. Searching for something – quite what, I'm not sure he really knows himself. Except he knows it's never what he's doing at the time."

"It *is* all about Charlie. That's why Dad is doing this," said Susan.

"I know," said Olivia. "He's paying Charlie back for all the missing years."

"A massive guilt trip," agreed Susan.

"But we shouldn't forget what they just pulled off together," said Fran. "It was incredible. It happened."

"Yeah," said Emma. "And Bristol is buzzing, I can tell you. Archie is beside himself about it. Totally inspired. Said he was going to join HOPE, and all his mates were too."

"But what will happen to Charlie now?" Olivia asked.

"I think he'll be OK, at least for now," said Susan. "He's in the custody of the Irish. They won't just hand him over. They'll expect some proper process. Extradition proceedings. Could take months. There's no love lost between the Irish government and the Authority. They won't go out of their way to help."

"A clever move by Charlie," said Emma. "And that protest in Gorey… I read that there's something big planned in Dublin tonight. My friends in the collective are talking about setting something up in Bristol. I just don't know how the Authority will react."

"I don't suppose the Authority knows," said Susan. "It's divided. Wembley showed that. They don't want to use force against their own people – they've always maintained that they are a democratically-elected government, that the only repression has been against subversives. They might lose the Americans if they clamped down too hard. They haven't got many other friends – except the money launderers."

"But can they afford to lose control?" asked Fran.

"No. But right now I think they'll play a wait-and-see game. A few known agitators and opposition politicians might be arrested, but they might just have to allow the people to protest, and hope it peters out after the initial excitement. If Charlie's stuck in legal proceedings, and the rest of HOPE have gone to ground, there won't be much leadership."

"Unless a new leadership emerges," said Emma.

"Yes," said Susan, "But that's where the selective arrests may come in. I'd warn Archie and his friends to be careful."

"Especially just before his A levels," said Olivia.

"Oh, Emma," said Susan, "If we can help at all…"

"I'm so glad I've got you all," Emma whispered, wiping a tear from her cheek. Fran embraced her. "Oh, Fran, we're talking about me when you've been through so much. That interview…"

"It was horrible."

"You were very brave," said Susan. "Speaking up for Charlie. The web is going crazy over you."

"It just came out that way. I hadn't planned it. I had a script – we all had scripts. I couldn't have done it without knowing Olivia was there for me."

"You were brilliant, Mum. So calm."

"But what was Charlie going to do when he saw that, Susan? We – I – must have been the reason he gave up. And poor Gabi…"

"How is she, Mum? She looked drugged up to the eyeballs."

"I think she was still on a lot of painkillers."

"And truth serum," said Fran. "She told me she'd had a talk with a nice man with tiny glasses. He said he just wanted to know how she was and if she remembered anything about Wembley. And if she knew where her friends would be, as he was worried about their safety. She said she couldn't remember much, so he said he'd come back when she was feeling better."

"Ugh! I know the man," said Susan. "A real creep."

207

"I think we all do," said Olivia. "What will happen to Gabi now?"

"I guess they'll question her more, at least to understand how HOPE managed to pull it off. The pressure may be off her a bit, now that Charlie's in custody. I'm sure they'll ask the Irish if they can speak to him. They'll want to track down the others. I assume they'll be in Ireland too."

"What if he handed himself in so the others could escape?" asked Emma.

"Good point," said Susan. "They could be anywhere, I guess."

"And James?" asked Olivia.

"I just don't know, Mum. It depends how involved he is in all this – especially whatever's going on within the Authority."

"I just hope he knows what he's doing," said Emma. "And what about Will?"

"Susan, you heard…" said Olivia.

"Yeah, when I had to talk to that creep yesterday morning. Henry Devereux-Duchamps no less. He said they'd tracked Will to Amsterdam, via Berlin. I don't know why he was there. Must have been a reason to get out of Ukraine."

"Maybe they were after him," said Fran. "If they knew what Charlie was planning, maybe they thought Will would know more. They might be a bit more uncomplicated in their methods of questioning over there."

"Poor Will," said Olivia. "I hope he knows what he's doing, too."

"We're doing a lot of hoping," laughed Susan. There was a pensive silence. It was broken as three teenage girls approached their table.

"Oh, Mrs Mowbray – and Fran, wow! – sorry to disturb you. We just wanted to say how much we admired you in that interview. You were both so strong. Really inspiring. And Charlie, he was so brilliant. We're having a candle-lit vigil for him, and for Gabi, at the Abbey tonight. We wondered if you could come."

They all looked at each other, and nodded. "We'd love to," said Olivia. "Only, Susan might not be able to, as she works for the government."

"Mum," declared Susan, "I wouldn't miss it for the world."

***

They continued talking into the late afternoon, sharing a bottle of white wine. There was so much to discuss. Their lives were intertwined, caught in the web of surreality spun by Charlie, and his father, James. The vigil planned for that evening in the Abbey grounds had given them heart. Young people were mobilising, taking action. HOPE had given them hope. And Olivia, Fran and Gabi had made things real, tangible. Their emotions were the emotions of everyone. Family, love, vulnerability. They had domesticised the fight between HOPE and the Authority. This could happen to anyone. And there was revulsion at the Authority's actions. The interview may have caused Charlie to hand himself in, but the exploitation of three women, all hurt in some way by what had happened, was shocking to many, even in a deeply cynical, detached age.

Michael and the two members of staff had just closed the café and were clearing up, when there was a knock on the door. They didn't respond at first, but the knocking persisted. Michael went up to the door and looked through the glass. Immediately, he unlocked the door and let the man in. He was in his thirties, dark-haired, unshaven. Well-dressed but a little dishevelled. He looked across at the table where Olivia, Susan, Fran and Emma still sat, with their wine glasses. Olivia was the first to cry out…

"Will! Oh, my darling!"

She rushed across the café to her son, standing in the doorway, and held him in her arms as the tears streamed down her face, meeting those falling from his eyes.

"I made it, Mum."

Another bottle of wine was opened, and another. Will asked for an
Orchard Pig, for old times' sake, and told his story, to gasps of
astonishment. The mysterious presence of James in the background
intrigued everybody. Even Will was unsure how much was down to
James and how much was pure luck. But he was back, and in one
piece. And his Dad had definitely got him back to England, from
Holland. He was worried about his friend Serhiy, who was the real
hero for him. He'd not been able to contact Serhiy since his escape
from Kremenchuk, and feared the worst. He didn't mention Hanna,
and Susan decided not to probe, that evening. He would mention it
in time, in his own time. She knew how her brother was.

The vigil took place in the grounds of the Abbey, candles and
incense sticks perched on top of the ruins. Being Glastonbury the
smells were varied and intense, and some were intoxicating. Some
hippies danced to mystical music, cheerfully ignored by the rest of
the gathering. A few hundred people, of all ages, but mostly in their
teens and twenties, had assembled. There were cameras and a local
TV crew. As darkness gathered, a local priest said prayers and asked
for Charlie's safe passage in the coming weeks. There were protest
songs – and calls for Olivia and Fran to speak. Olivia wasn't sure,
but helped by a gentle push from Susan, took to the makeshift stage.
There were tears in the crowd as Olivia spoke of a mother's anxiety
– and pride. She reminded the crowd of Gabi's plight and the
outrageousness of putting her before the cameras, as she recovered
from her injuries. There were boos at each mention of the Authority,
and chants of *We want HOPE!* And then Fran took the microphone,
to a wail of teenage approval. She described her ordeal as she was
taken to the hospital for the interview under threat of what might
happen to her parents, to her role at the National Theatre, if she
didn't cooperate. She lavished praise on Charlie and his idealism.
She reminded the audience about his message at Wembley and
urged people to join HOPE and start a movement for change. Her

acting instincts had kicked in – she was relishing this chance to express all the feelings she'd had to bottle up for so long.

I love you, Charlie Mowbray! The people of Glastonbury, the people of England, are with you and your comrades. Let there be hope across this land again. We want HOPE!

The crowd roared – even the hippies had been caught up in Fran's oration. The chants for HOPE grew louder. A couple of local policemen looked on, smiling. As Fran stepped off the stage, fist raised in the air, she was mobbed by the youngsters, wanting to hug her, take pictures with her. There were joyous scenes. A few came up to Olivia and asked if they could have photos with her too. She happily agreed. Susan and Emma stepped to one side, and looked around at the celebrations.

"So amazing," said Emma. "This really is the start of something. Archie tells me there's a gathering in Bristol too, down at College Green. It's spreading."

"Look over there," said Susan, pointing at a short man in a black tracksuit top, hood up, smoking a hand-rolled cigarette and clutching a can of lager. Much the same as the group of friends he was with. "It's Jack Oldfield. Shall we say hello?" The two women approached Jack. His friends saw who it was and melted away. Jack looked sheepish.

"Had to come down and pay my respects to Charlie," he said. "Cheers."

"What happened to your cheek?" asked Susan.

"Got hit by some fascist's beer bottle when we was celebrating Charlie's speech down at the Tor and Anvil."

"Yes, I heard there was a bit of a riot down there. You had to be involved, I guess."

"We didn't start nothing. But we fought back. Yeah, of course we did. We was HOPE."

"I'm sure you were."

"Give him a break, Susan," Emma whispered.

"Yeah Suze, give me a break. I'm with Charlie all the way. You know what me and him were like."

"How can I forget?"

"Look, I know me and Charlie sort of fell out, but I'm not one to bear a grudge. I'm with him all the way. He's my main man – always will be. If I can do anything for him, just let me know."

A thought occurred to Susan at that moment. "Did you have anything to do with the Authority before Wembley?"

"What? Whaddya mean?" Jack looked furtive.

"Like what did you know about the Wembley plans beforehand?"

"Nothing. Not much. I just heard something."

"You were telling all of Glastonbury that Charlie had plans."

"Maybe, but I didn't tell them any details."

"What details? What did you know? Tell me, Jack. It's important. It might help Charlie."

Jack hesitated. "Yeah, alright. When me and Charlie split – when he ditched me – I heard him and Rosa in the pub talking about Wembley, about a kidnap. That's all."

"You weren't with them? What were you doing? Stalking them?"

"No, not stalking. I just wanted to know why he had dumped me. He made a fool out of me. No-one makes a fool out of Jack Oldfield."

"Except Jack Oldfield… so you knew that they were going to kidnap the players at Wembley?"

"Well, yeah…"

"And did you tell anyone – other than the whole of Glastonbury?"

"I didn't tell anyone the details down here. You have my word of honour."

"Yeah, that's worth a lot. Who did you tell? You did tell someone – I can see it in your face, Jack."

"Just my supplier in the Met. That's all. I was angry, Suze. Charlie made a fool of me. I done wrong, I know, but he made a fool of me, said I was a fool."

"You are a fool. You told the Met? You could have had my brother killed."

"Yeah, but he wasn't, was he? The whole thing went off a treat. Except for the blonde girl. Gabi – that's her name. Out of her head in that interview, poor girl. Dunno what they've been feeding her with."

Susan looked like she wanted to strangle the hapless fool in front of her. She took a deep breath. She had run out of words. Emma intervened. "Jack, you have been even more of a tosser than you usually are. You could have had Charlie killed. Didn't it ever occur to you that if they had a secret mission planned, he had to keep the circle of people that knew very tight."

"Yeah, but I was always in his circle. He kicked me out."

"Jack, you are a motormouth – always have been. How could Charlie rely on you? You told the whole of Glastonbury that he was up to something. That just proves the point."

Susan could hold back her tears no longer. She wiped them away with her hand. Jack saw her doing it and moved towards her, arms out. She pushed him away. "Fuck off, Jack. Just go away. Never bother me and my family again. Never, you hear? We don't want you around."

"But…"

"Just go, Jack," said Emma. She took Susan by the arm and led her back to Olivia. She knew that Susan would need her mother's love.

Jack stood there, watching their backs. Rejected again. He looked down at his can and lifted it to his mouth. He drained it of its remaining contents, then turned to find his mates.

Chapter Fifteen. The Garden
(23-05-27)

"I just lost it. Something inside me snapped. I just wanted to smash up everything, just like I'd smashed up your lives. The only time I'd ever felt a rage quite like that was when Mum and Dad told us they were separating. Look how long that took me to get over. I would have wrecked everything in that room if the boys hadn't pulled me away. And then I just broke down and cried, and Rosa came to me – and saved me. And then a few hours later she threatened to kill me! What a world I created, Fran. What a world. But yeah, the moment I calmed down, I knew everything had changed. I couldn't go on, harming the people I loved most. Not for any cause. I haven't stopped believing, Fran, but something had to change. Then I thought about it for a few hours, and Dad called. But he didn't help – not that time. He didn't understand. No-one could understand. I knew what I had to do."

"It was so brave of you, Charlie. How did you know that Rosa wouldn't shoot?"

"Because she loves me, Fran. She's mixed up because the Cause means so much to her. But I knew she couldn't shoot. When I looked around she was sobbing into Dan's shoulder. My heart went out to her. But I had a higher love, and I had to follow it in the end."

Fran rested her head on Charlie's shoulder, as they sat on a garden bench in the sunshine, staring at the fuschias, a gloriously rich, dark pink, on the bushes either side of them. Ahead of them, a small pond, with a decrepit concrete elf casting its broken fishing line, teetering on one side; a craggy bird table overlooking the other. The water sparkled in the sunlight, its surface momentarily broken by the wriggle of a goldfish. As they sat there, briefly silent, the serenity of the moment felt like a journey into paradise.

Charlie was under house arrest in Dublin. It was a pleasant house arrest, in a large house in Sandymount, not far from the sea. He was allowed a walk along the beach with his security guard once a day and had full access to communications. The Irish government was playing hardball with the Authority, not least because a *Free Charlie Mowbray* movement had snowballed in Ireland, after that first protest in Gorey. Fran had been invited over to address a rally in the Garden of Remembrance, after a march along O'Connell Street. To her surprise, the Authority hadn't tried to stop her. Charlie thought there were a couple of explanations for that. First, the Authority had to behave impeccably if it wanted to get him back to England; second, his Dad was probably still pulling some strings, from somewhere. He'd been coy about his whereabouts when they'd spoken, but Charlie guessed it was Spain. Same as Rosa and the boys, who'd arrived safely in Alicante. Whoever his contacts were in the Authority obviously still had some clout. Otherwise, Charlie joked, Fran would just have had to rely on O'Toole smuggling her over in one of his jet copters.

"It's funny," said Fran, "I was always a bit of a sceptic about HOPE and your involvement, and here I am now, rallying the protesters with your speech from Wembley."

"You are the face of the revolution now, Fran."

"I'm not sure I want to be. I just want to get back to my acting."

"This is your act now, Fran. You're the voice of the youth. The moment you spoke up for me in the interview, you became a symbol of the resistance. I didn't take that in the first time - I was raging so much inside - but I've watched it so many times since. I love you for that, and so does everyone else."

"Do you love me, Charlie – still?" Fran looked up at him.

Charlie hesitated. "Fran, I've lost my way with these words. So much has happened to me. So much tension, anger, stress. Fighting, performing. I don't know who I'm being half the time."

Fran laughed: "*If you would put me to verses, or to dance for your sake, Kate, why, you undid me...*"

Charlie brightened, recognising the lines: "*For the one I have neither words nor measure, and for the other I have no strength in measure, yet a reasonable measure in strength. If I could win a lady at leapfrog...*"

"Oh, Charlie, ever the actor."

215

"Just like you then. Together we shall conquer the world stage. England shall be our Agincourt!"

"I'm scared, Charlie. I don't want to conquer anything. Remember what you said about a higher love. That's all I want in this world. It's time to stop being Henry the Fifth, Charlie. Time to start being yourself. That's who you are, Charlie. Olivia's son, Susan and Will's little brother. My…"

Fran sighed and looked down wistfully at her feet. A moment later, her gaze had turned to a look of astonishment, as Charlie leapt onto his knees before her, resting his elbows on her thighs, his hands clasped as if in prayer.

"Love, Fran. You were going to say love?" Fran nodded and smiled. "Fran, my darling. I can't be myself unless I'm with you. Will you help me be myself?" He paused. "Will you marry me?"

Fran's lips trembled. Her hands shook as she took Charlie's. Her eyes glistened. Charlie thought he could see the dazzle of the sun in the film of tears. And beyond, the infinite pools of blue, soothing, healing. The deep waters of his soul reflected back at him. He waited for the words he so needed to hear.

"Oh, Charlie, of course I will."

Printed in Great Britain
by Amazon